LETHBRIDGE-STEWART
MUTUALLY ASSURED DOMINATION

Based on the BBC television serials by
Mervyn Haisman & Henry Lincoln

Nick Walters

Foreword by Paul Finch

CANDY JAR BOOKS · CARDIFF
A Russell & Frankham-Allen Series
2015

Editor: Shaun Russell
Deputy Editor: Andy Frankham-Allen
Cover: Adrian Salmon
Editorial: Hayley Cox, Will Rees
& Lauren Thomas
Licensed by Hannah Haisman

Published by
Candy Jar Books
Mackintosh House
136 Newport Road, Cardiff, CF24 1DJ
www.candyjarbooks.co.uk

A catalogue record of this book is available
from the British Library

ISBN: 978-0-9933221-5-0

Plucking at the Nerves of an Entire Generation (Most of Them)

I first watched *The Dominators* when it was originally screened back in 1968. I was only four years old at the time, so my main memories of the story comprise flickering black and white images of the Dominators themselves in those startling costumes: the black-scale armour, the white body-plating with the raised, hump-like pad across the back of the shoulders, and of course the Quarks, those boxy, toy-like robots with their terrible singsong voices and all kinds of destructive capability.

I remember well the Island of Death, where the Dominators were trying to drill down into the planet's core. If memory serves, nuclear tests had been carried out there, leaving a grisly wasteland of bombed-out buildings and horribly blistered mannequins. As per the common tone of late-'60s *Doctor Who*, the atmosphere of this tale was unrelentingly eerie, the backdrop a blighted wilderness in which our investigating heroes were only one of several small parties vying for survival. I also recall some impressive explosions during the course of it, and several rather horrible deaths: people frozen screaming in the Quarks' death-ray, their faces then melting and running before my goggling eyes. Looking back on it, it was clearly the case that late Troughton-era *Who* was gradually upping the action stakes, almost as though in preparation for the arrival of colour and Jon Pertwee in the very near future.

However, one thing I definitely didn't pick up at the time, thanks again to my tender age, was the subtext.

It's a strange thing, but when you tell people who didn't experience the 1960s that you did, they automatically assume you'll remember it the way it's recollected on TV documentaries. Well, I'd love to be able to report that everywhere I went back then I was aware of Beatles songs on the radio (that much is probably true, actually), or that I was always overhearing adults discussing the Cold War, seeing hippies setting up peace camps in the local park, and that I lived on a street where the traffic was constantly disrupted by anti-Vietnam War protests. But alas, because I was only a child, I didn't. Everyday life was just everyday life, as far as I was concerned. You had no idea that you were living through historical events.

The upshot of all this is that at the time I wasn't really aware that *The Dominators*, written by Mervyn Haisman and Henry Lincoln, was actually a very clever *Doctor Who* story indeed, plucking gently at the nerve-strings of the period in that it presented the Dominators as the hard face of industry/militarism/capitalism (whatever you want to call it), a cold, functional group bent on pillaging natural resources and destroying anything they couldn't use, while the pacifistic Dulcians were very much the '60s love generation: bright, perky young things, idealistic, well-intentioned, and yet fatally naïve, completely unprepared for the threat of a genuine aggressor. The Doctor of course, as always, was the one in the middle, trying to find a happy medium.

But hey… the fact I couldn't make this connection at the time, doesn't mean you won't be able to this time. Because this book you're reading now, in a twist that completely delighted me, is set in precisely that era: the late '60s, with the protest movement still at full power and the anti-nuclear ticket a hot one. It even has its own desolate wilderness – Dartmoor. Though of course at the heart of this wasteland stands not the Doctor, but his unofficial deputy on Earth (at least, that's always the way I used to think of him), and another fine creation of Messrs Haisman and Lincoln, Alistair Gordon Lethbridge-Stewart, better known as 'the Brigadier', though for our purposes today he's still a colonel.

Now if there's one *Doctor Who* character who really brings that period alive for me, this is the man.

Lethbridge-Stewart didn't appear in *The Dominators*, of course. Though he was already known to the Doctor by this time, he wouldn't become a regular character for another year or so. But for me at least, there is no one else in *Doctor Who* that more embodies that turbulent time – when the show virtually fed on Quartermass-type fears about government corruption, spies, reds under the bed, pollution, alien invasion, etc – than Alistair Gordon Lethbridge-Stewart.

And what a complex character he was. In an era when it would have been easy to play to the gallery and present a senior military man as a humourless authoritarian, instead he was actually given a very human face (and this is due in no small way to the late, great Nick Courtney, who inhabited the character for so long and so convincingly). Conservative… yes; an establishment figure… yes. But an affable guy too, who was happily married and enjoyed the odd pint. In addition he was a master of his craft: a skilled and seasoned soldier, an inspirational leader, and a man who always acted in the interests of the many, or tried to.

His charming relationship with the Doctor totally derived from this. Though the Doctor was always the bohemian – in so many ways they were worlds apart (literally) – they bickered and fell out, yet maintained a working relationship and a mutual respect for each other, which in the long-run became a firm friendship.

But I doubt I need to say more. If you're already following these new novels, you won't need to be reminded about the nature of their hero. Suffice to say that here is the great man again: back in the midst of the Cold War, trying to steer a course between youthful rebels and shady industrialists, having to cope with less than helpful government departments and of course an extra-terrestrial menace, and this time with no Doctor to advise him.

Anyway, that's it for me. No more spoilers. Just sit back and enjoy *Mutually Assured Domination*. I certainly did.

Paul Finch, September 2015

Edge of Dartmoor

White. Everywhere white. A blank, patient, restless white. Through it two figures moved. They walked slowly, heads bowed to the humped grassy terrain over which their booted feet trod. They stumbled now and then, and stopped occasionally to peer around themselves, and argue. They were bare-headed and wore shorts as they had not expected to encounter such conditions at this time of year.

The smaller of the two tripped and almost fell. 'Keith! Let's face it – we're lost!'

'We're not lost, Marie, love,' said the other. 'As long as we keep going down, we'll be okay.'

'Rubbish! We're lost as lost can be!'

'We're not! See this stream? It's flowing downhill, as water does. If we follow it, it will lead us off the moor.'

Marie tutted and they trudged on through the whiteness in silence, Keith shouldering the rucksack that contained all of their gear. He didn't mind. It was one of her *conditions*, and he played along.

The mist fascinated him. It wasn't a complete blank; it contained whorls and swirls, like you were staring into slowly moving liquid. If you looked at one bit it felt like you were falling, or flying. *Far out, man*, he thought.

'It's your fault we're lost! We shouldn't have spent so much time on that blummen' rock!'

'Tor,' he corrected.

'Tor-ment, this is!'

'Come on, you seemed to be enjoying it up there sunbathing!'

She stopped and turned to him. Her pale face, framed by ginger curls, looked pinched and drawn. 'Sorry, Keith, it's just – this mist is freaking me out a bit.'

He smiled down at her. 'You know what the guide book said, love. "You can expect sudden fogs on the moor at any time of the year."'

'Oh nuts to your guide book!' With that Marie turned and stomped off into the mist.

Keith shook his head. He'd never understand chicks. Well, he'd never understand Marie, at any rate. She was younger than him – only nineteen – and worked full-time in Woolies. She didn't seem to understand the academic life, and she often laughed at his studies. Geology – just a lot of old rocks! *Is that what gets* your *rocks off?*

Marie screamed. The sound cut right through him. Keith stumbled towards the mist, but Marie emerged before he reached it.

'What is it?' he asked.

She pointed, grimacing. 'Monsters! Monsters in the mist!'

He looked in the direction indicated by her trembling finger. There did, indeed, appear to be shapes in the mist, standing off-white in the colourless air – shambling things, the size of shire horses, white, moving with a slow deliberation that unnerved Keith.

As the shapes advanced they seemed to shrink, and

slowly resolved themselves out of the blankness.

Relief struck Keith like the punchline to a joke. 'Sheep!'

Sheep: about a dozen of them, meandering slowly across the moor. Keith felt foolish – he should have remembered how mist magnifies objects. The creatures glanced at the two humans and ambled on, clearly used to them.

'Funny thing about sheep, it sounds like they are saying the word "baaa" instead of baaa-ing, if you see what I mean.'

Marie burst out laughing. 'God, Keith, you are weird!'

They hugged and clutched each other as they watched the sheep fade away.

Marie stood back from him, her face worried again. He'd never known a girl with such changeable moods. 'Thing is, we're still lost.'

'We're not lost as long as we follow the stream,' said Keith. They were back where they started, on opposite sides; he wanting to convince, she refusing to be convinced. *Thing is*, Keith thought, looking around at the unchanging, featureless void, *I'm beginning to wonder myself.* Perhaps they really were lost. You heard of people dying of exposure out here. In his mind floated a phantom headline in *The Mirror*: *Moor Pair Missing – Police Investigation Continues.* He shivered.

They carried on in silence down the slope, following the course of the stream. Which, after a while, vanished underground in a cleft of rock.

Keith stood staring at the tinkling water.

'Ooh! Lights!' Marie said.

Keith looked up to see her pointing. Some distance ahead of them, sharp points of light shone out through the fog. The lights suggested the boxy, regular outlines of warehouses. The sound of generators could clearly be made out – sound

3

carried a long way through mist.

Keith frowned. 'Don't remember seeing that on the map.'

'Not in the guidebook either, was it?' Marie's mood had lifted noticeably at the sight of something man-made, the promise of civilisation in the midst of the wilderness.

'No… Come on,' he said, but she'd already started striding down the slope in the direction of the distant cage of lights.

'We can ask the security guard for directions,' he shouted after her, wanting to assert control over events. 'He might even give us some tea from his thermos!'

'What if there's nobody there?' Marie called back over her shoulder. Trust her to see the cloud in the silver lining.

'You're everywhere and nowhere, baby,' Keith muttered. 'Well then,' he said, loud enough for her to hear, 'there's bound to be a road leading up to it, for deliveries and so on. We can follow that off the moor to Buckfastleigh.'

Marie said nothing – silence was her usual response to cold hard logic – and walked off down the bumpy hillside.

'*And it's hi ho silver lining*,' Keith sang to himself and set off after her.

The installation loomed like a leviathan out of the fog. A central block-like building was ringed by a number of smaller structures, all windowless, with bright searchlights at each corner shining out into the mist. Other smaller huts and outbuildings were scattered around the central structures, and the whole thing was surrounded by a high wire fence topped with barbed wire. More lights sat atop the posts supporting the fence, casting blue-white beams through the whiteness. A distant humming and a sharp, minty chemical tang laced the misty air.

As they walked up to the fence, Keith racked his brains as to what it could be. Some government installation, or something to do with the military? Could be – the place was lit up like a Christmas tree; whoever owned it clearly didn't care who knew it was there. It had to be pretty new, as it wasn't on the map or in the guide book.

But whatever it was, it represented civilisation.

The two hikers stood staring up at the fence.

'Looks deserted,' muttered Marie, some of her good humour deflated by the sight of the seemingly impregnable industrial fortress.

'Come on, let's find the main gate.'

They set off alongside the chain-link fence, but they walked the entire length of it without finding sign of an entrance. They did find, however, a sign with big white lettering on a red background, bearing the legend:

**DOMINEX INDUSTRIES
KEEP OUT!
TRESPASSERS WILL BE DESTROYED**

Keith snorted. 'Destroyed! Ridiculous. Someone's having a laugh.'

But Marie looked scared. 'Come on, Keith, let's get away from this place – I don't like it.'

But the sign annoyed Keith. The threat was so over the top. He felt, somehow, personally insulted. He walked up to the fence and kicked it. 'Hey, there's a loose bit here!'

At the base of one of the fence posts, the concrete had crumbled away from the pins supporting the wire. Keith pulled the chain-link back and the resulting gap was easily big enough to admit them.

'Keith, no… Let's try your other idea and find the road back to Buckfastleigh.'

'Nuts to that,' grunted Keith, who was already forcing his way through the gap. 'I want to meet these idiots and tell them where to shove their sign.'

With a final tug at the wire he was through. He stared back at Marie through the wire-diamonds of the fence. 'Well, come on!'

With great reluctance she followed him through and soon they stood on the fresh tarmac, in the glare of the lights. In front of them the grey corrugated wall of an outbuilding rose like a cliff face. Bright white searchlights blazed down at them.

Keith felt rebellious excitement well up within him. 'Right!' he said and strode off towards the outbuilding.

'Keith…' Marie trailed in his wake, hugging her bare arms to herself. 'This is stupid. I don't wanna be destroyed!'

'We won't be destroyed!' Keith scoffed. 'This is England; they can't shoot us just for trespassing.'

An enormous voice, seeming to come from all around them, bellowed, 'Stop!'

Keith and Marie froze, caught like rabbits in the headlights.

'Do not move!' The voice was male and sounded psychotically angry.

Keith found Marie's hand and gripped it tightly. 'Look, we're sorry! We'll just turn around and go away.'

'Please don't destroy us!' Marie wailed.

'Shut up!' Keith hissed. He called out over Marie's

whimpering, 'We got lost in the mist! We hoped you'd help us...'

His voice trailed off as, with a smooth action and a mechanical whining noise, a hatch in the corrugated grey wall opened, and two figures emerged. Two *things*.

Their bodies were robust grey blocks of what looked like lead, their heads spherical, split into textured octants, with crystalline spikes protruding from each side, fore and aft, and on top. They walked on shuffling shoebox feet, and from the front of their bodies, rudimentary, oblong arms extended, deadly looking apertures gaping at the ends. They were about five feet tall. The things, whatever they were, made constant burbling, chirping noises. They looked like oversized, demonic children's toys, or robots from a science fiction play on the telly.

'What the hell are they?' Keith cried, surprised at how loud and stupid his voice sounded.

The two improbable objects paused in their advance. They stood a few metres away, their blocky arms waving back and forth as if to swat flies. They looked ridiculous – but also somehow sinister. One of them – or perhaps both of them, Keith could see no mouths in those spherical heads – spoke, in high, piercing, almost childlike voices which made his ears hurt.

'Shall we destroy? Shall we destroy?'

'Affirmative!' the giant voice bellowed again, making Keith and Marie jump. 'Quarks – deploy and destroy! Destroy! *Destroy!*'

Keith and Marie watched as the body of the Quarks split open and they rose up on mechanical cantilever legs. A profusion of lethal looking protrusions bristled forth from their unfolding bodies.

The Quarks towered ten feet tall. They stepped forward in unison.

Keith unshouldered the rucksack and hurled it at the nearest Quark. It bounced off the gunmetal grey armature and fell away uselessly to one side. The thing didn't even seem to notice.

The bristling machines stepped closer, stooping over their prey. There was a cold, calculated precision to their movements. Keith found himself staring right down the barrel of what was unmistakably some sort of weapon.

No way. No *way*. No way was this it, no way was this the end of his life! What about his degree, what about his parents, what about Marie, what about the kids he suddenly realised he wanted to have?

Keith looked desperately at Marie, who was sobbing and trembling with fear like a cornered animal. He tried to find words of reassurance but all he could do was shout. 'Sorry! I'm sorry!'

Though the Quarks' forms had grown, their voices remained that of gleeful, cruel children. 'Destroy! Destroy!' they trilled.

Keith turned to run, yanking the shrieking Marie after him, but it was too late, far too late. Keith heard a colossal roar of energy, and felt an intense, burning fire engulfing him. He felt Marie's hand slip from his, heard her scream in mortal agony. He howled in helpless rage and searing pain as shuddering pulses of heat slammed through him. His last thought was of Marie's face, laughing in the sunshine.

*

'Quarks! Return and recharge!' the enormous, belligerent voice commanded. There was a note of pride, of satisfaction, of an appetite only partly sated, in its baritone rumble.

The Quarks regarded the smoking remains of the two organics, then retracted and reverted to their basic forms. Chirping and burbling happily to themselves, they waddled back into the outbuilding. The hatch whirred shut behind them.

Ten minutes later the mist lifted and it was once again a beautiful May day on the moor.

— CHAPTER ONE —

The Last Summer of Love

'And what of Miss Travers?' Colonel Alistair Lethbridge-Stewart asked, once he and Major General Oliver Hamilton had finished discussing the latest developments.

'She remains at the Vault until the time is right to bring her completely into the fold.'

Into the fold. An interesting phrase, Lethbridge-Stewart reflected, considering how long it had taken him to get Hamilton to open up. Although perhaps 'open up' wasn't the phrase, either. There was still much Lethbridge-Stewart didn't understand, not least the reason why Hamilton chose to keep his role in Lethbridge-Stewart's recent disappearance to himself.

'And the latest acquisitions? The Rutan technology is incontrovertible evidence of alien–'

'At the Vault, I'm afraid.'

That wasn't good news. Lethbridge-Stewart understood there was much going on at the Vault that was secret, and he'd been given more than enough indication to believe those secrets were not, despite what the Ministry of Technology claimed, for the betterment of British industry.

'Not the best result, sir, if you don't mind me saying.'

'Agreed, Colonel. But it's either that or the Foreign

Technology Division get their hands on it. The Vault is the best bet here; the most-secure facility in the UK.' Hamilton smiled, and lifted his small glass of whisky. 'Besides, at least if the tech remains at the Vault with all the other recent left-overs, Miss Travers can keep a close eye on it.'

That was true. Despite her sometimes abrasive and insubordinate nature, Miss Travers had proven herself many times over. But he doubted how much she could achieve alone; she herself had warned him against letting the Vault get the Rutan technology. But there was nothing to be done. Better the devil you know, he supposed.

'In the meantime,' Lethbridge-Stewart said, moving the subject on to the final piece of business, 'I have Corporal Bishop following up the leads Vice-Marshal Gilmore gave me in uncovering all information on the Operational Corps.'

'Good to hear.' Hamilton collected up the papers on his table and placed them firmly in a manila folder. 'I think that's all for today. We'll reconvene soon, once I've met with Bryden and Peyton.'

Lethbridge-Stewart finished the last sip of his own whisky and stood. He placed his cap on his head and offered a salute.

Hamilton stood and returned the salute. 'Dismissed, Colonel. But keep those eyes of yours peeled. Until the Corps is up and running we still need to remain on our guard.'

'Agreed. Colonel Grierson's suspicions continue to grow,' Lethbridge-Stewart said, referring to the CO of Chelsea Barracks. 'The excuses for my absences are becoming more and more transparent.'

'Not for much longer, Colonel. Not for much longer.'

*

Corporal Sally Wright knew something was up.

Her commanding officer, Major General Hamilton, had sequestered himself inside his office at Strategic Command all morning, ordering no interruptions, no visitors, no phone calls, not even if the bally bomb dropped. Well, maybe perhaps let him know if the balloon did actually go up. But otherwise the general had requested to be left completely alone. He hadn't even sent out for his usual mid-morning cup of tea.

Sally hated being left out of things, but she was a firm believer in the chain of command, and respected her senior officers. Well, most of the time. She entertained the idea, as she went about her duties, of barging in on some pretext or other, but dismissed the notion. It would see her on a charge. Perhaps Alistair would know what was going on. She'd tried his number at Chelsea Barracks, and his home number, but he was at neither. Which made her wonder if he was closeted in there with Hamilton – he'd been very secretive since meeting with Air Vice-Marshal Gilmore last week. But he couldn't be, she hadn't seen him come in to Strategic Command and his name wasn't on the sign-in sheet.

It was somewhat of a surprise, even a shock, therefore, when on one of her exploratory passes outside Hamilton's office, the door opened and Alistair stepped out, almost bumping into her.

'Oh!' he exclaimed, managing to look surprised, apologetic and furtive all at once. 'Sorry. I mean, hello, Corporal.'

'Hello, Colonel,' she replied as they began to walk along the corridor together. 'Forget to sign in, did we?'

He coughed. 'Erm, yes, something like that.' He drew her in to a side room full of filing cabinets, dust, and a musty smell. 'Look, I haven't been here, all a bit hush-hush, all right?'

'Is it to do with your meeting last week?' Sally kept her voice as innocent as she could.

Alistair's face reddened. 'I suppose I can trust in your discretion. Yes, it was. But I can't tell you any more than that.' He glanced at his wristwatch. 'Now I really must be getting on.'

She hated it when he was stuffy like this, looking at her and seeing only the uniform. 'What about Saturday night? We haven't had a night together since Dougie went back to County Down – a week ago.'

Alistair turned away. 'Can't. Things to do.'

'Dare I ask? Sunday?'

'It's difficult this weekend.'

She knew he didn't have another woman. That just wasn't him. Evidently whatever was going on between him and the generals was keeping him busier than usual. She knew Alistair well enough to know that he had to have time to think, to plan. He was terrible company if his mind was preoccupied – and it almost always was. Especially since he had returned from East Germany.

'Perhaps next weekend,' he muttered, slipping out into the corridor.

She followed. He was already heading down the corridor. She hurried to keep pace with him. 'Tell you what, I'll come round Monday and cook for you. Ratatouille. Your favourite.'

She caught him smiling briefly. Then the look of

preoccupation returned.

'It's a date?'

He turned to her, and there at last was that twinkle in his hazel eye. 'It's a date.'

Then he was gone, stepping briskly down the corridor. She watched him go with a sad, knowing smile.

London. Swinging London, a city of some eight million souls, swirling on the crest of a wave that seemed always just about to break. Carnaby Street and It Girls, the Rolling Stones and the Beatles, miniskirts and flares, absolute beginners and absolute chancers, Mary Quant, Jean Shrimpton, Steed and Mrs Peel, Jason King and Simon Templar. This was the face that London held up to the world: brash, outrageous, free, stylish, fearless, and now.

Then there was Harold Chorley's London.

The crowd surged up the staircase from Marble Arch tube onto Park Lane, an explosion of colour against the grey concrete. Long hair and beads and brightly coloured t-shirts, flares and flowers in their hair, spirits high and voices carrying like tinkling bells up into the endless blue sky. Some carried placards, some carried tambourines, some carried children; all carried hope. In their midst, Chorley carried a worn brown leather satchel and patches of sweat under both arms. Once on street level he shaded his eyes with one hand and shoved his way through the people with the other. The heavy satchel bashed against his hips. He ground his teeth as a bead of sweat trickled into his eyes. The rumble and blare of the traffic was like a pressure on top of his head. Cursing, he let himself be carried along with the crowd down Park Lane, the concrete and glass cliff-face of the hotel to his left providing some shade from the punishing June sun.

Chorley glared at his fellow travellers. The hair. The colours. The sense of somnolent, carefree iconoclasm. Hippies. *Am I the only square in town?* In his casual slacks and blue cotton shirt, with his short black hair and black-rimmed specs, Chorley knew he didn't fit in with 'Swinging London'. He'd become increasingly aware of this as the decade progressed. At first he'd felt uncomfortable, as he entered his thirties, seeing it as a sign that youth was leaving him behind. He had once, briefly, considered growing his hair, and had in fact developed a tentative set of sideburns, but the blistering remarks one of his coarser colleagues had put paid to that. Afterwards he had stuck to his own conservative style of dress, seeing it as a badge of professionalism, while other freelancers had succumbed to the siren call of the zeitgeist. Now, as the 1960s, the era of permissiveness and revolution, was nearing its end, his conservative image was one Chorley cultivated with pride. Looking around at all the colour and long hair, Chorley felt that he, not they, was the real individual, the real iconoclast.

The crowd moved, as if with one mind, down the wide thoroughfare of Park Lane and swung left into Upper Brook Street. Chorley let himself be swept along, noticing with satisfaction that – despite his appearance – no one was paying him any attention. He smiled – the first time he'd done so since the Redgrave snub. His journalistic invisibility was something he valued, though he had no idea how it had been achieved. Someone had once told him one that he had 'the glamour', but he didn't believe in the paranormal.

He bumped into a girl with blue beads in her blonde hair

who looked vacantly through him.

Well, *once* he hadn't believe in the paranormal. Now, he wasn't so sure. He didn't know what he believed in. He knew there was something beyond the here and now, existing to the side and in the shadows, beneath the streets of Swinging London, behind its brash optimistic façade. He knew because he'd… seen things. Things he would sooner forget, but there they were, in his mind, in his memory, never to be erased. And he'd tried to forget them, God knows he'd tried. At first with drink, but had given that up, not wanting to travel down the well-worn road of the alcoholic journalist. No, he'd seen far too many go that way, broken by fifty, dead before sixty. He just had to live with the things he'd seen, experienced. They were part of his life now. Part of his London. Harold Chorley's London.

And, thanks to his on/off partnership with Larry Greene, he didn't always have to bear the load alone.

He dragged his thoughts back to the here and now. He could almost feel the excitement of the crowd, like static electricity, as they neared their destination.

The United States Embassy was a gigantic concrete oblong, graceless and charmless, squatting between Upper Brook Street and Grosvenor Street, its stern façade partly obscured between sentinel maple trees in full summer leaf. Rows of rectangular windows gazed outwards, seemingly black, giving no indication of activity within. It had been built only nine years ago in the first flush of the concrete fervour of the '60s, and always reminded him of a stylised, brutalist cousin of the White House. Otherwise, the only clues to its purpose were the American flag flying above it, and the enormous, gilded eagle which spread its wings over the eaves.

Grosvenor Square Gardens was situated before the Embassy and it was here – in the area dubbed 'Little America' during the War – that the crowds were gathering to protest against the latest war, the United States' involvement in Vietnam. A cordon of police lined the side of the Embassy bordering the Square, a dark bar of authority drawn across the colour and the sunshine of the day.

Chorley allowed himself to be carried into the Square. The crowd thickened, pressing in from all sides. A long-haired youth reeking of patchouli oil bellowed 'US out!' mere inches from his left ear. But apart from the shouting, the atmosphere was relaxed, even party-like. He could hear the distant hectoring of a protestor over a crackling tannoy, and the surging roar of assent from the crowd. The burnt-sweet aroma of pot assailed his nostrils. Something else that had failed to keep the memories at bay.

The trim, prim gardens, the flower beds and pavements of Grosvenor Square itself were invisible – Chorley couldn't see the grass for bodies. He felt a spike of anger – then remembered his job. Hippies these may be, but they were real people, with real concerns about what was going on in Vietnam. And he was here to talk to them – Harold Chorley's Londoners. Real people. He tried to bury the memory of his encounter with Vanessa Redgrave that morning.

Along with a few other prominent celebrity activists, she had been addressing the crowds at Trafalgar Square, speaking out eloquently and passionately against the war. But when he had approached her, asking politely for an interview, she had declined. Moreover, she had clearly

17

enjoyed snubbing him. That was what had driven him here, he realised, to the middle of this colourful crush. Not professionalism, but wounded pride. That and desperation, a desperation borne of his continuing exclusion from the world of journalism on military orders. He almost hated himself for it – but not quite. If it landed him with a decent, saleable story, his true motives didn't really matter. He just had to get something in the bag, to wow the BBC and start pitching for the talk show which seemed with every passing week to become more and more elusive.

The crowd surged and roared and Chorley was barged almost off his feet. He clutched his satchel, hoping that the tape recorder in the front pocket hadn't been damaged in the crush, and pushed his way through the crowd, looking for some space. The clamour of voices and hectoring tannoy would make it difficult to make a recording. Perhaps a first-hand account of the demo from his point of view? He wondered how many other journalists were here. He thought he'd seen Steve Worman but couldn't be sure. Probably him and loads of others.

Chorley took his glasses off and wiped sweat from his eyes. When he put his specs back on he was greeted by the sight of a tall youth in a garish purple tie-dye t-shirt and jeans, his shaggy ginger hair swept back from a high, bony forehead, brandishing a home-made banner above the heads of the crowd. The banner bore the legend, crudely formed in blue poster paint and surrounded by blotchy representations of flowers and the familiar logo of the Campaign for Nuclear Disarmament:

DOMINEX OUT!

Chorley frowned. Dominex? Ah yes, the nuclear waste plant on Dartmoor. What was their beef with that? The nuclear issue had faded out of the public consciousness of late. The Cuban Missile Crisis, almost seven years ago now, had been the last big flap. Since then, the peace movement had shifted its focus onto the Vietnam War – as evidenced by the crowds surging and jostling around him. But clearly, some CND members still had their eye on the nuclear ball. He wondered if this was just the usual hippie anti-nuke stuff, based on what was in the papers already, or whether they had something new. Something that would make the disconnected pieces of information he already had into a story. The deal with the British Government, and the missing hikers. This could be a bigger story than the protest, if he could only get some verifiable information.

Chorley found himself automatically moving towards the youth, who kept on waving the placard, not noticing the journalist's approach. By his side was a small, dark-haired girl with watchful eyes. She had seen Chorley and was regarding him coolly and with clear suspicion. Chorley grinned, knowing how square he must look.

'Harold Chorley, freelance journalist,' he shouted when he got within earshot of the couple. He extended a hand but the gesture was not returned.

The tall ginger lad squinted down at him with clear disgust. He had small, rather piggy blue eyes and a large, expressive mouth. The girl's gaze had changed upon his announcement; there was now curiosity in her hazel eyes.

'Emma Hindmarsh,' she said. 'Freelance person.'

Chorley laughed politely and pointed to the placard, which the youth was still waving about. 'I'm curious about your sign. What has Dominex to do with Vietnam?'

Emma looked up at the sign. 'Mike!' she cried.

The youth made a face and brought the sign down. 'Sorry!' He rummaged in his rucksack, drew out a piece of card and some paper fasteners, and within a minute the sign read:

U.S. OUT!

Emma turned to Chorley. 'That's better,' she said. 'Honestly, you can't take him anywhere.' Mike glowered at them both.

Chorley stood with Emma and Mike for a moment as the crowd surged around them. Disconcertingly, he could see mounted police at the far side of the square. And when he turned around, there were some on the other side too. It looked like they were being boxed in. The mood of the crowd began to change, almost at once: shouts of anger, boos and catcalls were heard, and objects were thrown towards the mounted officers.

'What's your beef against Dominex?' said Chorley, painfully aware that he was trying to sound 'hip'.

'Nukes!' bellowed Mike, as if that was enough.

Chorley staggered as the crowd jostled him. 'Could you please elaborate?' No point trying to fit in with the vernacular.

Mike frowned down at him, as if he were a small child, or an idiot. 'Nukes are bad, man!'

Chorley realised that he wasn't going to get much more out of the chap. Probably stoned. He could see it in his watery blue eyes. He turned to the girl, Emma. Intelligence shone in her dark, watchful eyes. 'But aren't Dominex merely reprocessing nuclear waste?' Chorley asked. 'Isn't that a good thing?'

'Depends on what they are really doing down there. Some sources believe they're making nuclear weapons.'

Chorley snorted. 'Surely that's just paranoid conspiracy nonsense?'

'Hey, man, it's true!' Mike said, cutting in. 'They're gonna bring about the apocalypse!'

Chorley ignored him, addressing Emma once more. 'Do you believe that?'

She looked thoughtful. 'I need proof before belief. But I can't shake the feeling that they *are* up to something down there. Did you know that Dominex did a deal with Sir Anthony Bufton, the Energy Minister? Planning permission, tax breaks, grants, just so they could open this factory down in Devon. So is the Government covering something up? Perhaps they're building nuclear weapons using Dominex as a cover! And then there's those missing hikers. Something's going on. After this march we're off to Parliament Square to protest.' A playful smile. 'Man!'

Chorley found himself smiling back.

Then all hell broke loose.

Chorley felt an elbow in his back; someone stepped on his foot and a hand shoved him and sent him sprawling into Mike. It was like crashing into a tree. The two of them almost fell, Mike cursing, Chorley trying to fight down the panic that suddenly rose in him. He heard Emma scream. Getting back to his feet, still holding on to Mike, Chorley gazed in disbelief over the heads of the crowd. The mounted police were forcing their steeds into the mass of people, batons drawn and brandished, the horses' heads tossing, mouths foaming. Shrill whinnying merged with the roaring and screaming of the crowd.

A story, thought Harold Chorley. *Police Brutality in Peace Protest.* Panic took over. Had to get out of here. Had to get away, or he might not survive to tell the story. He turned against the tide of the crowd, but his satchel got caught in the morass and he was yanked backwards, once more cannoning into the towering ginger form of Mike. He glanced up into angry blue eyes, and realised that here was something he could use to his advantage.

'Mike! We've got to get out of here!' he yelled, shoving the fellow before him in the direction of what he hoped was the nearest edge of Grosvenor Square, in the opposite direction to the charging mounted police.

With Emma between them they shoved and struggled through the mass of bodies. The roaring and screaming was now deafening and Chorley felt his heart hammering in his chest. At one point he tripped and fell, but found himself immediately yanked upright by Mike. Somehow they managed to fight their way to the edge of the square, only to find a line of mounted police barring their way. Chorley looked desperately up and down – there was no way out – the police were deliberately bottling them in. I'm not one of them, he wanted to shout. I'm not a hippy, I'm a journalist, just doing my job. But then he glimpsed Emma's terrified face and felt instantly ashamed.

Directly in front of him a horse reared. Chorley could see the whites of its eyes, the foam flecks around its mouth. Clearly the animal was as terrified as the people, maybe even more so. Shoving Emma and Mike before him,

Chorley lunged past the horse and made a break for freedom.

Something slammed into the back of his head and stars exploded in his brain. He just had time to see Emma and Mike running from the square, past the police cordon and away, before Harold Chorley's London faded to black.

— CHAPTER TWO —

Dangerous Business

L ethbridge-Stewart stood at the window of his first floor office at Chelsea Barracks, looking out at the streets beyond the parade ground. It all appeared so reassuringly normal.

But of course appearances weren't everything.

'Police were forced to intervene when protestors stormed the Embassy gardens,' came the cultured voice of the BBC news announcer from the radio on the desk behind him. 'At the end of the altercations, over two hundred protestors were taken into custody.' The voice went on, describing the chaos that had erupted earlier that summer day in Little America.

First the riots in Paris, now this. The younger generation kicking against the establishment. Could hardly blame them, but it was still worrying. Would order ever really, truly be restored, he pondered. So many factors seemed to be ranged against the prospect of a lasting peace. The war in Vietnam, the reaction against it. Violence begetting violence. Then there was the stuff the public didn't see. The business with the Great Intelligence in London, and its tragic aftermath in Bledoe, aliens at Fang Rock, worlds where dead men still lived... And that wasn't taking into account all those encounters he'd read about in Gilmore's secret files. Taken together, the threats to world peace from both terrestrial and non-terrestrial forces were redoubtable, perhaps insurmountable.

Lethbridge-Stewart turned away from the window and switched off the radio news, which was now into the weather forecast.

Maybe not insurmountable. Not if you took action, if you did something about it. He thought back to his meeting with Hamilton the previous morning, and his brief encounter with Sally afterwards. She didn't seem to understand that he needed time to clear his head. Couldn't relax now, needed to think things through. At least they weren't meeting until Monday night. He'd be able to pay proper attention to her by then.

Lethbridge-Stewart sat down at his desk and, with a heavy heart, opened the latest service record from the list. So far the names provided by Hamilton were not inspiring much confidence. He reached for his coffee and took a sip. He frowned. Stone cold. How long had he been standing at the window? He was reaching out to buzz for Bishop to prepare a fresh pot when the external telephone rang.

He picked up the receiver immediately; hopefully it was Hamilton with good news. 'Lethbridge-Stewart?'

'Thank God you're there,' gasped a strangely familiar voice. 'You've got to help me!'

Lethbridge-Stewart sat up straighter in his chair. 'Who is this? How the devil did you get this number?'

'I'm an investigative journalist,' snapped the voice. Its owner must have realised his tactlessness, as he then coughed apologetically. 'I only have the one phone call. Please don't hang up. I've been arrested. The name's Chorley. Harold Chorley.'

Harold Chorley. Lethbridge-Stewart leaned back and gazed into the middle distance. Name was familiar. Oh yes – journalist fellow. Last encountered during the Yeti business in the Underground. Slimy sort of chap.

'What have you done?'

'I haven't done anything! I was in the wrong place at the wrong time. Occupational hazard. Grosvenor Square. I was trying to get out when some flatfoot coshed me with his truncheon and I woke up here!'

'Where is "here"?'

'West End Central Police Station.'

Lethbridge-Stewart knew the place. It was bang in the middle of Savile Row, just around the corner from Little America.

'Look, are you going to come and get me out or not?'

Lethbridge-Stewart bridled at the man's rudeness. 'No.'

'You're my last hope! And there's something else I want to talk to you about. I think I'm on to something.'

'Something?' said Lethbridge-Stewart. 'Meaning what, exactly?'

'Meaning something in your line, your area of expertise,' said Chorley, stumbling over the words. 'Look, I'd rather not discuss it in here!'

Damn the man. Lethbridge-Stewart was about to put the receiver down. But if Chorley really was onto something 'in his line', surely it was worth following up? Again he felt he was clutching at straws, chasing any hint of alien involvement, to get the extra evidence that Hamilton and he so badly needed. But what was the other option? Continue to read the service records of less than exemplary officers? 'Very well, Mr Chorley, keep your hair on. I'll be over within the hour.'

West End Central police station was a white-painted Victorian edifice slap bang in the middle of Savile Row. *Looks more like a hospital than a police station*, Lethbridge-Stewart thought as he pulled the Land Rover up outside the entrance. Normally he would have had Bishop drive him in the staff car, but Bishop was busy; besides Lethbridge-Stewart wasn't sure he wanted Chorley to learn more about his 'area of expertise' than was necessary. The man clearly knew more than he should already.

The station certainly had a severe, institutional atmosphere. He smiled as he imagined Chorley's indignation, could almost hear his voice: 'You can't do this to me! I'm a journalist!'

Lethbridge-Stewart stepped from the Land Rover and trotted up the wide steps to the station entrance, ignoring the microphones that were thrust in his face, smiling blandly and waving away the questions with a brown leather gloved hand. Typical; sight of a uniform excites the blighters. Surprising to see so many press – or perhaps not, given the shenanigans at the Embassy. How many was it? Two hundred arrested? Lethbridge-Stewart walked up to the desk sergeant, a portly man with curly black hair, who was leaning his red face on a ham-like fist. On seeing him the man sat up straight, his eyes widening. Lethbridge-Stewart was amused to see him raise his right hand as if to salute, then think better of it and rub his ear.

'Colonel Lethbridge-Stewart. I believe you are holding a journalist here? Name of Harold Chorley?'

'That we are,' said the desk sergeant in a lugubrious

Yorkshire accent.

'Under what charges?'

'Breach of the peace. Same as all the others.'

'Well, I'm here to take him off your hands.'

The desk sergeant shook his head. 'On whose authority?'

Lethbridge-Stewart had been ready for this. The police were all right in their way, but could be awfully obstructive when they wanted to be. And this chap looked the officious type, the type who played things strictly by the book.

'Mine. I am authorised to take him into military custody. Here are my papers.' Lethbridge-Stewart passed the desk sergeant his military ID and a letter signed by Hamilton. 'Mr Chorley is attached to my unit on work of vital importance to national security. His arrest puts us – puts you, rather – in a delicate position. He must be released so that he can assist us with this vital work.'

The desk sergeant frowned at the papers and returned them to Lethbridge-Stewart, regarding him thoughtfully. 'Very well, sir,' he said at length. 'But since Mr Chorley has been formally charged, certain bail conditions will need to be met.'

'I insist that the charges be dropped. I am confident that Mr Chorley is completely innocent. His involvement with my unit is of vital importance.'

The desk sergeant glared stolidly back at him. 'We will send him a letter outlining these conditions, and setting the court date.' With that he turned away from the desk and disappeared through an internal door panelled with wire-reinforced glass.

Bit of a mess, thought Lethbridge-Stewart. Dratted nuisance, that Chorley. Lethbridge-Stewart wasn't confident of Chorley's innocence at all, really. Wasn't even sure he could get the charges dropped. But, annoying though Chorley was, the chap might be on to something. Or he could be making it up, just to get out of nick. Lord help him, if that were the case.

Left alone, Lethbridge-Stewart sauntered around the reception area looking at the posters on the wall: 'A Thief Would Like Your Bike', 'Watch Out – There's A Thief About', 'Keep Britain Tidy'. All the usual warnings for the unwary public.

After a few minutes the internal door opened and the desk sergeant reappeared with Harold Chorley trailing behind him. The chap looked dishevelled and hot, but otherwise unharmed.

'Lethbridge-Stewart, thank God!' For a moment Lethbridge-Stewart thought the man was going to embrace him. But all that happened was a manly handshake. 'Mr Chorley, this good man tells me you were involved in a breach of the peace.'

Chorley glared at the desk sergeant, who glared back. 'Rubbish! Police brutality, plain and simple. I was just trying to get away!'

The desk sergeant's face turned a deeper shade of red, and he opened his mouth to speak, then clearly thought better of it.

'From what I hear, the protestors stormed the Embassy,' said Lethbridge-Stewart. 'The police were merely trying to contain them. Doing their job.'

'That's the truth of it, sir,' said the desk sergeant.

'How the hell do you know? You weren't there! I was there, Colonel – doing *my* job. I saw what happened.

Mounted police just waded into the crowd as if they were a field of corn! Women – kids!'

'Hippies,' the desk sergeant grumbled.

Lethbridge-Stewart stepped between the pair. Had to get Chorley out of here before he said or did something stupid. 'Yes, well, it's never easy to ascertain the truth of these things. Now we'd better get out of here before this chap arrests you again.'

They turned to leave. 'Stick to your bail conditions, Mr Chorley!' the desk sergeant called behind them.

Lethbridge-Stewart grabbed Chorley's arm and steered him towards the exit doors.

'Don't worry about any of that,' he whispered to Chorley, adding with a confidence he didn't really feel, 'We'll clear all that up for you.'

'Blasted police!' Chorley muttered as they descended the steps, once again battling through the journalists. 'I'm going to write a searing expose of police brutality!' he shouted.

'Yes, well, there's no need to get all Vanessa about it.'

'Don't mention her!' said Chorley with a vehemence that surprised Lethbridge-Stewart. 'She's the reason I've ended up in this mess!'

Lethbridge-Stewart opened the passenger door of his Land Rover. He was beginning to lose his patience. 'Just get in.' He got into the driver's seat. 'What's this "something" you've got for me?'

Chorley shook his head. 'Not here. Home.'

'I'm not some blasted chauffeur!'

'Please? I've been through hell and back.'

Chap doesn't know the meaning of the term, thought Lethbridge-Stewart. Never seen action. Probably never been

30

shot at in his life. But suffering was relative, and he really did look a mess. Lethbridge-Stewart was about to start the engine when he realised that he had no idea where Chorley lived.

'Where is "home"?'

'Chelsea. Cheyne Walk.'

Not too far, thought Lethbridge-Stewart. He gunned the Land Rover and drove off down Savile Row.

'Can you at least give me a general inkling as to what this is all about?'

Chorley was silent for moment. 'Does the name Dominex mean anything to you?'

'Dominex… yes. Something to do with the nuclear industry. They opened a plant down in Devon earlier this year. Remember seeing it on the news. Why?'

'On the demo I met two CND members, with an anti-Dominex banner. They'd clearly brought the wrong one to the march.'

'So?' Lethbridge-Stewart frowned in irritation. 'You have to expect CND to be against a company like Dominex, or anything with a nuclear angle.'

'As indeed they are. They seem to think Dominex are up to something more than just reprocessing nuclear waste.'

They were now heading west along Piccadilly.

'Something more?'

'Probably just the usual hippy paranoid conspiracy thing, but they reckon they're building nuclear weapons down there.'

Lethbridge-Stewart scoffed. 'The UK nuclear weaponry programme is closely policed and closely guarded and the supply of fissile material is *extremely* closely monitored. If anyone's building nuclear bombs anywhere we'd know about it before breakfast.'

'Even so, if nothing is going on, nuclear waste reprocessing is the most dangerous business on Earth. And the most profitable. The place is going to be well protected. Especially since the place has the blessing of the energy minister.'

'Quite right.' The open space of Green Park passed by to the left, glorious in the summer sunshine. 'Anyone trying to break in there would be met with ultimate force.'

Out of the corner of his eye, Lethbridge-Stewart saw Chorley turn to look at him. 'And that's it. I think that's exactly what happened.'

Lethbridge-Stewart almost swerved into a cyclist. 'What?'

'I can't be sure, but I have my suspicions.' Chorley fell silent, turning to the window to watch the park pass.

Lethbridge-Stewart drummed his fingers on the steering wheel. 'Well come on, out with it, man!' he finally snapped. 'What have you discovered?'

'The answer's in my flat. So is my whisky. I'll need the latter before providing you with the former.'

Bit early in the day, thought Lethbridge-Stewart, but after what the journalist had been through, he could hardly blame the fellow. He gunned the Land Rover along the A4 through Knightsbridge. And if what Chorley was saying was true, he'd probably need one too before the day was out.

Harold Chorley's Chelsea barracks was the neatest and tidiest bachelor pad Lethbridge-Stewart had ever seen, certainly tidier than his own Pimlico flat. Situated on the Embankment with a view over the river, it was a spacious rectangular studio flat with a small modern kitchen at one end, and a mezzanine bedroom at the other. Between these was a combined living and working space. The rear wall was almost completely taken up with shelving containing rows of indexed box files and filing cabinets. On the opposite wall, floor-to-ceiling windows gave out onto a view of the river and the ornate white towers of Albert Bridge. A desk was set up in the centre of the room. Elsewhere a garish orange sofa and a couple of easy chairs surrounded a glass-topped coffee table. There were two televisions in the alcove below the mezzanine and a record player and 8-track tape machine on a table beside these.

Once inside, Chorley made straight for the stylish, smoked-glass drinks cabinet and poured himself a stiff measure of whisky, which he downed with evident relief. He offered a glass to Lethbridge-Stewart as if only just remembering he was there.

'Thanks,' said Lethbridge-Stewart, accepting the offer and taking an appreciative sip. 'Rather spiffing place you've got here. Journalism game obviously pays well.'

'It does but it's not easy, the freelance life,' said Chorley, with an edge of bitterness. He put his glass down and went over to his files.

'Especially when you get caught up in civil disturbances.'

'*Especially* since my access has been so limited by your lot,' Chorley pointed out.

'Sorry, not really my department. Now, what have you got on the Dominex lot?'

Chorley took down a box file and opened it. It contained issues of a tabloid newspapers, and Chorley began rooting through. 'You will be able to quash those charges against me, won't you?'

'Absolutely,' said Lethbridge-Stewart. He took another sip of whisky and looked around the well-appointed, neat and tidy flat. It had all the appearances of a bachelor pad, but Lethbridge-Stewart had clocked that Chorley wore a wedding ring. He sensed problems in that department. 'No sign of the little woman?' he said as casually as he could.

Chorley grimaced as he sorted through the papers. 'Huh. No. We're separated. This is my little bolt hole.'

'I see...' Lethbridge-Stewart tried to picture Chorley and a dolly bird canoodling on the orange sofa, but the image wouldn't coalesce. Perhaps the man was so dedicated to his work that it had driven out any chance of personal relationships. That was good – in a way. Bad in another. Lethbridge-Stewart thought of Sally. A chap needed a woman's touch. Kept you on an even keel, stopped you going bananas.

Chorley selected a copy of *The Mirror* and began flicking through it. 'Ah – here we are.'

He handed Lethbridge-Stewart the paper and indicated a stark headline: *Moor Pair Missing – Police Investigation Continues*. The story concerned two young hikers who had gone missing on Dartmoor last week.

'They were last seen heading up to Black Tor, a mile from the Dominex installation,' Chorley said. 'They got lost in one of the infamous Dartmoor mists, and disappeared. Search parties were sent out. Found nothing.'

'Was this Dominex place searched?'

Chorley took the paper back from Lethbridge-Stewart and read from the story: '*The police made enquires of the nearby Dominex nuclear reprocessing plant, whose spokesman said that*

34

though unfortunately their own internal security team had not turned up anything they promised full co-operation in the investigation. As of now the couple are still missing.'

'So? People go AWOL on the moors all the time. Dangerous place. Or they may even have eloped, be alive and well and living in... well, you get my drift. I hope you're not wasting my time, Mr Chorley.'

'There have been other disappearances,' said Chorley. He had his hands in his pockets and was gazing out at the river. 'I don't have the cuttings, but I remember reading about two cavers going missing back at the end of March.' He turned to regard Lethbridge-Stewart with eager intensity. 'Three things. One, these were experienced, older chaps who knew the cave system like the backs of their hands. Two, they disappeared at about the same time Dominex opened for business. Three, the Dominex installation is almost slap bang on top of the caves in which they went missing!'

'So you think these cavers were trying to break in?'

Chorley nodded enthusiastically. 'The hikers, too. One of the missing people was Keith Johnson. Geography student at Exeter University, member of CND. They could have been using the cover of the mist to attempt a break-in at Dominex.'

Lethbridge-Stewart took another sip of whisky. 'Are you sure you're all right, Mr Chorley? Suddenly believing all these conspiracy theories?'

Chorley's face darkened in anger. 'Four people are missing, Colonel. Presumed and quite probably dead. Dominex are denying all knowledge.'

Lethbridge-Stewart considered. 'Or it could all be a

complete coincidence. The cavers could have fallen somewhere inaccessible, the hikers – well, anything could have happened. And even so, this sort of thing is a police matter, nothing to do with "my line of work" as you claim.'

'Trust me,' said Chorley, stepping towards Lethbridge-Stewart. 'Since that business in the Underground I've got a feeling for this sort of thing.'

Lethbridge-Stewart regarded him coolly. The chap was intelligent and determined, if a little highly-strung. And while the business with the Yeti had clearly had some effect, he seemed to be managing it well enough.

'And my instincts have been strong enough for your General Hamilton to block Larry and me from investigating your disappearance back in April.'

'My...?' This was news to Lethbridge-Stewart. He knew Hamilton still hid certain things from him, but he had no idea that Chorley had somehow been involved. Perhaps he should humour Chorley after all, see what else he could get out of the man. 'Nothing to stop you going down and investigating; keeping me informed of anything out of the ordinary you might find. Needless to say, we have not had this meeting. Total deniability. If anyone asks, I just dropped you home. Favour to an old associate.'

Chorley nodded wearily, despite the smile spreading across his face. 'I get the picture.'

Perhaps more than Lethbridge-Stewart did. He paced up and down in front of the picture windows. 'Be careful, Mr Chorley. Remember what I said about ultimate force. Don't get involved. Just go down, ask a few questions.' He stopped pacing and turned to regard the other man. 'Do your job. And if you do get in trouble, I've got your back. Just don't get in trouble in the first place.'

Chorley picked up the whisky bottle and refilled their glasses. 'A toast,' he said. 'To the beginning of a new working relationship.'

'A toast,' corrected Lethbridge-Stewart, 'to the conspiracy johnnies. May their theories have no basis in truth' – they clinked glasses – 'whatsoever.'

And to me getting to the bottom of Hamilton's secrets, Lethbridge-Stewart considered ruefully.

CHAPTER THREE

Harold Chorley Investigates

Harold Chorley couldn't sleep. Each time he dozed off he woke up convinced he was back in the nick. It was an uncomfortably sticky night, even with the windows open, and Chorley sweated and writhed into the small hours. He eventually dozed off at around 5am, when it was fully light outside, but drifted into a nightmare in which he was chased by black-suited demons on horseback, the fanged mouths of the steeds spitting foam and froth. After that he had given up and got out of bed and gone for a walk along the river to get his thoughts in order. It was a Sunday, so he took the chance to recover, have a leisurely lunch, make his plans for his investigation into Dominex, and have an early night.

The next day, Chorley rose at his usual hour of 7:30am and, fuelled by three cups of percolated coffee (an extravagance he could never forsake), he began his investigation into Dominex.

A quick ring-round of his contacts in the dailies revealed no progress in the case of the missing hikers, or the cavers that had disappeared months before. A press release from Dominex blandly promised further co-operation. A call to Companies House showed that Dominex Industries checked out: they were a registered company, incorporated 5th January 1968, address Gibby Combe Lane, Dartmoor

National Park. They were a subsidiary of a larger corporation based in Antigua, rather bombastically named Dominex 10 Galactic. Managing Director and Chief Executive: Mr Dominic Vaar. Probably Dutch, going by the name. And probably the founder, going by the company name. Chorley tried to phone the company but either got an engaged tone or a robotic voice that grated, 'Please leave your message after the beep,' then cut off.

To his immense luck Chorley managed to beard the bibulous and highly knowledgeable Percy Finch-Wright, Business Editor of *The Times*, in his Soho club at lunchtime. Over a lunch of indifferent grilled sole and a bottle of Rioja, Chorley listened to Finch-Wright chatter about the problems of new employers' liability legislation affecting British companies, the worry of exchange rates affected by the 'goings-on' in Vietnam, and the consequent fluctuations in the stock market. With this latter, Chorley saw his chance.

'I hear shares in Dominex are up five percent.'

'Dominex?' Finch-Wright frowned. He was a wiry, sandy-coloured gentleman in his fifties, who favoured tweed, pipes and bow-ties, and always looked as though he had just come back from a hearty walk in the country, involving at least one pub.

'The nuclear waste reprocessing company.'

'Ah.' Finch-Wright raised his gingery eyebrows and took another sip of wine.

Chorley leaned forward. 'Ah?'

Finch-Wright regarded him with a guarded look. 'Why d'you bring them up, out of the blue?'

'Because I think they might be up to something, possibly illegal, and I think they might be behind the disappearances.'

'Disappearances?'

'Four people have gone missing in the vicinity of Dominex.'

'Oh yes, yes, I remember reading about that. Dreadful business.'

'So do you know anything? Or have you been paid to keep mum?'

'I've never taken a bung, you should know that,' snapped the senior journalist. Then, less harshly, 'I know as much as you do, old chap.'

'I know only as much as is in the public domain,' retorted Chorley. 'Which is why I am here, talking to you – I want the benefit of your knowledge and experience.'

A slight frown, then a smile. 'Dominex. Nuclear waste reprocessing plant, run by, er, a Dutch fellow, I think. Generous business grants, pet project of the energy minister, what's his chops, Sir Anthony Bufton. Nothing unusual in that. Nuclear is up and coming, and we want to be ahead of the game.'

'Up and coming, and dangerous,' Chorley pointed out. 'Do you know what exactly they're doing? Any weight in the rumours that they're secretly building nuclear weapons.'

'If they are, how would we know?'

'How indeed. So you don't know anything?'

Finch-Wright leaned across the table. 'Only thing that's not widely known is that Dominex have developed this new process. Negative Mass something or other. Turns nuclear waste into energy, apparently. Don't ask me how it works. But it appears to.'

'No wonder Bufton's all over them.'

Finch-Wright nodded. 'Chap's over the moon. He's on

40

a *Panorama* Special tomorrow, the Dominex top dog is, you know.'

Chorley mopped up the last of his grilled sole. 'Well then. So no dirt on Dominex.'

'Bottom line is, Dominex are clean.' Finch-Wright stared levelly at Chorley. 'As clean as anyone dealing with nuclear waste can be.'

Chorley hesitated. Was this a hint? 'Thank you, Percy. You have been very helpful. And thanks for lunch.'

'Suppose I can afford to buy you freelance johnnies the occasional lunch on my salary,' muttered Finch-Wright, taking another sip of wine. 'I'm only sorry about the quality of the sole. I'll have a word.'

Leaving Finch-Wright snapping his fingers to summon a waiter, Chorley left the club and steeled himself for the next item on his list.

Shopping. A sadly necessary activity Harold Chorley hated. It got in the way of work, but there was no way around it: one needed things. And today, Chorley needed things he never thought he would ever need. Hiking boots, for one thing, and all the other paraphernalia needed for a long walk in the country. After finding a reasonably priced pair of boots that fitted him in Freeman Hardy & Willis, Chorley had bought the necessary Ordnance Survey in Foyle's and some other gear, then tubed and trudged back home, mildly frazzled. Coffee and a smoke set him right.

A quick phone call to the BBC revealed that the preview tapes for tomorrow night's *Panorama* Special were not available, so Chorley resolved to try to watch it, wherever he might be at the time.

41

Over more coffee he sat at his desk opposite his view of the river, immersed in an OS map of South Devon. The Dominex installation, of course, wasn't on the map (it was too new) but Gibby Combe Lane was there, branching off from the main road west from Buckfastleigh, and ending in nothing. Chorley marked it in red biro and put a cross where he supposed the Dominex installation might be. On the map, the green expanse of Dartmoor reminded Chorley strikingly of a brain, the roads across it like veins. The Dominex complex was only five miles out from Buckfastleigh. And Buckfastleigh was two hundred miles from London, a good four hours' drive, maybe more. Chorley glanced at the clock; it was only half two, so there was still a good six hours' daylight left, maybe more.

The nearest station to Buckfastleigh was Exeter, but after that, he would either have to rely on public transport or hire a car. Better to drive. For getting around London, Chorley used a lime-green Vespa scooter, bought before a certain section of youth society had appropriated them and made them 'cool'. This called for something with longer range; his sky-blue Hillman Imp; small, economical, and reliable.

In fifteen minutes he was packed and ready, and he set off, light of heart. He hadn't been down to Devon since his childhood years, holidaying with his parents at Sandy Bay in Exmouth or at some posh hotel in Paignton, and as he drove out of London the happy memories flooded back to him. He had to keep reminding himself that he wasn't going on holiday, he was about to investigate the most dangerous business on Earth. Still, as he bowled along the brand new M3 motorway towards Basingstoke, windows open, limitless blue sky above, he couldn't help singing along to the hits on the radio, nightmares of demonic horses completely scoured away by the brilliance of the June sunshine.

He followed the M3 down to Southampton, then the dual-carriageway A31, which ran north-east to south-west through the New Forest. Chorley felt strangely humbled as the countryside opened up around him. He'd spent most of his life in London, and yet here was all this beauty, mere hours away, spread out waiting for him. Perhaps, when he'd won the Pulitzer and retired, he'd move down here, with or without the wife.

He took the bypass around Bournemouth and reached Dorchester by 5pm. By his reckoning he was over half-way so he drove through the town and parked up in a lay-by, enjoying the view over the supine mounds of Maiden Castle while he ate the cheese sandwiches and drank from the flask of coffee he'd prepared earlier. Refreshed, he drove on through the alarming hills around Bridport and Lyme Regis, through the busy market town of Honiton, and the rural metropolis that was Exeter. From there it was a matter of some twenty-odd miles on the road bordering Dartmoor and then up on a curving lane overhung by trees, bright sunlight dappling the tarmac, onto the very edge of the moor itself, and Buckfastleigh.

Buckfastleigh was a small, compact, idyllic little spot, formerly a milling town populated by a few thousand people, bolstered at this time of year by the tourists attracted to such delights as the butterfly sanctuary, nearby Buckfast Abbey, and, of course, the moor. Chorley parked the Imp in a short-stay car park and got out, tired and sticky, rubbing his aching neck. Seven in the evening and the day was still hot, hot, hot. There was no room at either *The King's Arms* or *The Globe* but to his immense luck, considering it was the height of the tourist season, he found a tiny but workable single room at *The White Hart*.

The pub. The true centre of any community. Where you went to meet friends old and new. Where you went to drink, to celebrate your triumphs or drown your sorrows, or just drink for the sake of it. Where you went to impart your wisdom, tell saucy jokes, rant and rail, laugh and cry, kiss or fight. Where you went to get away from the wife. Where you went to get away from life. Where you went to play. Where you went when you wanted to find out things.

Harold Chorley sat at a corner table in *The White Hart*, with the remains of a gristly Cornish pasty and a half pint of best bitter before him, not even trying to blend in, waiting for one of the locals to notice him. So far, they were ignoring him so thoroughly he might as well have been invisible.

Situated in a side street off the main Plymouth road through the town, *The White Hart* was a staunchly locals' pub. It did not serve, and probably had never heard of, either Babycham or Skol. Its decor was a mixture of old and new – battered wooden furniture, horse brasses, and a stuffed fox in a glass box, mingling with Formica-topped tables, a fruit machine and a jukebox. The interior reeked of cigarette smoke both fresh and stale.

The landlord, Cyril, was a thick-set fellow in his sixties with white sideburns and a red nose, who had welcomed Chorley when he'd checked in an hour ago, and proved a pleasant enough, if taciturn, host. He now stood behind the bar polishing glasses and indulging in infrequent, lugubrious small talk with the three locals who were the pub's only other customers. It was only half seven in the evening, but it looked like these three chaps were as permanent a fixture as the poor old stuffed fox. Nearest to Chorley, perched on a bar stool, was a barrel-chested, bearded bloke in a plaid shirt, bare elbows on the bar, hands clasped around a pint pot, a roll-up drooping from his lips. He appeared to be staring furiously at nothing. Further along the bar, a thin old gent in an old-fashioned three-piece suit straight out of the last decade, with a glass of whisky on the bar before him and a cigarette in his mouth, propped up the bar. He would occasionally take the cigarette from his mouth, either to cough deeply and unpleasantly, or make some remark to no-one in particular about 'darned foreigners'. Finally, on the opposite side of the room, a red-haired man in a chunky blue jumper sat at one of the Formica tables, smoking a pipe, intent on the local rag.

Would any of these know, or even care, about Dominex? Chorley took a sip of his beer – Watney's Red Barrel, ubiquitous even in the sticks, it appeared. He didn't need the Dutch courage to talk to the locals, but how on Earth he was going to bring up the subject of Dominex – or indeed any topic at all – with such a bunch.

Fortunately the problem was solved for him.

The door banged open and a dishevelled, grey-haired fellow rolled in.

'All right, Josh? Usual is it?'

'Ar!' barked the newcomer staggering to the bar, against which he slumped, licking his lips. He wore clothes that looked like they had seen both World Wars, and an overcoat that appeared to be grown around him like a fungus. He glared around at the others, who appeared not to have noticed his dramatic entrance.

The landlord poured a pint of cider that looked luminous in the gloom. Josh grabbed it with a filthy-looking hand and took a hefty draught. He then subsided onto a bar stool and began muttering to himself.

Chorley narrowed his eyes. A gentleman of the road, or a local tinker? A smell wafted over him, redolent of pigs. Perhaps a farm labourer? These sorts always knew what was going on, at least within their own very small worlds. Could be a mine of information, if he could get any sense out of him. Chorley was about to rise from his seat when he realised that the man was staring at him. As their gazes met, Josh rose from his stool and staggered over to Chorley's table, carrying his pint pot, cider slopping around inside it.

Chorley sat back down. Above him, watery blue eyes gazed down out of a face with skin the colour of brick. 'Oo're you?'

Chorley said, languidly, 'My name's Harold Chorley, how do you do?'

'Oo ar? Oo ar?' crowed Josh, cocking his head to one side.

Chorley frowned. Was the fellow deaf? He leaned forward and said slowly and clearly, 'Harold Chorley!'

Every head in the pub turned to look at Chorley as if they had only just realised he was there. Which, indeed, they had.

'We don't like strangers pokin' their noses round 'ere,' growled the bearded, bull-necked chap on the stool at the end of the bar nearest to Chorley. 'Especially not Lunnon types!'

The dapper old chap glared at him, and the ginger-haired fellow in the blue jumper raised his eyes from his newspaper to frown suspiciously in his direction.

Chorley faced their angry scowls with practised professional equanimity and a wide, bland smile. 'Then you're going to love me. I'm a journalist. From London.'

CHAPTER FOUR

The Dominex Deal

'A journalist!' The old chap in the grey suit sneered. 'Now now, Sid, easy. His money's as good as anyone else's,' said Cyril the landlord, though his gaze told Chorley that he resented not being informed of his visitor's profession.

Josh had wandered off back to the bar, muttering to himself, his interest in this newcomer obviously at an end.

'What you doing down here then?' said the bearded man on the bar stool, who had swivelled around to regard him properly. 'Is it to do with them missing hikers?'

'In a way, yes,' said Chorley.

'Piskies!' spluttered Josh all of a sudden. 'Gordannum blasted piskies, dungoddem!' He flailed his arms and almost fell off his stool. Cyril nimbly rounded the bar to help him, and the bearded man – who Chorley had heard addressed as Phil – laughed heartily and somewhat cruelly.

Distracted by Josh's antics, Chorley hadn't noticed that the ginger-haired fellow in the blue jumper had left his paper and was now sitting himself down next to Chorley. Close up, Chorley could see he had intelligent eyes and the sensitive mouth of an artist or an epicurean. Those eyes were now regarding Chorley with steely interest.

'Harold Chorley, Ian Cawdery. We've had a lot of journalists in the town over the last few weeks. Doesn't seem like there is any more to find out about those missing hikers.'

'Piskies! Gordannun piskies!' spluttered Josh.

'What's he mean?' Chorley asked, thumbing his hand towards Josh.

'Local legend,' said Ian. 'It's said that piskies have the ability to summon the mists in order to confuse unwary travellers.'

A place like this was bound to be steeped in superstition, but Ian didn't seem the type. 'You don't believe that, do you?'

'No,' said Ian.

'So what do you think happened?'

'As I told the previous journalists, I don't know.'

'What do you do?'

'I'm a teacher. History.'

It was Monday, a school day. 'Why aren't you teaching?'

Ian Cawdery turned his head slightly away, then looked back at Chorley with a searching gaze. 'Do you have any new information on the disappearances? Has... Has something else come up? Is that why you're here?'

'I'm doing a report on Dominex,' said Chorley slowly, watching the faces of the locals staring at him.

'Gordannun bludgers!' Josh cried.

Phil swore, then took a deep pull at his pint.

Interesting.

'They seem about as popular around these parts as, well, journalists,' Chorley said dryly.

'It's no laughing matter!' The jovial landlord was jovial no more. 'We thought they'd bring in jobs. Jobs for everyone from here right down to Ivybridge and up to Okehampton and beyond!' If a pint glass could be polished in anger,

Chorley was watching it. 'And trade.' Cyril glared at Sid, Ian and the bearded chap.

Clearly Cyril had hoped for troops of thirsty Dominex workers banging his doors open at the end of their shift. Chorley had seen photos of the Dominex complex; it looked substantial, enough to house a considerable workforce. 'So what happened?' he asked. 'Did they bring in their own men from outside Devon?' He fixed his gaze on Sid. 'Or even from abroad?'

'It's worse than that!' Cyril snapped. 'Whole place is fully automated!'

A place that size, Chorley thought. *That is newsworthy in itself.* 'Has anyone actually been up there? Been inside?'

'Of course not,' said Ian scornfully. 'It's a nuclear waste reprocessing plant. Can you imagine the security?' He snorted. 'You should see the signs they've got warning people away. Totally over the top. But...'

'But what?'

Ian looked warily at Chorley, as if on the verge of some confession. 'What the hell,' he said eventually. 'They've never been found. The two hikers that went missing. You have to wonder...'

'And what about the cavers? The ones that vanished back when the Dominex place opened?'

As Chorley spoke Ian rose abruptly and walked off to the gents, leaving behind him an uneasy silence.

'What's his problem?' muttered Chorley. 'Weak bladder? Better lay off the ale, in that case.'

Cyril spoke softly, but with a hard edge to his voice. 'One of those cavers was Ian's brother.'

Chorley winced and sank back into his chair. He picked

up his glass but the beer tasted sour and foul.

Five minutes later Ian returned and, ignoring Chorley, went back to his pint and his paper. Chorley rose to go to speak to him, but a warning glance from Cyril made him sit back down again.

He glanced at the clock. Quarter past eight! He jumped up from his seat. 'Excuse me, could I have the telly on?'

There was a tiny black and white set on a shelf next to the dartboard. It looked as if it had never worked.

'Why, what's on?' said Cyril.

'*Panorama*,' replied Chorley. 'Something of local interest.'

Cyril shrugged. 'Be my guest.'

After a bit of fiddling and cajoling, Chorley managed to tune in to BBC 1, just in time.

The small black and white screen showed a TV studio, with the bespectacled, bow-tied figure of Robin Day sitting behind a desk, the familiar globe of the *Panorama* logo behind him.

'And now we turn to the nuclear issue,' said Day in his familiar, clipped tones. 'It's the youngest and most controversial industry in the world. And one of the newest players on the pitch is the international company Dominex, who earlier this year, in a controversial deal with the UK government, opened a reprocessing plant in Devon. And tonight on *Panorama* we are pleased to welcome the Chief Executive of Dominex, Mr Dominic Vaar, to answer our questions.'

The camera pulled back to reveal, sitting behind the desk next to Day, a hulking, dark-haired man in a business suit. His massive hands were clasped together on the desk in front of him. It looked to Chorley that he did not have the face of an executive, but of a fighter – no, it was more noble than that; of a Roman Emperor, one of the bad ones. Tiberius, maybe. His black eyebrows and wide, full-lipped mouth had a downward cast, and his dark eyes held the expression of one who had seen much and would tolerate little. Deep lines ran from his bullish nose to the corners of his downturned mouth, and across his low forehead. His thick black hair was combed into a neatness that it seemed to barely contain.

'Looks like a blooming Russki!' shouted Sid from over his pint.

'Welcome to *Panorama*, Mr Vaar,' said Robin Day with his customary smoothness.

For the briefest of moments, it looked as if Vaar was going to lean over and bite Robin Day's head off. Then that cruel, despotic mouth broke into a terrifying grin and Vaar spoke. 'It is good to be here, Robin.'

As was his style, Day got right on with proceedings with no further preamble. 'Director Vaar, Dominex has been in operation for six months now and has become the biggest nuclear waste reprocessing plant in the United Kingdom, with your Dartmoor plant reprocessing waste from Windscale, and you've recently started accepting waste from the fast breeder reactor at Dounreay in Scotland. What are your plans for expansion?'

'We will continue to accept waste from the developing UK nuclear industry, and hope to establish operations overseas,' pronounced Vaar solemnly. His voice was deep, predatory, sepulchral; the voice of a funeral director; the voice you'd imagine a tiger to have, were such beasts to magically acquire human speech, just before it ripped out your innards.

'With assistance from the government?'

Vaar's expression shifted. His eyebrows came down in a menacing glower. 'Your... *the* government has been most helpful in helping us establish our Dartmoor reprocessing facility, but, as you will soon hear, this is for the benefit of all.'

'Not everyone agrees with that, Mr Vaar. There have been concerns from groups such as the Campaign for Nuclear Disarmament about the safety aspects of your reprocessing activities.'

Director Vaar's mouth twitched, ever so slightly. Then that smile again. 'We are monitored by the UK Atomic Energy Authority, and they are satisfied that our processes conform to the most stringent safety standards.'

'I'm sure that will reassure all but the most determined of your opponents.'

Vaar frowned. 'Opposition is...' – he seemed to be searching for the right word – '...*inevitable* in an enterprise such as ours.'

'Quite.' Robin Day adjusted his glasses. 'Now, we understand that you have an announcement to make. Something of great import.'

'Yes!' Vaar thundered. Then he appeared to remember where he was, and said, more gently, 'Yes, Robin.' He turned to the camera, which zoomed in on his enormous, glowering face. 'We have developed an entirely new process, which we call Negative Mass Flux Absorption. With this, we intend to convert nuclear waste into cheap energy for the whole country.' Vaar nodded in triumph at Day. 'For the benefit of all.'

'Nuts to this!' The voice came from behind Chorley, from

bearded Phil, who, scowling angrily, leapt up from his bar stool and strode over to the television set, reaching out for the controls.

'How does this…' Robin Day began, before the channel abruptly switched with a staccato clicking hiss to HTV, where a football match was being broadcast.

'Hey! I was watching that!' said Chorley angrily.

'So?'

Chorley sighed. No point arguing. But at least he had seen the face of – well, not exactly his enemy, even if he did look the part. Chorley was well aware of the dangers of judging by appearances – even if, sometimes, he was guilty of it himself, he realised, remembering his reaction to the crowds in Little America. Despite Dominic Vaar's intimidating appearance, he seemed to be nothing more than a businessman. An entrepreneur, even, leading the field in the nuclear industry. 'Seems like a nice enough sort of chap,' he said to no one in particular.

'Looks like a Russki to me!' snarled Sid again, near enough for Chorley to smell the whisky on his breath.

'Yes, we know, you've said!' Chorley snapped. 'Actually, I think he's Dutch.'

'Still a blooming foreigner,' growled the gnarled old man as he staggered off to the gents.

Chorley retreated from the waft of disinfectant that issued forth, and decided to have another pint.

Even though Sally Wright had him all to herself for the whole evening, she still felt that a part of Alistair was on duty elsewhere.

She had turned up at his Pimlico pad at 6pm, exactly on

time, not merely to please Alistair, but because it was in her nature to be punctual, a habit reinforced by military training. Even if she tried, she couldn't be late. She had brought with her the ingredients for a Fanny Cradock ratatouille – quite a feat, considering how hard it was to get hold of aubergines these days – a bottle of red wine, and no expectations.

She busied herself in the kitchen while they talked shop, skirting around the issue of Alistair's meeting with Hamilton. Well, she didn't mind him having secrets from her, as long as they were military secrets. For the greater good, security of the realm, and all that. If he wanted to take her into his confidence, he would – if and when, and only on his own terms. It was no use her pressuring him, or trying to tease it out of him. Her training had taught her that, it was part of her sense of duty, to the Crown, to Alistair. What he needed was her support, her loyalty, and her culinary skills. Which, that evening, he seemed to appreciate, albeit in his usual distracted way.

Afterwards they sat down in front of the telly. Alistair was keen to catch the evening's broadcast of *Panorama*, while Sally was more interested in the exploits of *The Troubleshooters*.

Halfway through *Panorama* was an interview with the Chief Executive of the new nuclear reprocessing plant down in Dartmoor. Alistair leaned forward to watch; afterwards he leaned back with a deep sigh.

'I don't want to put two and two together and make five, but that man bothered you, didn't he?'

'What, Robin Day?' Alistair shook his head and cleared his throat. 'Terrible taste in clothes. Bow ties should only be worn by waiters and snooker commentators.'

Sally nudged him in the ribs. 'No, that director chap.'

Alistair looked away. 'Yes. Yes he did. Something about him.'

'It's not because he's foreign, is it? Dutch, I think. Surely not, Alistair!'

'Foreign? No…' Alistair stared into the middle distance, a shadow passing across his face. 'But if Director Dominic Vaar's a Dutchman – well, then I'm a Dutchman.'

Sally stayed for another couple of hours but never did get to the bottom of what Alistair had meant by that cryptic statement.

CHAPTER FIVE

Out on the Moor

Dartmoor crept up on you, then leapt out at you. At its edges, the countryside was idyllic picture-postcard England, all narrow winding lanes, high hedges, tiny villages and low, conspiratorial clusters of farm buildings. Even a mile or so into the moor, this rural serenity prevailed, and as Chorley drove out of Buckfastleigh, he wondered if he had taken a wrong turning. He passed fields with grazing cows, and distant views of the sort of patchwork countryside seen anywhere in the country. He wound through the tiny hamlets of Scorriton and Holne, three miles into the moor, and still all seemed pretty much the usual sort of countryside. After Scorriton, however, the road rose sharply, and the higher he got, the lower the hedges became, the wilder the trees seemed to look, and the blue sky seemed to get nearer and wider. Then he came to a cattle grid, and once across he was – suddenly – on Dartmoor.

It was like another world. On either side of the old grey road, the grass, cropped billiard-table short by countless generations of sheep, shone impossibly green in the early June sun. Bare rocks, scoured, pitted and weathered, were dotted here and there, between the fronds of bracken and great clumps of prickly gorse. The trees and bushes appeared theatrically windswept; their branches seeming to beckon or to warn. The land rolled away in blankets of brown and green. As he drove, slowed by awe at the solemn beauty of it all, it occurred to Harold Chorley that you could hide anything out here, do anything. This was a place of secrets. A place where the things beneath the surface world could surface. No wonder the locals talked of piskies.

Harold Chorley's Dartmoor.

Chorley took the Imp to the top of a rise and pulled in at a picnic area. He was not surprised to see that there were a few other cars and camper vans enjoying the splendour of the oh-so-brief British summer. Disembarking from the little car, Chorley ignored the shrieking children spoiling the immortal and immense natural beauty and gazed hands on hips at the undulating khaki landscape, every inch the experienced hiker surveying his route – or at least, he hoped. He ground his teeth as the children pointed and laughed at his tan-coloured shorts and his thin, pale legs. Well, what else was he supposed to wear on a blinding hot day like this?

Nodding and smiling to an old couple playing cards on a picnic table next to their olive-green Morris Minor, Chorley bent to adjust the laces on his hiking boots, hoping no one would notice their virgin state. He wondered who he was expecting to be watching him, but you could never be sure. He remembered Lethbridge-Stewart's warnings. The most dangerous business on Earth. Ultimate force.

Chorley spread his OS map on the roof of the Imp and frowned down at it, pretending to know where the hell he was. Well, that was the road out of Buckfastleigh, he'd come through those two villages, Scorriton was the second one, so he must be – he placed a finger on the map – right about there. And Gibby Combe Lane – marked in red biro – was, fortunately, the next left turning after this picnic area.

Right! Off we go!

Shouldering a small rucksack (also brand new) and popping a straw boater (from his college days) atop his head (the sun really was punishing), Chorley waved at the old couple, curled his lip at the pesky kids who were still laughing at his shorts, and strode off along the road, trying to whistle a carefree tune and almost succeeding.

Gibby Combe Lane, at the end of which – according to the Companies House records – lay the Dominex complex, was indeed next left, a few hundred yards past the picnic area. It led gently down into a shallow valley, then rose more steeply again to the horizon, sharply dark against the blue of the sky. Chorley set off down the lane, no longer whistling, concocting various stories in case he was questioned or challenged. He was a German tourist and he was lost, *danke schön*. Perhaps not, on second thoughts. He might be taken for a spy. Well then, he was a historian looking for the remains of a Roman hill fort. A history lecturer from Leeds. Could he do that accent? Best say he was from London, play to his strengths. Were there Roman forts on Dartmoor? He didn't know, and, hopefully, neither would anyone who challenged him. But weren't there Roman remains everywhere? Course there were. So, yes, he was Peter Carver, lecturer in ancient history from the City of London Polytechnic. On his hols poking about for some ancient ruins. He was not, absolutely not, Harold Chorley, journalist. Never heard of the chap.

At the bottom of the valley was a bridge over a stream which chuckled brightly and busily over exposed granite, and Chorley stopped for a drink from his flask (this time filled with iced water). Looking around, he saw he was utterly alone. No car had passed him, and he hadn't seen another soul since the picnic area. Good. But he still felt a shadow of unease pass across his mind. He thought of the missing hikers and glanced up at the sky.

It was absolutely clear, not a single cloud. Could a mist drop down even out of this beautiful blue? Even if it did, he'd be okay if he stuck to the road, he'd be able to follow it back to the picnic site and the Imp. Thus self-reassured, Chorley walked on, the shirt under the rucksack uncomfortably wet with sweat.

Soon he reached the top of the rise on the other side of the valley, and there it was: Dominex.

It lay at the bottom of the next valley, and somehow it looked mundane against the wild, alien landscape of the moor. Mundane, but massive. Even at this distance it was clearly the size of several football pitches. A central, grey, blocky structure was ringed with a series of smaller structures of various shapes and sizes. Gibby Combe Lane led right up to the gates of the installation. On the other side of the valley the land rose steeply to a brown shoulder topped with the strange, almost alien shape of a granite tor – Black Tor, according to the map.

There was no sign of movement or life, not even any sound.

Chorley set off down the lane, not even trying to whistle. His stomach growled – it was coming up to lunchtime, and the fry-up he'd had at *The White Hart* for breakfast only seemed to have made him hungrier. He produced a Scotch egg from his rucksack and ate it mechanically, eyes fixed on the Dominex complex as he approached.

This close, the place looked like some kind of technological castle, but still there was no movement, no signs of life.

I'm Peter Carver, I'm looking for this Roman fort and it looks like you bally fools have built this thing smack bang on top of it! He adopted an appropriate expression of indignation and marched up to the gates.

No patches of oil on the road outside or inside, so not much traffic. There was no gatehouse, just a pair of metal gates, bearing a sign which read:

DOMINEX INDUSTRIES
KEEP OUT!
TRESPASSERS WILL BE PROSCUTED

Low standards of spelling and grammar always depressed him. He shook his head sadly, before remembering he was not Harold Chorley, he was Peter Carver, and Peter Carver wasn't too bothered about bad grammar; he was more interested in looking for his Roman fort.

He began to lope theatrically alongside the chain-link fence, peering through, trying to discern some sign of life. But there was nothing. He gazed up at the shining towers and grey, block-like outbuildings. He could hear a distant buzzing hum, as of machinery. He began to get the distinct impression that he was being watched.

After walking aimlessly up and down the fence for a few minutes, Chorley as Carver turned abruptly aside and marched off with what he hoped would be seen as affronted dignity back toward Gibby Combe Lane. As he walked up the road he became aware of a low rumbling and chuntering coming from over the brow of the hill. It became louder and louder and a lorry appeared on the horizon, driving down Gibby Combe Lane, straight at Chorley. Another followed it, and another. Three lorries, painted a dull grey. Army trucks? They had the look of the military, but they bore an ominous yellow and black warning symbol on their doors. Chorley stood back from the road as the three lorries passed him, barely slowing as they neared the gates of the Dominex plant, which slid open with a painful-sounding squeal of protesting metal.

Chorley suddenly felt exposed, and cast around for somewhere to hide, but the clumps of gorse and bracken on the moor would barely hide a squirrel, let alone a journalist – or history lecturer. Then he thought, *why should I hide? This is public land. I'm not trespassing, so they can't 'proscute' me.* So he, as Peter Carver, stood waving at the lorries as they trundled past and through the gates, acting as if he were overseeing the delivery.

He watched the last lorry pass through the gates, observing the warning symbols on its rear. He fought a sudden impulse to run after it, but instead stood his ground and watched as the gates slid shut, wincing at the squealing noise they made. There was no sentry, not even a sentry box – the gates were automated. Controlled from within. Tiny black boxes perched atop the fence posts were obviously cameras, observing him, observing everything.

Chorley shivered. He watched the lorries until they disappeared around a corner behind a block-like grey building. The arrival of the lorries tallied with what he knew about Dominex so far.

He turned and walked back along Gibby Combe Lane, unable to shake the feeling that he was being watched.

When he got back to the picnic spot he saw that a VW camper van had parked next to the Imp. A dirty VW camper van, decorated with a swirling, floral pattern in every colour of the rainbow, which looked like it had seen quite some travelling. Pop music blared from the open windows. Of the old couple and the screaming children, there was no sign – in fact, all other vehicles had departed.

Chorley marched quickly up to the Imp, not wanting to endure the inevitable derision that would be heaped his way if the beautiful people clapped eyes on his shorts and his skinny legs. Not to mention his straw hat.

Too late! With a squeal of protesting metal the side door of the van slid open and a tall, ginger-haired figure in blue bell-bottomed jeans and a green tie-dyed t-shirt emerged. Chorley yanked open the Imp's driver door but something about the approaching shambling figure made him pause.

He looked familiar, but before Chorley could place the (unshaven) face he was seized and almost lifted off his feet in a massive bear hug. 'Hey, man!' growled a voice in his ear.

When he was returned to *terra firma* Chorley saw that others had emerged from the van, and were staring at Chorley with suspicious, if slightly vacant, expressions.

The ginger fellow turned to his comrades and spread his arms wide. 'Hey, guys! It's the journo!'

Chorley brushed himself down and adjusted his straw boater, which had almost been shoved off in the embrace. Suddenly he remembered. 'Mike?'

Mike – for it was he – was excitedly explaining to the others the events of Saturday. Chorley smiled at the small crowd that had now gathered around him – there were half a dozen of them – knowing full well how square he must look, feeling again that he, instead of them, was the true style revolutionary.

He found himself clasped again by Mike. 'This guy saved us. You saved us from the pigs, man!'

The events in Little America were a confused jumble in Chorley's memory. 'Did I? I think you're rather overstating it.'

Mike shook his shaggy head. 'No, man, if you hadn't shoved us past those horses we'd have been arrested!'

He was just about to ask where Emma was when she appeared, stepping lightly down from the van. She was barefoot, and wore a long white dress patterned in pink and yellow flowers, fastened at the waist by a wide daisy-patterned belt. The sun shone through her dark hair, making it appear golden. Chorley felt the world fall away from beneath him. He put his left hand in his shorts pocket, to hide the wedding ring.

'Hello, Mister Freelance,' she said with a cheeky smile, extending a hand.

Not knowing what to do or say, he took her hand, and bizarrely felt the urge to bow and kiss it, but turned the gesture into a nod. He managed to say 'Hello' and then remembered his knees. 'Under cover,' he muttered.

'Obviously.' Emma frowned in concern. 'Hey, we looked for you after it had all died down but couldn't find you.'

'Yes, well, I was carted off to the nick!' Chorley said, suddenly reminded of the whole hellish experience. He fervently hoped Lethbridge-Stewart was busily getting that breach of the peace charge quashed. 'What are you doing down here?'

Mike grinned. 'We're gonna take our protest right to the doors of Dominex, man!'

There was a chorus of 'Yeah' from the others.

'Did you see the lorries just now?' said Mike, his smile turning into a scowl. 'Taking their filth up onto the moor!'

There were rumbles of assent from the others.

'You said you were under cover,' said Emma. 'So are you here to investigate Dominex?'

Chorley hesitated, decided on a half-truth. 'Just following up on the missing hikers' story. And having a bit of a holiday. So... what exactly does your protest involve?' He imagined the ragged bunch storming the implacable Dominex fortress and had to suppress a laugh.

'We're holding a midnight vigil right outside their gates. Light some candles for those disappeared hikers.' Emma's face brightened. 'You should join us.'

'Maybe.' Chorley felt that he should warn them to stay away from Dominex, but there really didn't seem to be anything to warn them about. Despite his instincts, it looked like this was going to be a non-story. He watched as two of the hippies started building a fire at the edge of the picnic area. Wasn't that forbidden? He didn't have the heart to remonstrate with them. What harm could it possibly do? 'Anyway, I'm back off to town to write up my notes.'

'What? All the way to London?'

Chorley waved an arm vaguely in the direction of Buckfastleigh. 'Oh, somewhere local.'

Emma and Mike exchanged glances and Chorley

imagined them in *The White Hart* and the reaction of Sid and the others. It seemed he had found people even less welcome round here than he was.

'We'll see you later then,' said Emma with a smile.

'Yeah, later, man!' beamed Mike. He'd certainly changed his tune. He must have really believed that Chorley had saved them from prison. Although, as a certain sweet-acrid smell reached his nose, perhaps there were further reasons.

Chorley fumbled with his keys but managed to drive away without further embarrassing himself. The vision of Emma, her lithe body clad in that floral dress like some summery goddess, her calm intelligent eyes and patient, welcoming smile, floated before him as he took the road back down from the moor.

Perhaps he would turn up for the midnight vigil, after all.

CHAPTER SIX

Your Future is Our Business

It was a glorious summer day and Lethbridge-Stewart sat in his office in his shirt-sleeves, wishing he had the chance to get out of the Barracks and enjoy the weather. No chance of that – far too much to do. He had spent most of the morning reviewing deployment orders given by Colonel Grierson for the various Guards regiments that were stationed at Chelsea Barracks, and going through more names on Hamilton's list, half-expecting – *half-hoping* – Chorley to phone in from his Devon investigations at any time. At eleven o'clock he brewed some coffee and picked up the phone himself. He dialled a number first given to him by Mr Benn, which he had since committed to memory, and the phone was answered promptly.

'Anne Travers.'

'Good morning, Miss Travers. Lethbridge-Stewart here.'

'Colonel, always good to hear from you. Did you receive my report?' Lethbridge-Stewart said he had; it had arrived direct at his front door this morning. He had read it over his morning tea before heading off to the Barracks. It confirmed everything she had told him about the events at the end of April. 'However, that's not why I called. I need your scientific advice. It's about this nuclear waste recycling company, Dominex.'

'Reprocessing,' Miss Travers responded absently. 'Thanks, Len, if you could put that there.' The sound of movement on the other end of the line, then her voice became clearer again. 'Sorry about that, Colonel. What about Dominex?'

'It may be nothing. Just want to understand what they're about. Saw the head honcho on *Panorama* last night, talking about this new process they've got, absorption something or other.'

'Negative Mass Flux Absorption, yes, I read about it in the *New Scientist*. They say they can turn nuclear waste into energy.'

'Is that possible?'

Miss Travers was silent for a moment. 'Tricky.'

'Well, can it be done?'

'Not by any process I know of. You see, nuclear waste remains radioactive for hundreds, thousands of years. There's no way to get rid of the transuranic heavy elements, and render it safe.'

'Not by any process *you* know of. What about other experts in the field?'

'They're all stumped too, even at the British Nuclear Defence Control Centre. They are dying to investigate it but Dominex are keeping it secret.'

'So you could say it's at the cutting edge of technology.'

'You could say that it's leaving the cutting edge of technology standing at the starting line with its shoelaces tied together.'

Lethbridge-Stewart thought of the heavy, cruel features of Director Dominic Vaar. He thought of Harold Chorley and the missing hikers. He thought of the protestors and the conspiracy theorists. He closed his eyes. 'Could you even say that it's beyond the technology of our planet?'

'You could. Or it could *just* be a wonderful new process that some genius in Dominex has thought up and is guarding from the rest of the scientific world. I can hardly blame them.'

'Quite. You've heard the conspiracy theories, I take it?'

'That Dominex are making nuclear weapons?'

'Yes. Is that possible? To make nuclear weapons – from nuclear waste?'

'It... might be. But it's pointless, and dangerous. No one would bother. Reactor-grade plutonium, for example – found in spent nuclear fuel rods – is far too dangerous to work with. You'd have to reprocess it to separate out the plutonium, and that would create fission products so radioactive and volatile that it's just not worth the risk. Better to make weapons-grade plutonium in the first place.'

'You mentioned reprocessing – that's exactly what Dominex are up to.'

'Yes, but to reprocess reactor-grade plutonium; it's too risky.'

'But if they had superior technology, unknown to us?'

Miss Travers sighed. 'We're at risk of seeing aliens in every shadow, Colonel. But, given the last few months, I have to say, I can't rule it out. But it's very, very unlikely.'

Lethbridge-Stewart thought of Chorley, down in Devon, nosing around and asking questions. He thought of Dominic Vaar refusing to be intimidated by Robin Day. 'I do hope you're right, Miss Travers. For all our sakes.'

When Chorley got back to the pub, it was as if nothing had

changed. Perhaps it never did. Perhaps if were to return in a decade, or somehow travel ten years into the past, he would have found them the same way: Sid would still be propping up the end of the bar, Phil still mumbling into his pint, Cyril polishing yet another glass. Chorley bought a half of lager and retreated to the far side of the saloon, where Ian Cawdery was sitting with his newspaper. The teacher gave Chorley a hostile glare, seemed to think better of it, and nodded curtly.

Chorley sat down opposite him. 'Look, I'm sorry about earlier. I didn't know.'

Ian shook his head. 'No, it was my fault. I over-reacted. You weren't to know. But grief – it does things to you that you don't expect. I find myself going for long walks at night, talking to Matthew.'

The rawness of Ian's emotion, his honesty, made him feel uncomfortable. Chorley had been young when his parents had died, and had never experienced bereavement in his adult life. He'd never been close to any of his colleagues, except Larry Greene; he wasn't sure how he'd cope with losing Larry completely.

'Can I buy you a pint?' Chorley asked.

'Better not,' said Ian. Chorley realised that the man hadn't moved from the pub since before lunchtime. He must have put away, what, five, six pints?

Ian took a final swig at his beer, draining the glass. 'It helps. For a bit.' He lapsed into a forbidding, impenetrable silence.

Chorley thought for a moment. 'Maybe I will have that pint, after all. No, put your money away, I'll sort myself out. Sure I can't tempt you?'

Ian gave the smallest of nods, his eyes lost in memories of the past.

That was all Chorley required. He needed to draw this fellow out, find out more about his brother and what had happened to him. He returned to the table, setting the pints down gently on the beermats. He sat supping in silence for a while.

'So, was Matthew a regular caver? Only been caving once myself. It was enough. Wookey Hole.'

A flicker of interest. 'Amateur hour.'

'Oh, I know. Still, it was enough for me. Managed to fall and twist my ankle. Had to be carried out on a stretcher.'

'Put you off for life, did it?'

'Well, yes,' said Chorley, feigning awkwardness. 'Don't really like to talk about it. But I've always been a bit claustrophobic.'

'At least you got out alive,' said Ian with feeling. He took a deep pull of his pint, then sighed. 'Look, I'm sorry, I'm being rude. Must have been a terrible experience for you, especially if you're claustrophobic.'

'That's okay, I wasn't meaning to equate my experience with your loss. I mean, a twisted ankle… it's nothing.'

Ian was staring into space again, lost in reminiscence. Eventually, he spoke.

'It was my fault. Well, partly. Matthew and his friend Adrian came down to see me and do a spot of caving. I'm a pretty experienced caver myself, so all three of us were going to go down into the caves beneath Black Tor.' He paused, gazing into the distance. 'I wouldn't be speaking to you now if I had gone with them.'

'Why didn't you?' Chorley prompted gently.

Ian shifted uncomfortably. 'I had an argument with Matthew about his lifestyle, his choice of friends. It was the drink…' Ian stared at his pint intently. 'I got drunk, said stupid things I regret. The morning after, I woke up with a stinking hangover, to find they had gone. No note, nothing. They'd taken their kit, so I knew they had gone caving. They never came back.' Ian seemed to fold in on himself, holding his head in his hands.

Chorley knew the rest. Search parties had been sent out, gone down into the caves, but had found nothing, and the case has officially been closed. Out of respect, the caves had been sealed off; presumably they still were.

Unbidden, Chorley rose and asked the landlord for a double whisky.

'You should leave him be,' whispered Cyril as he poured the drink. 'He's been through enough without you sticking your nose in.'

'Sorry,' muttered Chorley and returned to the table. 'Here, drink this.'

Ian downed it automatically. It seemed to revive him.

'You can't blame yourself,' Chorley began hesitantly.

'I can. And I do. If only there was something I could do…'

'Look, some people I know are holding a vigil up there tonight. In memory of the missing hikers. If you wanted…?' Chorley tailed off.

Ian rose unsteadily to his feet. 'Thanks, but no thanks. I'll deal with it in my own way. Even if it is the wrong way.' He reached again for his glass, grumbled at its emptiness, and staggered out into the night.

Chorley half-rose to follow him, but caught Cyril's

disapproving gaze and thought better of it. Perhaps a quick progress report to Lethbridge-Stewart? But he had nothing to report – yet. Hardly worth bothering the chap. Perhaps another pint.

Back in London, Lethbridge-Stewart was conducting his own investigations into Dominex.

He started by visiting their London offices, which were housed on the penultimate floor of a shiny new glass and concrete office block in Victoria. If the receptionist, a young, pretty blonde in specs and chic Mary Quant dress, was surprised by the sight of his uniform, she didn't show it. She merely requested politely that he take a seat while she found out if anyone was free to see him.

The plush reception area was silent, furnished with blocky sofas and decorated with what, Lethbridge-Stewart assumed, were examples of modern art: squares of canvas upon which geometric designs intertwined in a way which foxed the eyes. To avoid looking at these, he picked up one of the magazines that lay stacked in neat piles on the smoked-glass coffee table. Except it wasn't a magazine, it was Dominex Industries' prospectus. The cover showed green fields under an unrealistically blue sky and bore the legend: *Dominex – Your Future is Our Business.* A glossy affair full of corporate speak and facts and figures about nuclear waste reprocessing, all of it beyond him. He flicked through its heavy pages looking for a biography of Director Vaar. Nothing. He tossed it back on the table.

'I see you're admiring our brochure.'

Lethbridge-Stewart looked up to see a slim young chap in a grey suit and pale blue kipper tie emerge through the inner door, hand outstretched.

'Yes, I was.' Lethbridge-Stewart rose and they shook hands.

'Jack Redmond, Chief Administrator for Dominex Industries.' His grip was firm and dry, his gaze calm and collected.

'Colonel Alistair Lethbridge-Stewart.'

Redmond gestured for him to sit. 'Can I get you anything? Cup of tea, coffee?'

'No, thank you, I'm fine.'

Redmond sat on the edge of the sofa, hands clasped loosely in his lap. 'May I ask what the purpose of your visit is?'

'Security.' It was vague, but it was also true. 'I'm heading up a taskforce concerned with monitoring the security of the nuclear industry.' That bit was not at all true, but Lethbridge-Stewart hoped it would fly.

Redmond frowned. 'This is news to me. We are already closely monitored by the Atomic Energy Authority.'

'I am well aware of that, Mr Redmond. It was the AEA chairman himself, Sir Edwin Plowden, who set up this taskforce. Something with a military remit. Dangerous business you're involved in, after all. Lots of people would be interested in taking you down. Competitors, for example. And then there's the terrorism angle. You have sufficient fissile material to cause us great concern, should it fall into the wrong hands.'

Redmond bristled. 'Security is our paramount concern, and our Dartmoor operation is impregnable.'

Touched a nerve there. 'Perhaps so. There are, however, other concerns about your operation down on Dartmoor.'

'You mean the missing people?' said Redmond blandly.

Lad is sharp, Lethbridge-Stewart thought. 'Indeed. Within the last four months, four people have gone missing in the vicinity of your plant.'

'We have already issued a statement concerning that. I drafted it myself. And we will continue to co-operate with the proper authorities.'

There was an edge to the last two words that Lethbridge-Stewart chose to ignore. 'I'm glad to hear it. We're still concerned, however, that due to the extreme secrecy of your process, there is something you're not telling us.'

'Colonel Lethbridge-Stewart, I say again, we have co-operated fully,' said Redmond hotly. 'Dominex has nothing to hide!'

'What's your background, Mr Redmond?' said Lethbridge-Stewart smoothly. 'How did you come to work for Dominex?'

Redmond smiled, not at all caught out by the abrupt change of tack. 'Came here straight from University. Sheffield. It's very exciting working for such a brave, new industry.'

Lethbridge-Stewart glanced over at the blonde receptionist. 'Are you all graduates here?'

'Oh yes, except for the chief executive and other directors.'

'Have you ever seen this chief executive?'

Redmond frowned. 'Of course! Director Vaar has an office here, on the floor above.'

Lethbridge-Stewart glanced up at the tiled ceiling. 'What do you know of your director's background?'

'He grew up on a small farm in, now let me see, one of

those Eastern European places. I can't quite recall. Very hard to pronounce.'

Not Dutch, then. 'Have you ever wondered why he decided to come to this country with his process, rather than remaining behind the Iron Curtain?'

Redmond beamed a corporate smile. 'Director Vaar was able to secure very generous funding from the UK Government.'

Lethbridge-Stewart wasn't sure he cared for the insinuation. 'Any chance of a meeting with the director?'

Redmond smiled, but there was steel in his gaze. 'I'm afraid not, Colonel.' He rose smoothly from his seat. 'Now, if you'll excuse me, I have very many pressing duties to which I must attend.'

Back at Chelsea Barracks, Lethbridge-Stewart called the office of Sir Anthony Bufton.

'The Minister of State for Energy's office?' The voice was crisp, officious, male and middle-aged.

'Yes, I'd like to request an urgent meeting with the minister.'

'Who's calling, please?'

'Colonel Alistair Lethbridge-Stewart.'

'And what's the matter you'd like to discuss?'

'Dominex.'

There's was the merest pause. 'Let me check the minister's diary.' There was the gentle knock of the receiver being placed on a desk. A polished oak desk, no doubt, thought Lethbridge-Stewart. He'd had experience of dealing with these Civil Service johnnies before. Had to be patient. Wheels of bureaucracy turned very slowly. And they never told you the whole story. The brief pause after he'd mentioned the name Dominex, however, had spoken volumes. Touched a nerve there. Dodgy dealings?

The PA's voice broke into his thoughts. 'I'm very sorry, sir, but the minister's diary is completely full for the next three weeks.'

'This is a matter of National Security.'

'Really.' The PA did not sound impressed, or convinced. 'Sir Anthony is personally involved with Dominex, as you know. He was behind their grant application. He believes totally that Dominex are working for the best interests of the country. If there are any concerns about National Security, then this is the first this office has heard of them. Would you care to elaborate?'

The voice was now icy, challenging. *Perhaps I've gone too far.* But he couldn't turn back now. 'Not over the telephone. I really would prefer a face-to-face meeting with the minister.'

The PA's voice dripped with false politeness. 'I do apologise, but as I just said, the minister is fully booked for the next three weeks. If you would care to put your concerns in a letter, I will pass it to him for his consideration in due course.'

'Thank you. I will.'

There was a *click* and the line went dead.

Lethbridge-Stewart had no intention of writing a letter, of course. For one thing, there simply wasn't time. Chorley was down there in Devon poking around – and how he wished he was there with him – and he needed gen on Dominex *now.*

— CHAPTER SEVEN —

The Quarks Attack

A t 9pm, after an evening meal consisting of yet another Cornish pasty, Chorley drove back onto the moor, leaving his wedding ring on the bedside table. It was still light, and would be for almost an hour yet. He reached the picnic spot, expecting to find the VW van, but it was not to be seen. The place had been reclaimed by the straights who were there to enjoy the spectacular sunset over the moor. The only sign of the presence of the hippies was a charred black circle on the grass where they had made their fire.

He drove on, down Gibby Combe Lane and up the other side, and then over to where the Dominex complex sat enigmatically in its valley. Even though it wasn't yet dark, lights were on all around the perimeter fence and on the main buildings. And there, to the left of the main gates, Emma and Mike and their gang had set up camp. The VW van sat at the centre of a circle of two-man tents, their canvas adorned with flowers, rainbows and the familiar CND logo. A small fire sent smoke up into the clear sky. Figures sat around the it; others danced in the orange half-light. As Chorley drew near, they waved.

He parked the Imp a little distance away. The smell of pot and woodsmoke that met his nostrils as he got out made the night seem exciting, enticing. Emma ran out to meet him. She was still wearing that white floral dress, still barefoot, as the night was warm.

'Come and meet the gang!' Emma took him by the hand and led him to the circle of tents. She paraded him around as if he was some sort of prize specimen. As well as Mike there was a lugubrious-looking chap with long brown hair called Nigel, two skinny girls of about Emma's age called Daisy and Denise, a youth in leathers called Dave, and an older fellow with grey in his beard, all in denims, called Barry. Apparently there used to be an Owain, but he moved on with a girl called Jennie some time ago. They either seemed extremely interested to see him, as in the case of the two girls, and Barry and Dave, or completely uninterested, as in the case of Nigel.

Chorley took a seat by the fire and accepted a can of lager from Mike. He indicated the Dominex installation which towered over them. Next to the mis-spelled warning signs they had taped their 'DOMINEX OUT!' sign. 'You've got a bit of nerve.'

'Have we?' said Emma. She laughed. 'We're not trespassing, so we're not gonna be *proscuted*!'

He watched the two girls dancing with Dave and Barry. 'Seems a bit jolly for a vigil.'

'We're gonna light the candles at midnight. Until then, it's party time! Let your hair down!'

'I haven't got any hair to let down,' retorted Chorley drily.

This prompted a laugh. 'Well, you should grow it, man! Lose the square image.'

'I would, but it's for the job. I did try once. But my hair doesn't grow down, it grows out, into a sort of Afro.'

Emma laughed. 'Wow! That would be so cool. You should do it.'

What the hell was he doing, blabbing on about his hair? But in Emma's presence, he felt that he could say anything. Something about her made him want to open up. She was different to the others. He got the impression that the others didn't really care about the missing people, or indeed Dominex; they just wanted an excuse to party. But after talking to Emma for a while, he found that she was deeply committed to the CND cause. He also discovered that she and Mike used to be a couple, but had now split up, and this news stirred him more than it perhaps should have. He told her about the interview with the Dominex CEO, and about his plans to provide free energy via some new process. 'So they're doing good,' he concluded.

'Or it all could be a smokescreen, to disguise their real intent – building nuclear weapons.'

'Do you really believe that? Honestly?' asked Chorley.

'I don't know,' said Emma after a moment's thought. 'It's more that I don't trust nuclear power. It's just too dangerous, the risks far outweigh the benefits. I mean, even if Dominex aren't building bombs, just storing waste, it leaves them open to attack. What if someone decided to turn that place…?' She waved a hand over at the Dominex plant, the chainlink fence gleaming steel under the perimeter lights. '…into a giant bomb?'

Chorley shifted uncomfortably and took another swig of lager.

'And the waste itself is deadly. Despite what Dominex claim, there's no way to totally get rid of it, let alone turn it into energy. It causes cancer, poisons the land. It's our duty as humans to protect the planet.' Emma gazed into the darkening distance.

By now it was 10pm and the last vestiges of light were fading from the sky. The outline of a story began to form in Chorley's mind. *Nuclear Power – Everything You Wanted to Know But Were Afraid to Ask*. Sounded good. Or maybe something on the counterculture, to make people realise that these hippies were real people, not just idle layabouts. Some of them even had jobs – well, one, anyway; Dave was a car mechanic from Crediton.

'I know it's for your job,' said Emma out of the blue. 'But you look so totally square.'

Her accent was Home Counties, even posh. What was she doing hanging around with this lot?

'What brought you here, Emma? Apart from the protest, of course. What's waiting back home? Husband? Job?'

For a moment Chorley thought she wasn't going to answer, but she threw her head back and affected an even posher accent and said, 'Oh, I'm a spoilt little rich kid. My dad's a senior police inspector and my mum's a lawyer.'

'They must love all this.'

'They tolerate it. They think it's a phase I'll soon grow out of. When, of course, it isn't. Oh, I love them, but they're so blind to what's going on in the world. Which is worrying, given their careers.'

'Do you still live with them?'

'I stay with them from time to time. They keep my room for me. The family home is this massive pile in Hastings. But since dropping out of uni I've been staying with friends, in squats, even sleeping in that damned van.'

'What were you studying before you dropped out?'

Emma gave an uncharacteristically bitter laugh. 'Law, at London. That's where I met Mike. He was studying politics.' She gazed wistfully at the lolloping figure of Mike as he danced with Daisy and Denise. 'He got me into all this. We both dropped out and have been hanging around with this lot ever since.'

She's what, twenty-one, twenty-two? Chorley thought. He was old enough to be – well, if not her father, then certainly her older brother. Her square, boring older brother.

'What about you? How did you end up being a journalist?'

'A lifelong desire to tell the truth.' It was his stock answer, and it was almost true. There was that, but there was also the desire to always be the centre of attention. He was a narcissist, and he knew it – so what, so be it, there were much worse character defects. 'And of course there's the glamour and adventure of it.' He gestured at the dancing girls, the flickering flames, the sullen men and the van.

Emma laughed. Chorley hoped she was laughing with him, not at him.

He was desperately casting about for something excruciatingly witty to say when he realised that the singing and dancing had stopped. Everyone was staring over towards the Dominex plant.

Mike ran over to them. 'Hey guys! There's something in there!'

Chorley sprang to his feet, as did Emma. They both looked towards the gates. A few yards beyond them, two blocky shapes were shuffling forward. Because of the bright perimeter lights and the steel rails of the gates, Chorley couldn't quite make out any detail. Then he remembered what Cyril had said about the plant. Automation. 'Guard robots?'

The others, except Barry and Nigel who were standing back by the fire, had run up to the gates and were calling to the approaching figures.

'Get back!' cried Chorley.

With a rasping squeal of protesting aluminium, the gates slid open sideways, revealing the true shape of the advancing figures, outlined clearly in the bright sodium lights.

They were short, barely five feet high, with bodies the size and shape of small refrigerators, on top of which sat spiked, spherical heads. From their bodies, rectangular appendages protruded. If they were guard robots, they didn't look very formidable. But something about them scared Chorley. They were strange, they were sinister – they were *other*. They were from that other world, the one below the surface, from whence the Yeti had come with their glowing eyes, shattering roars and suffocating web guns.

'What are they?' cried Emma.

'I don't know, but I suggest we get the hell out of here!' Grabbing Emma's hand he retreated back towards the VW van.

Lethbridge-Stewart sat at a corner table in a Soho pub with Doug Scanlon, Senior Systems Engineer at Global Power, opposite him.

'Damn Dominex.' Scanlon took a deep pull of his pint.

It was late, gone 10pm, but it was the only time Scanlon had been available. He'd had to attend an evening dinner with some potential investors – investors Global was desperate to secure. Lethbridge-Stewart had spun him more or less the same story he'd told Redmond.

'Damn Dominex,' said Scanlon once more.

'Do they really pose that much of a threat?'

'Are bears Catholic?' Scanlon was a slight, hunched, wiry fellow in his late forties with thinning sandy hair and pale blue, slightly bulging eyes that reminded Lethbridge-Stewart of poached eggs. He wore a shabby tweed jacket and old school tie. 'The blighters waltz right into this country and the energy minister rolls right over waving his legs in the air. Before you know it, bang! Massive base down on Dartmoor and all the funding they need.'

'Well, you can see why,' said Lethbridge-Stewart, sipping his pint. 'I need hardly tell you that the nuclear industry is still really in its infancy, and you can't blame the government for wanting to take advantage of Dominex's new process. Negative Mass, er, whatever it was.' Lethbridge-Stewart noticed Scanlon's expression. 'Sorry, I'm a military man, not a scientist.'

'Negative Mass Flux Absorption, they call it.' Scanlon banged the table with a clenched fist. 'Ridiculous! Never heard anything like it. Can't find out anything about it, either.' He leaned across the pints to Lethbridge-Stewart, those bulging eyes bulging even more. 'I can count on your confidentiality?'

'Of course.'

'Industrial espionage is a fact of life. Everyone accepts it. But our chaps haven't found out a damned thing about Dominex or their process. Of course, they haven't patented it – if they did, then it would be public knowledge, so no problem. But they haven't. So short of going down to Devon and breaking in to the place, we're stumped.'

Lethbridge-Stewart coughed. 'Well, quite. Do you have

84

any view on the conspiracy theories? That Dominex are building nuclear weapons?'

Scanlon laughed. 'No! How could they be? If they were assembling fissile material, we'd know. Or rather, the AEA would know!'

'But this new process. You say you don't know anything about it.'

Scanlon waved a hand dismissively. 'Utter rubbish. Dominex may be giving our shareholders sleepless nights – and me, for that matter – but building nuclear weapons? On Dartmoor? For a start, why?'

Lethbridge-Stewart sipped his pint thoughtfully. The fellow had a point. But no smoke without fire. 'There's another security aspect I'm interested in. The missing people.'

Scanlon shook his head. 'Can't see it myself. Dartmoor's notorious for disappearances. Those mists! Especially the inexperienced.'

'But the two missing cavers were experienced men.'

Scanlon shrugged. 'Caves are dangerous places.'

'Their bodies were never found.'

'Not surprised. Plenty of places for bodies to fall into oblivion, underground lakes, rockfalls, and so on. Look, I'm not being callous. I really don't think Dominex – jammy blighters though they undoubtedly are – had anything to do with it.'

Lethbridge-Stewart finished his pint. Time to head home. It had been a long, interesting, though ultimately rather fruitless day. He stood up. 'Thank you for your time, Mr Scanlon.'

Scanlon didn't rise, but offered his hand. 'If you do ever

find any dirt on Dominex, let me know. I could do with the laugh, if nothing else.'

Chorley watched aghast as the two robots marched out of the complex. The two girls, Daisy and Denise, were dancing directly in the path of the advancing robots, laughing and throwing clumps of earth at them. The things appeared oblivious. They stopped a few yards outside the gates.

Then they spoke, in harsh, shrill, piercing voices.

'Depart! Depart! Or we will destroy!'

Mike roared with derision. 'We're not going anywhere, mate!'

One of the things extended an arm. There was a blinding flash, a sizzling roar, then an ear-numbing thump. Chorley flinched as the ground in front of Mike exploded, sending him flying backwards. The girls screamed and ran for the safety of the van, where Barry and Nigel had already taken refuge.

'We will destroy!' shrilled the robots.

All of a sudden it became horribly clear what had happened to the missing hikers – and to Ian's brother and his friend.

The things advanced, coming between Emma and Chorley and the van, which was already pulling away from the scene. Chorley grabbed Emma's hand and dragged her in the other direction, towards his car. There was another sizzling roar, and something like a firework soared past Chorley's left ear, half-blinding him, making his head ring.

Then the Imp exploded.

A blooming orange fireball, a wall of heat and Chorley was blown back onto the grass, Emma landing heavily on his arm. Stunned, disoriented, half-blinded and half-deafened, Chorley lay in a timeless limbo as the world raged around him. *My car! My car, the blasted things have killed my car!* And then the urge to flee, to survive, got hold of him, and sucking in great burning lungfuls of air, he hauled himself to his feet, pulling Emma with him. They clung to each other, staring in disbelief at the burning wreckage of what had once been Chorley's Hillman Imp.

'Destroy! Destroy! Destroy!'

Chorley screamed, not caring how scared he sounded. The things were right behind them. And as he watched, their casings unfolded, and they rose up on cantilevered legs. Their torsos opened, and fearsome-looking weapons bristled forth. The things were now twelve feet tall.

They strode forward in unison.

'Destroy! Destroy! Destroy!'

Chorley turned and ran, heading for the van, which was now a hundred yards ahead. As he neared it the door opened and the figure of Mike appeared, beckoning him onwards. His legs pumping and his chest on fire with pain, Chorley sprinted across the moorland grass, slamming into the side of the van as it slowed. He felt strong arms hauling him inside. He fell with Mike into the van, and remembered Emma, remembered with shame that burned hotter than the flames that in his panic he had forgotten her, he had left her to those things…

He twisted around to see Mike hauling Emma aboard. She was sobbing with fear and Mike hugged her as he drew the door closed.

'Everybody in?' yelled Barry from the driver's seat.

'Yeah!' cried Mike. 'Step on it, man! Get us the hell outta

here!'

Barry needed no further encouragement. Chorley hauled himself up to stare out of the rear window. The remains of his car were still burning, and the two guard robots stood over it, arms extended, for all the world as if they were toasting crumpets in the flames. As he watched, they folded up back into their original, stocky forms, and began to waddle back towards the Dominex installation.

Chorley began to shudder with delayed shock.

Now he had a story, all right. One hell of a story.

In the heart of the Dominex installation was a circular, domed control chamber. Although brightly-lit, it also, curiously, appeared dark and oppressive. The floor was a disc of clattering black iron grating, and the walls and ceiling were made of transparent material behind which a smoky, inky, gaseous substance ebbed and flowed. In the middle of the chamber stood a raised dais of shining steel, bordered by railings, in the centre of which stood a squat apparatus, topped with a glass dome that was filled with softly glowing crystalline tubing. Against the curving wall on one side of this stood an ovoid star-map, and the other a bank of instruments set into tomb-like control panels, above which hung a circular screen. The screen showed the burning remains of a car, and the retreating shape of the VW van.

Standing watching the screen, a satisfied smile on its ghastly, cadaverous face, was a hulking humanoid figure. Fully seven feet tall, its long, muscular limbs were clad in close-fitting metallic plating that shone bluish purple in the harsh lighting. Its arms hung poised by its side, as if it carried two rolls of invisible carpet under each arm, and ended in massive, black-gloved hands, each one looking big and powerful enough to crush a human head. On its feet were thick-soled black boots, around its body, a shell of ridged jet-black armour that completely hid its neck, giving the creature a hunched, towering aspect.

Its face was heavily browed, with deep-set, red-rimmed, greenish eyes and white, leathery skin that gave it the appearance of an animated corpse. Its receding hair was black and cropped closed to the skull. Its voice was a stentorian, husky bark. 'Quarks! Retract, and return!'

'Probationer Azbo! What is the meaning of this?' bellowed a similar, but deeper voice from the far side of the chamber, where another towering figure had entered. This one was taller, its hair fuller, its face squarer and more imperious. Its lips were curled in a snarl of barely-controlled wrath, and its eyes burned with an implacable yet calm hatred.

'Navigator Deka! The Quarks were repelling some more trespassers.'

Navigator Deka strode up to Probationer Azbo. 'Have any more humans been destroyed?'

Azbo shook his head. 'No! Only one of their vehicles.'

Deka turned away, seething. 'That is fortunate.' He swung back to face his subordinate. 'But your conduct remains highly unsatisfactory!' He thrust a gloved hand towards the screen. 'You are once more wasting vital Quark power! You know the dangers of working with a squad of low-powered Quarks. Remember Dulkis!'

Probationer Azbo did not need reminding of that shameful historical incident, but nodded dutifully anyway.

Deka ranted on. 'And your actions will only attract

unwanted attention. It is what the inhabitants of this world call "bad public relations". Remember you are still a probationer, and your only function is to obey! No more destruction!'

'Command accepted.' Azbo's low-browed face took on a sullen aspect. 'But Navigator Deka, why must we hide? Why must we wait? That is not the Dominator way!'

'How many more times must I advise you?' snarled Deka. 'This is a new phase of our operations.'

A door slid open and the two Quarks entered, burbling happily, their mission to repel the trespassers complete.

'Quarks! Recharge!' barked Deka.

The squat robots emitted a warbling burble and their arms swung back and forth furiously – a quirk Dominator engineers had been unable to eliminate – as they recharged themselves.

'Quark energy must not be wasted! It must be conserved until Project M comes to fruition.'

'Project M,' muttered Azbo. 'I cannot see what is wrong with our usual mode of operation.'

'Director Vaar must be obeyed!' thundered Deka. 'Project M is our main priority!' He continued in a more conciliatory tone. 'If Project M fails, we will revert to our standard mode of operation. Until then...'

'Until then...' rumbled Navigator Azbo.

Deka narrowed his eyes. This probationer was proving to be unruly. His subordinate's performance would reflect badly on himself, so it was up to him to keep Azbo on mission. If he became too rebellious, however, he would have to be destroyed. Nothing could be allowed to endanger the mission. 'Until then we proceed with Project M. What is the current status?'

Azbo turned, swivelling like a turret, and scanned a display. 'We are now at eighty percent.'

Navigator Deka smiled a ghastly smile. 'That is good. Fleet Command are getting impatient. A few more consignments and we can begin the conversion.'

He moved to leave for his private chamber, then paused, remembering something.

'Have you altered the signs?'

Azbo nodded curtly. 'Yes, Navigator. They now read, "Trespassers will be pros – *proscuted*".'

'Excellent,' hissed Deka. 'See, Azbo, the value of research! Sometimes the best weapon is intelligence, not might!' So saying he stomped from the control chamber.

Probationer Azbo's lips curled in a sullen sneer. No, the best weapon was *always* might. He turned to monitor the Quark power levels, which were now almost back up to one hundred percent. Azbo's eyes glowed. Lurking in here like cowards – whatever the navigator said – was not the Dominator way. Azbo's black soul seethed with the urge to destroy.

Back in his flat, Lethbridge-Stewart prepared himself a nightcap, and reflected on his researches of the day. So far so – nothing. Well, not quite. He'd found out that Dominex employed university graduates who were keen to join the burgeoning nuclear industry, but who knew next to nothing about the man they worked for. Nothing Redmond had told him had rung any alarm bells, though – except maybe his inability to remember the name of his director's home town. But even that was not so unusual. These Eastern European places were hard to pronounce. He had trouble himself.

As for the minister, perhaps he really was busy for the next three weeks. Or perhaps he did have something to hide. Impossible to know, to penetrate the Civil Service smokescreen.

And Douglas Scanlon had told him nothing. In fact, despite his disdain towards Dominex, he had positively pooh-poohed the idea that they were up to anything illegal, or had anything to do with the disappearances.

Sitting down in his favourite easy chair, Lethbridge-Stewart picked up the Dominex prospectus. 'Your future is our business.' He sipped his whisky. A bland corporate phrase, for sure. But he couldn't help feeling there was something jolly sinister about it.

Chelsea Barracks at the dead of night could be quite a spooky place, but Lance Corporal William Bishop didn't let that bother him. With the radio on blasting out the Beatles or the Stones no spook would ever dare poke its ectoplasmic conk through the wall. Not that Bishop believed in that sort of thing – certainly not after recent experiences at Fang Rock. But some of the stuff he was reading – well, it set the imagination running, didn't it? The stuff the Operational Corps had got up to. The now-historical events they'd had a hand in. All in a day's work, he supposed. And his day's work – his evening's work – was to redact all these classified files, on all four of the Corps, into one readable report for Colonel Lethbridge-Stewart. His heart wasn't in it; he'd been expecting action and adventure and excitement. He'd certainly found that on Fang Rock, but he'd been wounded in the process. He supposed that was part of the reason Lethbridge-Stewart had him reading through classified files – not to say that Bishop failed to see the importance of such a job. But still, he was a soldier, not a clerk who enjoyed dusty office dullness and routine. 'You can learn a lot from the colonel,' Major Edwards of the Black Mafia had said when his transfer had been made official. 'Keep close to him.'

That afternoon Lethbridge-Stewart had come steaming into his office and demanded to know how Bishop was getting on with the job. 'Be ready for you tomorrow, sir,' he'd said. Which was why he was here, now, late Tuesday night, rather than in *The Blue Posts* with the lads. Redacting classified files, whilst singing along to the radio to keep the spooks – the supernatural kind – at bay.

It must have been around half ten, as he was redacting some information on Air Vice-Marshal Ralph Cochrane and the Fourth Operational Corps' role in the infamous Dambuster Raid of '43, while singing along to *The Israelites* by Desmond Dekker, that he realised the inner office phone was going off. Quickly rising from his chair he strode over and pulled open the door, feeling slightly foolish. How long had it been ringing, drowned out by the music and his singing?

Bishop stepped over to the desk and grabbed the receiver. 'Yes?' he asked, wondering who would have the colonel's direct number.

'Who the hell is this? Get me Lethbridge-Stewart!' screamed a voice in his ear.

— CHAPTER EIGHT —

Into Darkness

Darkness. Silence. Darkness save for splashes of torchlight lighting up surrounding walls of rough red sandstone. Silence save for the scrape of boot on rock, ragged breaths and hushed voices, the drip of water on ancient, cold stone. Darkness and silence and the chill of subterranean air across their faces, like the touch of a ghost, the sweat on their brows intensifying the coolness. Darkness and silence and chill on the skin, but bodies hot and prickly with exertion. Pain from the crouching, pain from the crawling, pain in the back and the neck, pain in the knees and the elbows. Pain upon pain.

People do this for fun? Lethbridge-Stewart thought as he squeezed himself through a particularly narrow gap, gasping with the effort. Each to their own, and all that, but it wasn't his bag. Never did like being underground. Underground… A flashback of tunnels and glowing web, of shuffling, brutal killers, of choking death and no way out.

The unforgiving yellow beam of Lethbridge-Stewart's helmet light illuminated an unglamorous rear view of Ian Cawdery's worn brown corduroys. 'Are you all right up front?' he called, partly to distract his mind from the memories. His words echoed briefly and faded away.

'Yeah,' came an exhausted voice.

Grunting, he twisted around and called back in the other direction. 'Are you all right back there?'

'No!' The word bounced around the narrow tube of rock like a marble hurled by a petulant child.

Lethbridge-Stewart sighed. 'All right, let's take a break!' he called out.

Mr Cawdery stopped and turned, the beam of his lamp making Lethbridge-Stewart squint. 'You chaps okay?'

'I'm okay,' muttered Lethbridge-Stewart, shifting around to face the third member of the party. Harold Chorley crouched a little distance back down the tunnel, a picture of dejection, his glasses reflecting the beam of Lethbridge-Stewart's helmet light.

'Mr Chorley, do keep up,' snapped Lethbridge-Stewart.

'Can't I go back?' cried the desponded journalist. 'I don't like it down here. It's dark. It's cold. And I'm claustrophobic. You don't need me. And if I go back I could guard the entrance!'

'Mr Chorley, you're the one who dragged me all the way to Devon!' snapped Lethbridge-Stewart. 'It's on the strength of your report that we're down here in the first place.'

'I should never have got involved,' said Chorley. 'You were right, it is the most dangerous business on Earth!'

His voice was wavering. He was on the edge of panic. Lethbridge-Stewart had seen this sort of thing before, many times, in the heat of battle. It wasn't cowardice, it was a natural reaction to danger, to stress. Panic. Shell shock. Battle trauma. Quite soon, Chorley would be useless – worse than useless: A liability, a burden. A risk. He could put all their lives in danger.

'Please let me go back!' wailed Chorley.

Though in Chorley's case it might well be cowardice. He regretted his earlier harsh words. What the man needed was reassurance, encouragement. 'Mr Chorley, remember you are a journalist. Remember your professionalism. You are essential to our mission. Your powers of observation are vital.'

'It's great to feel wanted,' whined Chorley sarcastically.

Lethbridge-Stewart struggled to contain his frustration. 'You've seen these robot things. We haven't. So you'll be able to warn us.'

'You don't need me for that!' snorted Chorley. 'I've described them to you – and it's not as if you'd mistake them for anything else!'

'You have a point. Robots are robots. We're not going to miss them.' Lethbridge-Stewart thought for a second, then reached into his jacket pocket and drew out a silver hip-flask. If this didn't work, he'd send the man back – but it usually worked. 'Take courage, Mr Chorley.'

Chorley grabbed the flask and gulped down almost half the contents. 'Sorry,' he gasped, passing the flask back to Lethbridge-Stewart. 'It's just – these caves. Never liked being underground. Claustrophobic. And it reminds me of – somewhere...'

Their eyes met.

'Here, can I have a sip of that?' Ian asked.

'Sorry, medicinal only,' said Lethbridge-Stewart, slipping the flask back into his pocket.

It had all started with the panicked phone call from Chorley on Tuesday night. Lethbridge-Stewart spent most of the evening missing Sally (she was out with friends) and had an early night, but found himself unable to sleep, his mind going over the meetings of the day, and unable to stop wondering about how Chorley was getting on down in Devon. When the call came from Bishop, Lethbridge-Stewart felt almost as if he had willed it into being.

'Harold Chorley on the line for you, sir,' Bishop had said. 'And he sounds… *freaked!*'

Freaked was just about the measure of it. Chorley was near-hysterical, babbling about killer robots and the loss of his car, and it was all Lethbridge-Stewart could to do calm him down. He sounded drunk – but Lethbridge-Stewart supposed he could hardly blame the fellow, after what he'd been through. Or rather, what he said he'd been through. Lethbridge-Stewart gathered from Chorley's garbled report that he had been 'hanging out' with a bunch of hippy youths and CND protestors. Lord alone knew what had really gone on. But Lethbridge-Stewart decided to give Chorley the benefit of the doubt and hot-foot it down to Buckfastleigh.

First thing the next morning, he made straight for Fugglestone, foregoing breakfast, intent on briefing Hamilton on developments.

The general listened patiently while Lethbridge-Stewart relayed Chorley's garbled field report. At the end of it Hamilton got up, walked over to the decanter on top of his filing cabinet, and poured them both a stiff measure of whisky.

'Little robots that transform themselves into giant robots, that blast Hillman Imps to smithereens?'

Lethbridge-Stewart took a sip from his glass, despite the earliness of the hour. 'Could be the work of extra-terrestrials, sir. Just what we're looking for. Dominex could be a front for alien activity. Evidence!'

Hamilton raised his eyebrows. 'And you say Chorley was hanging around with counter-cultural types? And he sounded drunk? And you're giving credence to his story?'

'He's excitable but he's not likely to make something like that up. He's a professional, like us. Different field, but all the same.'

'I have plenty of reason to doubt that, Colonel.'

Hamilton was referring to the way Chorley had tried to expose the truth of the London Event, the way he had brought in that Larry Greene chap, and left him out to dry when the authorities came down on them both. Nonetheless, Lethbridge-Stewart liked to think everybody deserved a chance to change, and he wanted to believe this was Chorley's.

Lethbridge-Stewart raised his glass again, but thought better of it, he had a long drive ahead of him. Instead he put the glass on the edge of Hamilton's desk and placed his gloved hands either side of it, leaning in, holding Hamilton's gaze. 'Let me take a squad down, sir. Get in to the Dominex place, have a proper look round.'

Hamilton shook his head, his eyes never leaving Lethbridge-Stewart's. Was there something reticent about his manner? 'Afraid the place is out of bounds. Orders from above.'

When it was clear that Hamilton wasn't going to elaborate, Lethbridge-Stewart straightened up. 'Could you be more specific, sir? Orders from who, exactly? High Command?'

'Higher even than that. Our political masters. Sir Anthony Bufton, more exactly.'

Lethbridge-Stewart sighed. 'Let me chance a guess. Dominex are the golden boys of the power industry, so it's hands off.'

'Precisely.'

Lethbridge-Stewart sensed unusual anger in that single word, but Hamilton's face remained calm.

'Dominex are world leaders in nuclear waste reprocessing, and Britain is grateful that they have decided to locate here. Inward investment, future prosperity, jam tomorrow, all that. You know the score, Colonel. Hands off. No go.'

As Hamilton spoke Lethbridge-Stewart felt his own anger surge within him; he forced himself to control it, channel it. 'Sir! There have been four deaths in the area since Dominex "located" in this country. And now this incident – whatever the reality of it. We must investigate!'

'Colonel, I understand how you feel, but please confine yourself to the facts. Four people have been reported missing, not presumed dead – not yet, anyway. And those two young hikers could well have run off together.'

'With respect, sir, the cavers went missing months ago, and if they were alive, they would have turned up by now. As for the hikers, if they have indeed run off together, why have there been no reports of them turning up elsewhere? Let me take a small team down, have a discreet look round. We don't have to go battering on Dominex's door.'

Hamilton patted his desk with a meaty hand. 'Out. Of. Bounds. We have to follow orders, Colonel, you know that. Chain of command.'

Politics more like; not something Lethbridge-Stewart had any interest in getting involved in. Although he doubted he'd have a choice the further he and Hamilton went with the Operational Corps. 'What do you suggest we do? Nothing?'

Another shake of the head, another sip of whisky. Again Lethbridge-Stewart sensed hesitancy in Hamilton's manner, as if he were holding something back. 'Far from it. We get Chorley back here and debrief him, then we'll see. In the meantime we'll let the police get on with their investigations into the missing persons and leave Dominex well alone.'

Stalemate. Lethbridge-Stewart knew Hamilton was right. But there was something in the older man's expression, a slight... an oh-so-*very* slight raise of the eyebrows and tilt of the head. Was it a look of resignation, or welcome?

Lethbridge-Stewart carried on regardless. He had nothing to lose. 'Chorley sounded in no fit state to travel, sir. And his transport has been taken out of action, whether by transforming robots or not remains to be seen. Would it be out of order if I sent someone down to Buckfastleigh to pick him up?' He paused, holding his breath.

Hamilton picked up a pencil from his desk, then put it down again on the other side of the blotter. 'I suppose not.'

Those three little words were all Lethbridge-Stewart needed. 'May as well go down myself. I can debrief him down there, and make some careful enquiries around the local area.'

'Don't see why not,' said Hamilton. He leaned forward slightly. 'As long as you stay away from Dominex.'

'Right. I'll drive down right away.' As if hearing this, Lethbridge-Stewart's stomach rumbled in protest. 'Spot of breakfast first, though,' he muttered to himself.

'If you're going to the mess hall, do try the sausages.

100

Delicious!'

'Right.' Lethbridge-Stewart smiled at the informality, but the moment had, seemingly, passed. Instead Hamilton rose from his desk and fixed Lethbridge-Stewart with a stern glare.

'Now, Colonel, you do understand that Dominex are absolutely out of bounds?'

'Yes, sir.'

'I don't like it either but those are our orders. So be damned careful, and if you find anything, any evidence of alien activity, I'll be listening.'

'Thank you, sir.'

'Let's just hope it really is just a load of – hash smoke.' Hamilton grinned but the warning stayed in his eyes.

Lethbridge-Stewart almost responded with 'no smoke without fire', but thought better of it. He made his farewell and went to the mess hall.

The sausages were, to his surprise and dismay, disgusting.

He'd filled up the Merc and barrelled down to Buckfastleigh that blazing June morning, not bothering to stop for lunch, and arrived at 2pm, ravenously hungry. He met a visibly frazzled Harold Chorley at *The White Hart* pub, where he wolfed down a nasty but necessary pub lunch of gristly steak pie and chips garnished with a sardonic clump of cress, and listened while Chorley re-told his story, every now and then stopping him for clarification.

'These robots – can you describe them in more detail?'

'You're going to think I've been smoking something.'

'Well, you have been associating with, shall we say,

counter-cultural types.' Lethbridge-Stewart glanced around the smoky interior of the pub. 'Talking of whom, are they still around?'

Chorley shook his head. 'Not after what happened last night. Gone down to the coast, I think.'

'Pity. They might have been able to help with my enquiries. Talking of which, you were describing these... robots?'

Chorley hunched forward over the table. 'Yes. Well. If you believe me or not, this is what I saw. There were two of them...'

Lethbridge-Stewart listened to the description. It sounded like nothing he had ever encountered, but also like something that wouldn't be beyond the capabilities of an Earth-based company to manufacture. Especially one who could make energy – or, allegedly, weapons – from nuclear waste. Rather bizarre to use the things as guard dogs, though. But then Lethbridge-Stewart recalled the most improbable part of Chorley's story, the part he found hardest to believe.

'And you say these things – changed? Grew bigger? How?'

Chorley spread his hands. 'They – opened. Like a Swiss Army Jack-in-the-Box.'

Lethbridge-Stewart tried to picture the scene. 'Why would they do this?'

Chorley looked as if it had never occurred to him. 'What do you mean?'

Lethbridge-Stewart pushed his half-eaten meal away. 'Let's suppose Dominex have the capability to build autonomous, offensive-capability robotic units. Why give them the ability to transform in this way? From small, rather comical-looking things, by the sound of it, into fearsome tank-like affairs?'

'Search me,' said Chorley. 'Maybe it's a sort of Trojan horse effect. If they look funny – and they did, in their small form – people won't take them seriously. And then – wham! That's pretty much what happened up on the moor.' Chorley shuddered.

'Maybe. Or perhaps it's a transportation issue – smaller units would be easier to carry over long distances. Interstellar ones, for example. And then, maybe also a power conservation solution. They only expand to their full size when they need to, and other times stay in their original forms.'

'I could murder a pint,' muttered Chorley.

'So could I, but we've got work to do. Now, describe their firepower. How many shots did they fire, and what did it look like?'

'Two, or at most three. It was – it was like a blinding beam of orange light. Hurt the eyes. They blasted my car!' Chorley's voice rose with the memory of the indignity, and the regulars turned to look at him, shook their heads and turned away.

'Keep your voice down!' hissed Lethbridge-Stewart. 'How much do this lot know?'

'Nothing, I've not said a dickie bird. They just think the hippies and I had some sort of hash-fuelled orgy up on the moors. Chance'd be a fine thing.'

'Sounds like some sort of projected-energy weapon,' said Lethbridge-Stewart. 'I'd have to ask Miss Travers, but I'd imagine it would be the sort of thing you could make, if you had the know-how, from nuclear waste.'

'So you don't think they're – alien?'

'Just keeping my options open, Mr Chorley. One thing is bothering me, though. Why now?'

'What do you mean?'

'I mean, why go on the offensive now? We can pretty much assume Dominex are up to no good, so–'

'So why not send a squad up there, storm the place?'

Chorley clearly wanted revenge for his dratted Hillman Imp.

'Because, one, orders from on high. Dominex are out of bounds. I don't like it, but those are the orders – that's why it's just me down here, not a whole squad. And two, we don't know what we're up against yet, not fully – we don't know how many of these robot things are up there. Which brings me back to my point. Why reveal their hand so soon? Why attack a bunch of innocent – well, fairly innocent – civilians? Makes no military sense at all. Such an action would only draw unwanted attention – which it has.'

'Perhaps we were just target practice,' said Chorley morosely.

'Some sort of test? Could be. Are Dominex so confident of government protection that they think they can go around blasting merrily away at a bunch of hippies? And if it's a test – what are they planning? Invasion?'

'Search me,' said Chorley. 'Whatever it is, it can't be good.'

'Whatever it is, the answer's in that plant. We've got to get in there, somehow.' Lethbridge-Stewart lapsed into thought while Chorley went to the bar.

Too risky to go marching about the moors, not with all the disappearances, and now these robot things waddling about. A more subtle, covert approach was called for.

Chorley brought back a pint of brown ale for each of them. *Well, one won't hurt*, Lethbridge-Stewart thought, and took an appreciative sip. It was of better quality than the pie had been. 'You say you've met the brother of one of the missing cavers?'

Chorley had already downed half of his pint. 'Yeah. Ian Cawdery.'

Lethbridge-Stewart leaned back in his chair. 'So… that's where we start our investigation. The caves.'

Ian Cawdery was an understandably morose, rather stout fellow, who had quietly agreed to assist them if it helped solved the mystery of what had happened to his brother. In his small, tidy kitchen that smelt of cinnamon and pipe smoke, Ian had spread out a home-made map of the caves and talked them through the route his brother had taken. The same route they were going to take. From a crevice in Black Tor it proceeded underground for a mile to almost directly underneath the Dominex plant.

'We'll need warm clothing and boots, which I have in your size, I think, sir,' Mr Cawdery said in his soft, cultured voice to Lethbridge-Stewart. 'Harold, I see you have some walking boots – brand new, they look. Well, they'll have to do. We'll also need caving helmets with torches; again I can provide those.'

'What about rope?' asked Lethbridge-Stewart.

'Won't need it, thankfully. Over the mile, the tunnel declines about a hundred feet, but it twists and turns a lot so the descent is quite gentle, except for a few steep bits. It's narrow and there's plenty of hand-holds, so we won't need to use any specialist caving equipment.' Cawdery glanced at Chorley as he said this. 'The ceiling's not very high so we'll be crawling most of the way, except for the end when it opens up a bit. Believe me, that'll feel like a relief.'

'But we'll be able to do it, despite not being experienced cavers?' asked Chorley.

'Yes, it's amateur hour, remember?'

'And this tunnel passes directly beneath the Dominex plant?'

'Yes, right through the Bishop's Chamber. That's more or less smack bang under the Dominex place, about a hundred foot or so down.'

'And did your brother get as far as that?' asked Lethbridge-Stewart gently.

Mr Cawdery shook his head and stared down at the map. 'We don't know. They just didn't come back. Not a trace was ever found.'

The three men stood in uncomfortable silence. Chorley shot Lethbridge-Stewart a glance that clearly said *and we're going down there?*

Lethbridge-Stewart broke the silence with a tactful cough. 'Right, men,' he found himself saying, as if the journalist and his teacher were soldiers under his command. 'We may as well start immediately.'

Lethbridge-Stewart had driven them up to the moor and they parked up in a secluded, overgrown farm track on the far side of Black Tor, avoiding Gibby Combe Lane and the Dominex plant. En route Chorley had concocted a cover story for them; he was Peter Carver, archaeologist, giving his two friends Barry and Alex a tour of the local caves.

Lethbridge-Stewart didn't think this would wash with any malevolent transforming robots they might encounter, but he kept the thought to himself. He already sensed an edge of panic to Chorley's voice.

By the time they got up to Black Tor they were sweating under their jumpers and thick trousers, but Mr Cawdery assured them they would be grateful for them once underground.

Black Tor itself stood like a stone sentinel atop a ridge strewn with smaller stones amid long moor grass yellowed by the summer sun. The slope up to the peak of the ridge was shallow, but on the leeward side it sloped sharply down to the valley where the Dominex plant lay. Lethbridge-Stewart gazed down at the harshly illuminated complex, a manifestation of the modern world on the ancient moor. What secrets lay within? He remembered Director Dominic Vaar on *Panorama* telling the world of the benefits that Dominex would bring. Cheap energy for all. He recalled the company's mission statement: *Dominex Industries – Your Future is Our Business.* Again he was struck by its ominous, sinister aspect, the threat veiled under the assurance, the promise within a promise that said, *we'll get to you in time, all in good time…*

He walked back round the other side of the tor, where Chorley and Cawdery waited. Above them, the tor glowered, an impossible-looking pile of massy granite stones, its smooth surfaces giving it the appearance of a giant clenched fist. At the foot of the tor, Cawdery stopped, leaning forward to move aside a clump of bracken, revealing a triangular niche formed by the angle of two stones and the ground. Tattered police tape hung like bunting around it.

He turned and regarded the two men solemnly. 'This is where Michael went. From where he never returned. Let's hope we have better luck.'

Lethbridge-Stewart winced and glanced over at Chorley. The man's face was pale and drawn. 'Ready?'

'No.'

'That's the spirit!' Lethbridge-Stewart followed Ian Cawdery into the tunnel.

— CHAPTER NINE —

A Deadly Discovery

O n they went, down and down into the dark. After about half an hour Cawdery called out for a rest, so they stopped beside an impressive array of stalagmites that resembled the pipes of an enormous subterranean organ. The other two men were plastered in red clay, and Lethbridge-Stewart supposed he must be too. The cool underground air was rich with the smell of it.

'Are we almost there? Not that I'm in any hurry to meet those things again.' Chorley said this with a grumble, but the tremble in his voice had disappeared; the whisky had done its job.

'Not even half-way,' Cawdery's voice echoed back. 'Steep bit ahead. Turn around – it's feet first.'

'Right.' Lethbridge-Stewart turned around, gasping as he squeezed his body in the confined space. Now it was Chorley's rear end he was staring at. At Cawdery's word he moved backwards, knees dragging on the gritty floor, until Cawdery told him to stop.

'You're at the edge now. Just ease yourself over and slide down – there's a ledge about ten feet below. That's where I'm standing now.'

Lethbridge-Stewart did so, Cawdery's arms gripping Lethbridge-Stewart's torso as he lowered himself down the final inches.

Chorley's head appeared over the lip of the drop, the beam of his helmet light shining in their faces, dazzling them.

'Come on, Harold, it's not far!' Cawdery seemed to be relishing his position as experienced cave guide.

Lethbridge-Stewart was glad that, so far at least, the man was untroubled by thoughts of his brother, but that sort of goading wasn't going to help Chorley in his precarious state.

'Turn round and slide yourself down. I'll catch you!' called Lethbridge-Stewart.

Chorley's head disappeared and his booted feet appeared over the edge. Brightly illuminated by Lethbridge-Stewart's helmet light, the soles were hardly marked, the uppers scuff-free.

'How much did these set you back?' Lethbridge-Stewart asked as he helped Chorley slither down the drop and into a standing position.

'Can I claim expenses?'

Making jokes was a good sign – or perhaps it was the whisky talking. Whichever it was, Chorley was holding up okay. 'Right, on we go,' said Lethbridge-Stewart.

And on they went, crawling on all fours, and at one point slithering on their bellies, worming their way through a narrow, winding throat of stone. After an interminable time, Cawdery called for a halt.

'Are we there *now*?' came Chorley's voice from behind Lethbridge-Stewart.

'Almost,' Cawdery called. 'I've stopped because we're coming to the bit where you can stand up and walk.'

'Thank God for that!'

'That *is* a relief!' Lethbridge-Stewart agreed.

'In fact we can walk all the way to the Bishop's Chamber,' Cawdery added.

'Well, let's get going.' Lethbridge-Stewart's lower back was beginning to complain and the sooner he stood up, the better.

'Okay, but before we do, I've got to warn you, watch out for Smackhead Rock.'

'What-head what?' Lethbridge-Stewart spluttered.

'Smackhead Rock. A big lump of black limestone jutting down from the ceiling about half-way along. It's caught the occasional caver off-guard. If you're not looking for it you could bang your bonce. Hence the name.'

'We'll be okay, we've got helmets on!' Chorley blustered, clearly keen to get on.

'Even so, could still give you a nasty knock. Like I said, watch out!'

'Why don't they just, well, get rid of it?'

Cawdery shot Chorley a withering look. 'You don't go messing about with Mother Earth's innards just for your convenience.' So saying he continued on down the tunnel.

'Let's hope that's a message Dominex have taken to heart,' said Lethbridge-Stewart, following after the history teacher.

Navigator Deka entered his private chamber. It was a sparse, bare room with a cabinet resembling an upright coffin in one corner: his recharging unit. Dominators had no need for sleep, or food; these puny dependencies had been genetically engineered out of Dominator physiognomy. A brief period of recharging from their power sources every hundred cycles was sufficient. It was not Deka's time for recharging, however; he headed instead to his personal comms console. He tapped in a sequence of symbols on the chunky keyboard and the image of Director Vaar appeared on the circular screen.

'Report!'

Navigator Deka began speaking in the native Dominator language but was immediately cut off by Vaar.

'Use English only!'

Deka cursed himself. 'I am sorry, Director.'

'It is imperative that you speak the native tongue at all times. It is a vital part of Project M! Should the humans overhear us speaking our own language, it will arouse their suspicion! So use English at all times – even when conversing with Deka! Even when issuing orders to Quarks!'

Deka frowned, considering this excessive. Learning the native language had been difficult – even with advanced Dominator learning machines – and sometimes he and Azbo stumbled over Earth words. But the Director had to be obeyed. The chain of command was sacrosanct. 'Command accepted, Director Vaar.'

Vaar nodded, his lips curling in a snarl. 'Now, report!'

'We are now at eighty percent. Full capacity will be reached within three, maybe four cycles. Conversion can then begin. Capability is expected within six cycles, deployment within seven.'

Director Vaar nodded in satisfaction. 'That is excellent. All is proceeding according to schedule.'

'There is, however, one risk. A minor risk, but a risk nonetheless.'

'Have any more humans been destroyed?' Director Vaar

snapped with unbridled anger.

'No, Director Vaar, but Probationer Azbo continues to stray off mission. He constitutes a risk to Project M. His actions could lead to undue attention being focused in our direction, and the discovery of our plans. He may therefore have to be destroyed.'

'Manage that risk, Navigator Deka. The Probationer is your responsibility. I shall return shortly to oversee the final stages of Project M.'

The screen went blank.

Deka turned and stomped from his chamber. Perhaps he should destroy Azbo now, eliminate the risk. But the Probationer was needed to manage the Quarks. Soon, however, it would not matter. Project M would soon come to fruition, and they could leave the remains of this world behind them and rejoin the Fleet.

It was certainly a relief to stand up, though the tunnel was narrow so they had to keep to single file. After a hundred yards Cawdery called a halt and pointed up to the ceiling. Lethbridge-Stewart shone the beam of his helmet light in the direction indicated. There, jutting down from the red sandstone roof of the tunnel, was a black lump of rock shaped like a crooked elbow. Once caught in the beam of a torch it was unmissable, but if you happened not to be looking in that direction – ouch. Lethbridge-Stewart made sure to bend down as he passed under Smackhead Rock, motioning Chorley to do the same.

After another fifty or so yards the tunnel ended in blackness where it opened out into the cavern Cawdery had called the Bishop's Chamber. A hundred feet above their heads, Dominex were going about their business, hopefully unaware of the presence of the three explorers.

They moved into the cavern, the beams of their helmet lights lancing into the darkness, illuminating undulating walls of striated red sandstone, and freakish formations of stalagmites and stalactites.

'Some interesting structures here!' Cawdery's voice, which, despite the circumstances, sounded genuinely enthusiastic, echoed horribly loudly.

Chorley grabbed his arm. 'For God's sake, shush!'

Cawdery ignored him. 'What's that?' He said, training his light on the nearside wall of the cavern. Something metallic glinted in the beam.

The three men strode over, their beams gradually revealing a neat stack of barrels ranged against the wall of the cavern. Lethbridge-Stewart shone his torch right and left, up and down, and did a quick calculation. At least a hundred – and it looked like there were more behind.

Each of the barrels bore an ominous yellow and black warning symbol.

'So this is where they're keeping the waste,' Lethbridge-Stewart muttered.

'Christ!' Chorley hissed. 'Just chucked down here like this? Is it safe?'

'Not my field, I'm afraid.' Lethbridge-Stewart thought back to his chat with Miss Travers. It was common practice to store nuclear waste underground. But how much, and how far underground? He remembered her mentioning a depth of a hundred metres – not feet. But that was for high-level waste. Or was it intermediate? He wished he'd brought Miss Travers with him – even though this wasn't the sort of place you'd bring a woman. Still, she'd survived much worse.

While Lethbridge-Stewart pondered, Cawdery wandered off to the far side of the cavern.

'Hey! Look at this!' he called.

Lethbridge-Stewart and Chorley turned and went over to where the teacher was standing, pointing at the wall of the cavern. The section he was indicating was not sandstone or clay, or any type of rock. Set into the cavern wall was a shining sheet of silver metal, a yard and a half wide and two yards tall.

Lethbridge-Stewart was about to say 'It looks like a door' when with a powerful electric thrumming sound the door – for that's what it was – began to slide slowly and smoothly upwards. Bright white light shone out from the widening gap.

Lethbridge-Stewart turned to motion his men to retreat but Chorley was already hot-footing it back towards the tunnel entrance. As Lethbridge-Stewart watched he tripped and fell before he could make good his escape. Cawdery was running in the other direction – towards the stack of nuclear waste barrels. Chorley was curled up on the floor of the cavern, grimacing and clutching his ankle.

Now the door was fully open and the cavern was flooded with light.

Lethbridge-Stewart pressed himself back against the wall as a strange procession emerged. First came a trolley bearing two barrels of waste. Its wheels squeaked alarmingly in the sudden silence. Pushing this trolley with two of its block-like arms was, clearly, one of the robots Chorley had described.

It was even more comical than Lethbridge-Stewart had

imagined. It walked, or rather shuffled, on block-like feet the same size and shape as shoeboxes. Its legs were stocky ribbed tubes of some rubber-like material – Lethbridge-Stewart remembered how Chorley had described the thing growing, transforming, and he could well imagine those little legs extending. The rectangular body, the same gunmetal grey as the rest of the thing, had rounded edges, and bore an incongruously municipal aspect. Its spherical head, slightly sunken into the body, was divided into octants by encircling metal bands. The lower octants were metallic grilles, while the upper four contained clusters of odd tubular metallic formations that shone in the bright artificial light. Five crystalline spikes of shining white jutted out from the junctures of the metal bands – two fore and aft, two left and right, and a longer one on top. As it waddled along pushing its load the thing burbled happily to itself.

Compared to a rampaging Yeti, or a murderous Rutan, the thing looked harmless, like an overgrown toy. But however odd it looked, Lethbridge-Stewart reminded himself, this thing was dangerous, deadly – a killer. Its appearance might even count as a military advantage. An enemy might be disarmed and amused by the sight of it – at their cost.

He watched it amble across the centre of the cavern towards the stack of barrels where Cawdery was hiding. Another trolley emerged from the entrance, again pushed by one of the strange little robots, and followed after its companion, chirruping merrily away to itself. The first robot was almost at the barrels. The robots hadn't seen Cawdery – yet. Or Chorley, who still writhed in agony clutching his ankle. Damn the man! Dratted liability – but Lethbridge-

Stewart checked himself, ashamed. Chorley was a soldier injured in the field. A soldier under his command. He was responsible.

Options flashed across his mind in seconds. Could he risk a dash across the cavern, scoop Chorley up and make a break for it back down the tunnel? But surely the robots would see them. And how fast could he go, bearing an injured man? Let alone get through the narrow tunnels with him. Too risky. Lethbridge-Stewart shuffled along the cavern wall and risked a glance through the door from which the robots had emerged. He saw a shining bright corridor leading to another set of doors. A lift? Perhaps he could slip inside, get into the Dominex plant. He looked over at the robots. Both of them were now at the barrels and were shuffling around to unload their trolleys. He made a move towards the corridor – but his duty to his men pulled him back. He couldn't leave them.

The robots were now busily unloading the barrels, grasping them with their block-like arms and hauling them into place. Now was his chance. He ran over to where the injured Chorley lay.

'Intruders! Alert! Intruders! Alert!'

The voices were shrill and piercing, all at once ridiculous and terrifying. Nothing human would speak like that. Nothing with a soul. Nothing with a sense of compassion or mercy.

Lethbridge-Stewart swung around. The two robots had abandoned their duties and had now turned to face him. Their block-like arms pointed straight at him. He could see the muzzle of their energy weapons.

Cawdery broke from cover, from behind the barrels

where he had been hiding, and made a break for the tunnel entrance.

A thunderous baritone voice bellowed from an unseen speaker. 'Quarks! Destroy! *Destroy!*'

'Watch out!' cried Lethbridge-Stewart.

'Destroy! Destroy! Destroy!' trilled the robots in chilling unison.

Twin beams of orange energy engulfed the running man. Cawdery shrieked, twisted and fell. Acrid smoke lifted from his blackened, charred corpse.

Something happened inside Lethbridge-Stewart. A switch clicked. A line was crossed. A decision made. No going back now. Dominex were the enemy, no doubt about it, and they had to be stopped.

The two robots – Quarks, the voice had called them – had turned back to face him. They were emitting a shrill burbling sound and their arms were waving furiously, as if they were trying to warm themselves. Why weren't they firing? Never mind why – now was his chance. He ran back to Chorley.

'Leave me – save yourself!' cried the journalist, but it sounded to Lethbridge-Stewart as though he was quoting a war film.

'Not a chance!'

A searing explosion just above his head, and a shower of stone and grit tumbled about them both. Staggering, half-blinded by the dust, Lethbridge-Stewart found himself at the mouth of the tunnel. He stumbled blindly within, and turned to see Chorley still prone in the cavern, the two Quarks shuffling towards him, their arm weapons waving bizarrely from side to side.

Again, why did they not fire?

A blinding flash, a thunderous crash and the entire moor seemed to fall on Lethbridge-Stewart. He felt a sharp pain as something glanced of the back off his head. Stars burst in his vision. He fell backwards, coughing and spluttering. Where was his helmet? Must have been knocked off. He flailed in complete darkness.

Silence, apart from the trickle and chatter of small falls of gravel.

Lethbridge-Stewart slid a box of matches from his pocket, congratulating himself for his forethought. But what the tiny flame revealed made his heart sink. The way back into Bishop's Cavern was completely blocked. No way back. He had no choice but to leave Chorley to the Quarks.

Two men down in a matter of minutes.

Lethbridge-Stewart staggered against the wall of the cave and saw stars again. Must have had a nasty knock. He stood for a minute, composing himself, planning his next move. Well, he couldn't rescue Chorley. And Cawdery was beyond help. It was obvious now what had happened to his brother, and the two hikers. Enough evidence now to shut Dominex down, whatever the orders from above.

Lethbridge-Stewart straightened up and brushed himself down. He set off back along the tunnel at a run, full of purpose, intent on getting out and reporting back to General Hamilton.

He ran straight into Smackhead Rock. His forehead connected with the arm of black limestone, pain and light exploded in his head, and he fell unconscious onto the floor of the tunnel.

CHAPTER TEN

Prisoner of the Dominators

In the control chamber, Probationer Azbo monitored the delivery of the new consignment with sullen impatience. As he watched the Quarks busily working on the screen, his giant hands curled slowly into fists, and muscles in his enormous arms and legs twitched spasmodically. All this pushing and pulling and unloading and checking and waiting – it was not the true Dominator way! Navigator Deka had drummed into him often enough the concept of the 'greater glory', but it had failed to stick inside Azbo's cavernous, monomaniacal mind. Azbo longed to destroy! But if he did destroy, he himself would face destruction, and that would mean he would not be able to destroy because he, Azbo, would not exist. Azbo shook his head, as if to rid himself of such troubling thoughts.

Frowning furiously, he concentrated on the Quarks as they unloaded the barrels of waste, and tried to stay – what had Deka said? – 'on mission'. Eighty percent – soon they would have enough to commence conversion, and initiate the final stage of Project M. *The sooner the better*, Azbo thought lugubriously. They could then return to the fleet and continue with their mission of universal domination. His thoughts passed over the event horizon of the black hole of his mind, and Azbo once more gave himself up to fantasies of death and destruction. Slowly he brought his two fists together in front of his massive chest, like two cannonballs kissing, the gloved fingers creaking as they clenched.

A movement on the screen caught his dark eye. A human – running about in the waste chamber! Without a second's hesitation, he hit the comm switch and bellowed, 'Quarks! Destroy! *Destroy!*'

He observed with satisfaction as the two Quarks blasted the human to extinction. A warm, soothing feeling thrilled through his body, from his feet, up his legs, through his groin and stomach and black, black heart to just behind his eyeballs. His heartbeat thudded in his chest as he saw two more humans in the chamber – one clearly damaged, the other confronting the two Quarks. Foolish, feeble creature! It would soon be destroyed, once the Quarks had recharged. Ah yes – Azbo grinned as one of the Quarks blasted the ceiling of the cavern above the human, sending rubble crashing down around it. Quarks were playful beings at heart, servile to the Dominators of course, but in the execution of their duty they often showed admirable cruelty.

'*What is the meaning of this?*' roared a voice from behind the Probationer.

Azbo whirled around to see Navigator Deka striding towards him.

Harold Chorley cringed on the floor of the cavern while the two Quarks waddled towards him. *This is it*, he thought. *The end. Blasted to ashes by these devilish robots!* Horribly, he could still smell the charred remains of Ian Cawdery. Now the same was going to happen to him. Would it hurt? He closed his eyes, and waited for his whole life to flash before him, but all he could think was, *my ankle hurts I don't want to die they killed my car now they're gonna kill me—*

But then, jolting him with surprise, the baritone voice that had ordered the Quarks to destroy spoke again.

'Quarks! Do not destroy. Do not destroy!'

Relief surged through Chorley. Relief which turned to terror as the voice bellowed, 'Bring the human to us!'

Deka bore down on Azbo. 'I have already warned you against wasting Quark energy in this way! Project M must not be jeopardised!'

'Yes, Navigator Deka.'

Deka shouldered Azbo aside and hit the comm switch. 'Quarks! Do not destroy! *Do not destroy!*' He swung back to face the glowering Probationer. 'The more humans we destroy, the more undue attention we will attract. Already, the human military have been witnessed visiting our London base.'

Azbo clenched his massive fists. 'But Navigator Deka, that was just one man.' His lips curled in a grin of lust. 'And we can crush any force this planet could raise against us! Are we not Dominators?'

'You are not yet a full Dominator, remember that, *Probationer* Azbo!' Deka snapped. 'Also remember the mission. We are not here to conquer. Or destroy! We are here to complete Project M. Only when that is complete can we go on to the glory of conquest! So, obey!'

Azbo frowned, and shook his head as if in confusion. 'But Navigator, these creatures were trespassing!'

'Negative!' A giant finger pointed at the screen. 'This

creature has probably come to investigate the disappearances of the others. Which were a result of your actions, Probationer Azbo.' He hit the comm switch again. 'Bring the human to us!'

'I apologise, Navigator Deka,' rumbled Azbo with mountainous insincerity that Deka ignored, but noted.

'Director Vaar will be extremely disappointed to learn of this wastefulness. He returns to the base shortly to oversee the final phase of Project M.' Deka stomped around the control chamber, his footsteps thudding like announcements of doom. The Probationer's performance was his responsibility, so Azbo's errors would reflect badly upon himself. Deka came to a decision, and stopped pacing to face his subordinate. 'Your performance is extremely disappointing, Probationer Azbo. You are failing to exhibit the appropriate expected behaviours. However, I will give you one more chance, because you are needed for the successful completion of Project M. Any further waste, any further disobedience, and you face immediate destruction!'

Azbo's eyes burned with rebellious fire, but he intoned dutifully, 'Yes, Navigator Deka.'

'We will bring the creature in for interrogation.' With that Deka strode from the chamber. But something Azbo had said suddenly struck him. He turned back. 'Azbo, you said "these creatures" – there were more than one?'

'Yes, Navigator Deka – the Quarks destroyed one, we have captured one other, and yet one more has escaped.'

'You should have informed me of this! If it manages to get back to its fellows – the attention it could bring would be catastrophic for Project M.'

'It should be hunted down and destroyed!' thundered

Azbo. 'Let me send a consignment of Quarks–'

'No!' bellowed Deka. But wait... Azbo's response, predictable though it was, contained a valid point. The creature could be hunted down and destroyed before it was able to report to its fellows. But that would waste valuable Quark energy, when they were so close to one hundred percent completion. An idea struck him. 'There is another way, a way shown by Director Vaar.'

'Another way?' Azbo rumbled, clearly unable to entertain any other concept than destruction.

'Director Vaar has connections with the human authorities. It would be easy for pressure to be exerted in the right places. Any report this escaped creature might make could be dismissed as the ravings of a lunatic. The time for a confrontation can therefore be delayed, and perhaps never come, before the completion of the final phase of Project M. I will contact the Director immediately so that he can make the necessary arrangements.'

Azbo seemed to visibly deflate at these words. 'But, Navigator, the risk! Surely it would be better to destroy! Is that not the Dominator way?'

'Obey! Obey!' yelled Deka. 'I have already warned you. The purpose of a probationer is to obey!'

'Yes, Navigator Deka.'

'So obey me now – and prepare the Mentotron!'

Azbo's green eyes gleamed cruelly. 'Command accepted!'

Chorley tried to crawl away as the two Quarks shuffled towards him, their cuboid arms extended as if to crush him in a quadrilateral embrace, but the pain in his twisted – broken perhaps – ankle made him grimace with agony, and he could only manage to slither a small distance away. Suddenly the Quark on the left retracted its concertina-like legs until its body was resting flush with the dusty ground. From its casing two shining silver prongs emerged, extending at ground level. The Quark slid smoothly towards the prone journalist and Chorley squirmed as he felt the prongs slide under his body at hip and shoulder. The Quark lifted him up as if he were a pallet of goods; it was a fork-lift and this was a warehouse, not a nuclear waste storage area. In this undignified manner, Chorley was unceremoniously dumped in one of the now-empty nuclear waste trolleys. One of them pushing their captive in the trolley, the two Quarks headed back across Bishop's Cavern towards the silver door through which they had emerged. Chorley felt a stab of anger. These blighted things had killed Ian, blasting him out of existence! And clearly they had also killed his brother and the missing hikers too.

'Where are you taking me?' he demanded.

The Quarks completely ignored him.

He had a pretty fair idea where he was going, though – right into the centre of the Dominex plant, to meet the masters of these strange little robots. Alien robots? So alien masters? He remembered Director Vaar on *Panorama*. Fellow looked foreign, maybe Slavic. But an alien?

Chorley winced as they went over a bump and his ankle banged against the side of the trolley. They were almost at the silver door now. Chorley fought down a rising tide of panic by telling himself that he wasn't just on his way to certain danger, but on his way to a story. Oh yes – if he ever got out of this alive, he'd have one hell of a story.

The Quarks wheeled him through the door and along a

short corridor of shining silver metal that had a faint sweet smell of oil. From his position on the trolley he was almost at ground level and had a very limited view of his surroundings. He could see the feet of the first Quark shuffling along ahead of him and if he craned his neck he could see the spired, spherical head of the Quark pushing the trolley, and the ceiling of the corridor, which was inset with circular glowing light panels which activated and dimmed as they passed by.

There was another painful bump and they stopped. Then the floor juddered and there was a sense of movement. From what he could gather they were now in a lift, heading up towards Dominex.

Chorley tried to compose his thoughts, and he ran over his cover story again. Peter Carver, in search of Roman relics. Totally innocent.

The lift came to a jarring halt which made Chorley think it wasn't built for transporting things that could feel pain, and he was wheeled along another corridor and around several corners until he was rolled into a small room that had the dimensions of a prison cell. There he was left, trolley and all.

The Quarks waddled off, burbling and chirruping, apparently pleased with themselves for a job well done.

Chorley lay on the trolley staring at the grey metal ceiling with its single circular light panel. After a few minutes his impatience and curiosity got the better of him and he sat up and slid into a sitting position, gingerly putting his injured foot on the floor. He winced. The pain was worse than ever. No chance of running away, then. Or even standing up.

With a hiss of hydraulics that startled Chorley, the door

slid open and a towering, terrifying figure entered the cell.

Fully seven feet tall, it had limbs like tree-trunks encased in plated black leather. It wore a ridged black shell of shiny blue-black armour, built up around the shoulders, making it look as though it had no neck. Its face was leathery, pale, and totally without mercy, green eyes gleaming with savage cruelty below a low forehead topped with receding black hair that gleamed like tar in the artificial light.

'You have been found trespassing on Dominex property!' it rumbled in a voice that seemed to shake the walls of the cell. 'You will be destroyed! No – you will be... proscuted. But first – you will be questioned!'

Before Chorley could process any of this, another figure shoved its way into the cell. This one looked like the older, cleverer brother of the first. The two... men? ... stared down at Chorley, still prone in the trolley.

'Stand!' the new arrival bellowed.

Chorley gazed helplessly up, it felt as if he was lying at the bottom of two statues carved into a cliff face. 'I can't!' he wailed. 'My ankle.'

'It appears to be injured,' the first muttered.

'Scan!' the second ordered.

The less hirsute one went to a panel on the wall and removed a device that, bizarrely, resembled a futuristic hairdryer. Chorley cowered as the nozzle was pointed in his direction, and closed his eyes, remembering Ian Cawdery, expecting obliteration.

Instead, he heard a voice rumble, 'Slight fracture to the talus bone.'

'Initiate regeneration!'

The hairdryer device emitted a low hum and Chorley felt

a globe of heat close around his foot and ankle. There was a moment of pain so intense that Chorley couldn't even scream, then it was over, leaving a pins-and-needles tingling.

'Now! Stand!'

Gingerly, Chorley did as he was ordered. The pain in his ankle had completely gone. 'Hey, you could market that, make a fortune,' he babbled.

The pair ignored him, regarding him with baleful, impatient glares. Now he was standing up, they still towered over him. A knot of fear tied itself in his guts, and yet he felt a sense of elation. He was on to something, something big. As big as the business in the Underground – maybe even bigger.

'You're aliens, aren't you?' he said softly.

'I am Navigator Deka, this is Probationer Azbo. We are Dominators! Masters of the Ten Galaxies! We have subjugated thousands of races – Bandrils, Tivolians, Gonds, Gurdels, Monoids – all have quailed before our might!'

'And you're here to "subjugate" us?'

Probationer Deka leaned down so his face was inches from Chorley's. 'Our purpose here is for us to know and you... to not know.'

'Touché. Hang on – if you're aliens, how come you can speak, and understand, English?'

'Silence!' Probationer Deka bellowed so loudly that the walls of the cell seemed to reverberate like a ringing bell. He swung around to face Azbo. 'Is the Mentotron prepared?'

'Yes, Navigator Deka.'

'Then bring it in.'

'Command accepted.' Azbo left briefly to return wheeling a compact, domed device borne on a trolley. From the side of the machine, wires protruded. It looked ominously medical.

Chorley backed up against the wall of the cell – and found himself slammed back against it, as if by an invisible hand. 'I can't move!' he yelled.

The two Dominators ignored him, instead busying themselves with their strange device. Shortly Azbo approached him, trailing two wires from the machine. These wires ended in sticky pads and Chorley could do nothing but grimace in dread as the Dominator attached them, with curious delicacy in spite of his massive gloved hands, to Chorley's temples.

Chorley blinked away tears as he watched Azbo step backwards and stand, before him, arms folded, nodding in satisfaction. Deka flicked a switch on the strange machine and there was a low droning hum of power. Chorley opened his mouth to scream – but there was no pain, only a slight tingling at the temples where the wires were attached.

Deka moved to stand beside and slightly in front of his subordinate. 'Name!'

Chorley desperately recalled the cover story. 'Peter Carver.'

The machine emitted a harsh buzz and sparks of agony shot through Chorley's head.

'You lie!' roared his interrogator. 'If you answer falsely, the Mentotron will detect it, and you will suffer!'

'You might have told me that before we started.' Sweat trickled into Chorley's eyes and he couldn't even move to wipe it away.

'Now. Name!'

'Harold Barrington Chorley.'

'What is your function?'

'I'm a journalist.'

'Explain! Expand!'

For alien conquerors they're a bit dim, Chorley thought. 'I report on events, happenings...'

'For what purpose?'

Chorley felt a disorientating mix of exasperation and fear. 'Well... to tell the people of this planet what's really going on.' Their blank stares emboldened him. And he was deep enough in now that the truth wouldn't hurt – in fact, quite the opposite. 'Take this place, you lot down here with your robots. I came down here to find out what was going on' – there was a tingle in his temples – 'okay I was sent down here to find out what was going on. And if I'd managed to get away, your game would be up, mush!'

Azbo stepped towards him, his fists bunching into cannonballs. 'You must be destroyed!'

'Silence!' bellowed Deka. He was staring at Chorley with a thoughtful expression in his deep-set, red-rimmed eyes. 'You... take information, and spread it to the rest of your kind?'

'That's about the size of it.' Chorley didn't like the way Azbo was staring at him, or the way his massive black-clad fingers were twitching.

'Enough talk,' growled Azbo. 'Let me destroy this worm!'

'Silence!' barked Deka.

Again he leaned down so his pale, leathery face was inches from Chorley's own. His breath had a sour chemical smell. Chorley tried to cower away but was unable to move even an inch.

The Dominator's green eyes burned with malevolence.

'This function you speak of may be of use to us.'

Chorley swallowed. His mouth was dry. Deka's words rattled around in his head. Realisation dawned. 'Are… are you offering me a job?'

— CHAPTER ELEVEN —

Tactical Retreat

Cold earth pressed against his face. Inside his head, pain. Churning, throbbing pain. The man lay prone and broken, his mind desperately trying to reassemble itself. Broken shards of memory lay scattered across a black, blasted plain.

His mind's eye picked up the nearest piece, the better to examine it.

Darkness. Cold rock all around. Stacked racks of poison. A silver gateway – was that what he'd passed through? A gateway to this nether world? The gateway opening. Things emerging – panic – hiding. Then – something his mind shied away from, a piece chipped off the shard. Then running, scrambling, and falling rocks and choking dust. Then no way out and running, running again and then sudden, head-splitting pain and then – nothing. The nothing had lasted for an unknowable time, and was a shard of memory the man would never recover. The next piece was jagged, and it hurt to handle.

Whiteness. Wandering. Lost in a white formless nothing. Dead. Had to be. Dead and stumbling around limbo. Hell's waiting-room. Tottering seemingly forever, a lost, wounded soldier on the last battlefield of all. Then tripping, falling, landing face down, his head once more exploding with pain.

There were further shards, out of reach for now. He lay there, the whiteness all around him, the pain within him, the world seeming to bob and recede away from him and then return and wash over him like a tide. He felt sick. He was sick. He vomited up bile onto the – the grass? Yes. It was grass. Though his vision blurred with every throb of his head, he could see that it was grass. Short, wiry grass. His head swam. Were there lawns in limbo?

A strange sound echoed around him. Wheezing, mechanical. He blinked. There, an oddly familiar blue box seemed to stand on the grass before him, disappearing on the wind.

He felt simultaneously microscopic and the size of the entire universe. Green grass, like the green, green grass of home. But this was not home. It was–

The shards began to move together, sliding back into place like the pieces of a broken mosaic.

Chorley's panicked phone call. The argument with Hamilton. Out of bounds. I'm going anyway. The dreadful sausages – burned, burned, the horrible smell of burned meat–

The long hot drive down. The dreadful steak pie. Chorley. Cawdery and his brown corduroy trousers–

A lancing beam of orange light – the screams of a man in mortal pain – the horrible smell of burnt *flesh*–

The caves. The tunnel. Smackhead Rock (his head seemed to pulse with renewed pain at the memory). Bishop's Cavern. The barrels. The silver door. The silver door opening and–

The little robots.

Terrible mechanisms of destruction.

The Quarks.

The enemy.

The deep, belligerent voice ordering destruction – the voice of the enemy.

Dominic Vaar being interviewed by Robin Day on *Panorama* – the face of the enemy.

Lethbridge-Stewart lay face down on Dartmoor as the memories cascaded through his mind, finding their places like ball bearings settling into holes. His head rattled and clattered, a juddering, mechanical vibration that–

That wasn't inside his head.

It was coming from outside – from the real world!

Lethbridge-Stewart rolled over and sat up, a hand going to his head which pulsed with renewed stabs of pain.

He squinted into the mist. There was something there – something square and bulky – casting two beams of light out into the mist, its engine turning over.

Then, a voice.

'Hey, man, are you okay?'

Lethbridge-Stewart allowed himself to be helped to his feet. 'Thank you,' he muttered, swaying unsteadily as he regarded his rescuers. There were two – a gangly youth with a mass of curly ginger hair, and a small, slight girl with a kind, watchful face. A short distance beyond them stood a camper van, its engine turning over, the twin beams of its headlamps lancing out like searchlights into the mist. He winced as the pain in his head throbbed as if his skull was fit to crack.

The girl stepped forward to steady him. 'Come on, let's get you inside.' She began to lead him towards the van.

'What are you doing wandering about out here, man?'

said the youth, ambling along beside him.

The image of the Quarks blasting Cawdery into charred oblivion flashed through his mind. He shook his head to dispel it. 'Lost... fell over. Dratted mist.'

'Yeah, you have to be careful, they can come down really suddenly, even at this time of the year.'

At the van the youth reached in and killed the engine. The silence was abrupt and alarming. Lethbridge-Stewart let them help him up and into the van. It was like crawling into a cosy cave. Rugs and cushions were strewn everywhere, the interior light bathed everything in a warm orange glow, and there was the unmistakable aroma of hash smoke. And as he watched, the ginger youth sat down opposite Lethbridge-Stewart and took a massive drag on an enormous roll-up. The fumes drifted over towards Lethbridge-Stewart and he could not help but inhale. His head swam as if he was on the deck of a small boat on a storm – but the pain ebbed away almost to nothing. He glanced at his watch: almost 10pm. He must have been out for hours.

'Here you are.' The girl brought him something and he sipped without even asking what it was, only discover that it was coffee. Bitter, delicious coffee.

Lethbridge-Stewart sank back in the seat, feeling the tension seep slowly out of him.

'Let's have a look at that head.' Lethbridge-Stewart let the girl examine him. 'Doesn't look serious. Better get it checked out though, you might have concussion. What exactly happened to you?'

'I was exploring the caves,' he said guardedly. 'Must have banged my head, wandered back out on the moor.

Lucky you found me.'

'Too right!' said the youth. 'Dangerous out there – especially near that Dominex place, man!'

Realisation dawned on Lethbridge-Stewart. 'You – you were with the journalist? Harold Chorley? When his car was attacked and destroyed?'

The youth frowned suspiciously. 'How do you know that, man?'

Lethbridge-Stewart realised that in his relaxed state, he had said more than he had wanted to. 'You're Mike, and you're Emma?'

'Yeah!' There was an edge to the youth's voice. 'How do you know, man? Have you been spying on us?'

Emma put a hand on Mike's arm and he sank back into his seat. 'How do you know us? Are you a friend of Mr Chorley's?'

'You could say that,' said Lethbridge-Stewart. He came to a decision. These people might be what you would call 'hippies', but Lethbridge-Stewart didn't like to put people in boxes. *Dangerous to judge the book by the cover.* And despite Mike's paranoia, probably caused by the hash, they looked like decent people. *Though they'd never make soldiers, they were against Dominex, so the enemy of my enemy, and all that.* 'I'm an associate of Mr Chorley's. I've come down here to investigate his report of what happened last night.' He glanced around the interior of the van. 'I thought there were more of you?'

'Huh!' Mike took another drag on the blunt.

'There were, but the rest of us didn't want to come back, so they've gone on to Plymouth,' Emma explained.

'And why have you come back?'

136

'We couldn't leave Harold in the state he was in.'

Mike grimaced. 'We *could* have.'

Emma elbowed him in the ribs. 'So, we've come back to see how he was. We were going to camp out on the moors but this mist came down and we found you. So how is he?'

'How is who?' The hash smoke was making Lethbridge-Stewart's head swim again.

'Harold!'

'Ah.' Lethbridge-Stewart looked from one to the other of them. The last he'd seen of the man was prone on the floor of Bishop's Cavern with a broken ankle. He suddenly felt cold as he realised that Chorley could very well be dead. 'Oh. Er...'

'Is he all right?'

Lethbridge-Stewart looked from one to the other. Time for the truth; well, a version of it, at least. 'He's missing. Missing in action. I'm Colonel Lethbridge-Stewart and I'm the head of a task force investigating Dominex for possible illegal activities.'

'I knew it!' Mike shouted jubilantly. 'They're making nukes down there, aren't they? In the caves under the moors!'

'I'm afraid I cannot give you any detail – it's classified. But I can tell you that Mr Chorley, a local man, and I went into the caves earlier today. The local man was killed by the very things that attacked you last night. And Harold Chorley is missing.' Lethbridge-Stewart pictured Chorley prone on the floor of the Bishop's Cavern, unable to run. He'd have had no chance against the little robots. 'Presumed, I am very sorry to say, dead.'

They sat in silence for a while.

'They – they killed him?' said Emma in a whisper.

'Not just him,' said Mike, anger in his voice again. 'The missing hikers, remember?' He jumped up, almost banging his head on the ceiling. 'So what's the plan, soldier man? Are you gonna go in, storm Dominex?'

Emma shushed him again. 'Perhaps we should try talking to them, you know? Diplomacy.'

Mike snorted.

'I'm inclined to agree with Mike,' said Lethbridge-Stewart. 'From what I have seen there is no negotiating with forces like this. You've seen them in action. Do you really think those things, and the people behind them, would listen? No, they must be fought. But the plan for now is a tactical retreat, to our base of operations.' His head was beginning to throb again, and he felt drained of energy. 'I need to rest before I make my next move.' Which would be a report to Hamilton and a demand for an immediate investigation of Dominex, he decided.

Emma frowned. 'Base of operations?'

'The pub, *The White Hart*.'

The pair stared at him.

'Well, come on man! I'm commandeering this vehicle for military purposes.'

Mike sneered. 'This is a caravan of peace, man!'

'Try telling that to the things that killed Mr Cawdery, that attacked you, that could be out and about on the moor – looking for me!'

Without a further word of protest Mike scrambled into the driver seat and started up the engine.

Their arrival back at *The White Hart* caused quite a commotion. Word had somehow got round about their caving expedition, and Lethbridge-Stewart was beset with questions, mainly about the whereabouts and wellbeing of Ian Cawdery (no one seemed to care about the fate of Harold Chorley).

Mike and Emma had retreated to a corner table and were trying, and failing, not to be noticed. A whiskery old chap had joined them and was chattering gibberish that seemed to both confuse and alarm them. Lethbridge-Stewart found himself in the bar surrounded by a throng of well-oiled locals (it was now near last orders) all of whom were glaring suspiciously at him.

'Where's Ian? What have you done with Ian?' The question came from a ruddy-faced individual chewing on a roll-up.

'Yeah, what have you done with Ian?' said another.

There were shouts of agreement that had a dangerously aggressive edge. The last thing Lethbridge-Stewart needed was to inform this rabble about the death of their fellow drinker. They'd probably storm up to Dominex with blazing torches.

Time to take control. He raised his hands. 'Silence!'

Silence fell, from the look on their faces more out of surprise than obedience. Before anyone had a chance to speak up, Lethbridge-Stewart went on.

'I am Colonel Lethbridge-Stewart and I am leading an investigation in this area, the details of which are at present classified.'

'It's Dominex, ain't it?' shouted the red-faced fellow.

'That information is classified.'

Roars of disbelief and anger. Lethbridge-Stewart's head throbbed. He was tired and hurt. He needed to recuperate, but first, he had to get things under control.

'What about Ian? You went down the caves with him, we all know that. And now he's missing! Like his brother!'

'The location of Mr Cawdery is classified,' said Lethbridge-Stewart.

There was an uproar, which he let surge around the crowded bar for a few moments. Then someone shouted, 'We'll call the police! Someone go get Sergeant Samuels!'

'I urge you not to call the police!' Lethbridge-Stewart shouted. 'I will talk to your Sergeant Samuels in the morning to ensure he is fully briefed. But this is a military operation, under military jurisdiction. I am the officer in charge, and the situation is under my control.'

'You declaring martial law?' asked the red-faced chap, leaning so close to Lethbridge-Stewart that he could smell his beery breath.

'If the situation demands it, then martial law may be an option. At present–' More shouting. Lethbridge-Stewart raised his voice. 'At present, let's just all calm down, go home and get a good night's sleep.'

'Not until you tell us what's happened to Ian. And your journalist friend!'

An expectant silence fell. No way out of this. A version of the truth would have to suffice. 'Both are missing, presumed dead.'

Gasps and cries of incredulity.

'What? How? What's killed them?' said the red-faced fellow.

'Don't say it's classified!' someone else shouted.

'It's that Dominex lot!' cried another.

'Silence, please!' Lethbridge-Stewart waited for the

clamour to die down once more. 'They accompanied me on a mission into the caves to investigate reports of illegal activities. We were met by enemy forces and were attacked. I managed to escape but Mr Cawdery and Mr Chorley, well, I believe they are both now dead.'

'What is this enemy? Russkis?' asked an old fellow in a flat cap.

'Enemies of the realm, that's all you need to know. I really can't tell you anything else, but please, you must trust me that I will sort everything out.'

'Last orders,' said the landlord, almost apologetically.

'The drinks are on me,' said Lethbridge-Stewart. This earned him a few grudging nods. Attention shifted from Lethbridge-Stewart to the bar, but conversation remained heated. He went to join Mike and Emma who were engaged in rather incoherent conversation with the whiskery old fellow.

'Meet Josh, he's a wizard!' said Mike with a smirk.

'Oo ar? You bin chasin' gordannun piskies?'

'Not exactly.' Lethbridge-Stewart did his best to ignore the old chap.

'Who are these enemy forces?' said Emma, her face serious. 'Are they anything to do with Dominex?'

'You know what I'm going to say to that.'

'Classified.'

'Correct. Now if you'll excuse me, I have a rather important telephone call to make.'

'Hamilton here. Is that you, Lethbridge-Stewart?' Despite the lateness of the hour, the general sounded fully alert and awake, as if he'd been sitting beside the phone waiting for

141

Lethbridge-Stewart's call.

'Yes, sir. Sorry to report, those sausages were disgusting. Even sorrier to report, this line isn't secure. I'm calling from *The White Hart*, Buckfastleigh. I'm phoning in my report.'

'Did you discover anything?'

'I've got evidence, sir. Hard evidence, of just the type we've been looking for. But it's come at a cost. A local chap has been killed and I fear the same has happened to Chorley.'

'Dashed sorry to hear that.' Hamilton's voice remained calm, betraying no emotion. 'Go on.'

'I've seen these transforming robots – Quarks, they're called. They're what did for this local chap, and now pretty obviously, the missing cavers and hikers. And Chorley's car, for that matter.'

'Best stick to the facts, Colonel, not conjecture.'

'I've seen these Quarks kill, on the orders of a voice I believe belonged to the management of Dominex.'

'Now, steady on!' Hamilton snapped, irritated. 'Just give me the facts, Colonel. What exactly happened down there?'

Lethbridge-Stewart gave a brief but detailed account of his fateful exploration of the caves. 'So Chorley's either dead, or a prisoner,' he concluded. 'I strongly suggest we send a force in there, forthwith, and blast our "hands off" orders.'

Silence. Lethbridge-Stewart imagined he could hear the machinery of Hamilton's mind ticking over.

At length he said, 'I'm sending a squad down.'

Lethbridge-Stewart almost swooned with relief. The pain in his head returned, a sudden stab, reminding him that he badly needed to rest. 'When... when will they get here?'

'They'll travel overnight and be with you by the morning.

The White Hart, you say?'

'Yes, sir.'

'They should be with you by 9am. Be ready.'

'Don't worry, I will be.'

'Whilst you're waiting, liaise with the local police, try to keep people away from the Dominex plant, but try not to cause a panic. And have a pint, old chap. You've earned it.' The line went dead.

A pint. Just one wouldn't hurt, might even help the pain in his head – as long as he stuck to just the one. A pint and a good night's sleep. And in the morning – at last – engagement with the enemy.

— CHAPTER TWELVE —

The World's Strongest Man

The gunmetal grey Mercedes Benz cruised effortlessly through the London streets. Its tinted windows were all wound fully up despite the heat of the June morning, completely hiding the occupants from view. No one paid any attention to this remarkable vehicle, because such a thing was a common sight in the capital. To the person on the street, plush, expensive cars were as much a part of London traffic as red double-decker buses or black cabs. They were the vehicles of the rich and the famous. Movie stars, businessmen, politicians, oil sheikhs – behind those inscrutable panes could be any one of these.

This particular vehicle did indeed contain one of this breed – the chief executive of a major company. Nothing unusual about that.

Director Vaar gazed from the rear-seat window at the milling masses of humans, in their vehicles or on foot, coming in and out of buildings, going about their business, completely oblivious to the presence in their midst. His lip curled in a snarl of satisfaction and contempt. How easily these creatures had been duped. How easily they had been bought with promises of free energy. He thought of the energy minister, his lined, eager face glistening with a sheen of sweat. His greed, so naked and obvious, so easy to exploit. This race, this human race, were mere worms, fit only to be crushed underfoot by the boots of the Dominators. They truly deserved the annihilation that was coming their way on completion of Project M.

The car extricated itself smoothly from London like a knife being slid out from a wound. It was shortly on the M3, in the fast lane, a silver bullet, a silver rocket. Despite himself, Vaar could not help but admire the engineering skills of the humans that had designed and constructed the Mercedes. True, it was only a primitive motor vehicle, bound forever to the skin of this world, and it could only traverse terrain specially constructed for it, but in its brutal, simple way, it was beautiful. Given time – many centuries, Vaar considered – the human race might escape the confines of their world, and go on to be an intergalactic power in their own right. They might even become a worthy foe for the Dominator fleet! Vaar laughed aloud at the thought; a short, harsh bark. Anyway, it would never happen. The human race would not develop beyond this present era – Project M would see to that. No, the pinnacle of human ingenuity and engineering was this Mercedes Benz W115 with its 2-litre internal combustion engine and grey finish that reminded Vaar of the colour of the outer shell of a Quark. Perhaps, when the time came to leave, he would take the vehicle with him.

Compared to those of the Dominators, however, the achievements of the human race were nothing. Mere twitches of blind infancy. Vaar leaned back in his seat, closed his eyes, and thought of the long, long journey he, and his people, had undertaken.

*

145

The Mercedes had left the motorway and was now speeding down a lesser road towards the county of Devon and the moorland on which the Dominators had established their base. Vaar gazed out of the window at the green English countryside as it sped past and considered his responsibility for the success of Project M. The usual Dominator modus operandi was to send a ship with two Dominators and a consignment of a dozen Quarks to assess a planet for its suitability for conversion into fuel, and its inhabitants as a slave force. The Dominant Echelon had, however, decreed that new methods needed to be found, in order to keep the fleet fully fuelled. So Director Vaar had himself come up with Project M. A radical, dangerous project, fraught with risk, but Vaar had convinced the Echelon that he could manage that risk. The key selling point of Project M was its power management ratio. For a minimal input, the output was far in excess of usual Dominator schemes.

And so Vaar had come to the planet Earth with a Navigator and a Probationer and a consignment of Quarks, and set Project M in motion. Now it was very near completion. Director Vaar allowed himself a smile as the Mercedes wound its way up the narrow lanes towards Dartmoor.

'Driver! Play music.'

Presently the car was filled with the strains of Holst's *Mars, Bringer of War*, Director Vaar's favourite piece of Earth music, which he admired for its technical brilliance in much the same way as he admired the Mercedes. It also reminded him of one of the Dominator Martial Anthems, only it was less strident and bombastic.

The driver was a Dominex employee, who – like all of

the rest of his race – had no conception of the true nature of his employers. Dominex employed about a dozen staff, all of them based in their London offices, all employed in the necessary but tedious activities of finance and accounting and the like. None of them worked or were even allowed into the Dominex plant on Dartmoor. That was fully automated – all the work was done by the Quarks. An unavoidably necessary use of Quark power. Director Vaar had assessed the risk of using conditioned human slaves in the plant, and graded it red. The mind, even the primitive human mind, was a tricky thing to control, conditioning had been known to slip, and if the humans ever found out about the true nature of Project M, Dominex would be shut down. Better to use the reliable Quarks. Even so, the power output was negligible against the massive power gains of Project M.

With the music still playing, the Mercedes drove smoothly up to the gates of the Dominex plant, where it stopped.

Vaar opened the door and swung his massive frame out of the car. He smoothed down the creases on his business suit.

The driver, a small, fair-haired human male, was looking expectantly up from the open window.

Vaar composed his leaden features into a smile. Soon, this human would be dead, along with all of its kind. Vaar had no further use for him, but he felt a twinge of sadness at the thought of the destruction of the Mercedes. 'You have done well. A very… pleasant journey. Now, return to London, and await further instructions.'

Director Vaar watched as the car moved off down the

lane, and out of sight over the brow of the hill. *Instructions that will never come*, he thought. He would never need the services of the driver again. He was here now and here he would remain, to oversee the very final phase of Project M.

He swung back round to face the gates which opened in front of him, then strode through into the Dominex plant. He walked down the main thoroughfare, lined with featureless concrete buildings, towards the centre of the installation. There stood the largest building, an enormous fortress-like construction of grey concrete. It housed the Dominator control room, and at the far end a special chamber in which Project M awaited completion.

Director Vaar walked up to the only door in the vast wall of the structure, which opened as he approached, and he strode through. He walked down shining metal corridors and into his personal chamber. It contained his recharging unit, a desk, and a steel-shuttered cabinet, nothing more. Scowling, he took off his business suit and tossed it on the desk. Hopefully, he would never need it again, but on second thoughts, it was probably prudent to keep it in storage, in case there was need for further diplomacy. So he hung the suit up, rather prosaically, in the steel-shuttered cabinet, which also contained trophies of his conquests: the skull of a Valethske general, a carpet fashioned from the hides of Ogrons, the scalp of a Monoid.

Director Vaar donned his Dominator armour, sealing himself into the metallic plates and fastening the outer shell around his massive shoulders.

Although the humans had never posed any threat to him, he felt better, safer, more potent once encased in the protective cladding of a Dominator. But even without such

148

armour, he would still be able to crush a human to death with his bare hands. They were so frail! Frail, and doomed to fail. He had witnessed, on television, a programme called *The World's Strongest Man*. Muscled specimens of humanity had lifted prodigious weights with much grunting and straining. Some, indeed, bore shoulders that resembled the mighty neckless shoulders of a Dominator, but even these specimens would be no match for Vaar. He admired himself in a panel of polished metal. Surely he, Vaar, was this world's strongest man!

Banishing such prideful thoughts, he turned his mind to Project M, and stomped back along the corridor to the control chamber, in which Navigator Deka and Probationer Azbo stood awaiting his command.

There was no time, or need, or inclination for pleasantries. 'What is the status of Project M?'

'One hundred percent,' stated Deka. 'Conversion is now in progress. We will have capability within four cycles.'

'That is excellent. You have done well.' He bore down on Azbo. 'Your behaviour, Probationer, has constituted a risk to Project M. You have wasted Quark energy. You have brought undue attention to us by needlessly destroying several humans. Fortunately for you, there has been no delay to the schedule. But if the humans attack us in force now, they could prevent the deployment of Project M. Should this occur, you will be destroyed. Fortunately, again, you are needed for the success of Project M.'

Probationer Azbo's eyes gleamed dully. 'Yes, Director Vaar,' he mumbled.

Vaar swung back round to Deka. 'Bring in the captured human!'

Deka pressed a button on the console and a door slid open. A human male stepped through, followed by one Quark, its primary weapon deployed. The Tellurian moved with a sleepwalker's gait and its face bore a glassy, faraway expression.

'He has been programmed in a way which will mitigate the risk of further undue attention from the humans,' said Deka.

'Good!' Director Vaar turned to the human. 'Name!'

'Harold Chorley.'

'Function!'

'Press and Public Relations Officer for Dominex Industries.'

'Loyalty!'

'To the Dominators.'

'Is there any risk of his programming slipping?'

'Minimal,' Deka answered. 'Should he show any signs of independence, the Quarks have been ordered to destroy him.'

'Yes, destroy!' growled Azbo, clenching his fists enthusiastically.

'You have already been warned, Probationer!' bellowed Vaar. 'Now, we must deploy this programmed human properly. We will use the medium of television, as we did before, to convince the humans of our benign motives. Prepare a Quark with video recording facilities!'

Deka bowed. 'Command accepted.'

'Now take me to the launch chamber. I want to see the missiles with my own eyes.'

Director Vaar strode along the central corridor of the main

Dominex building, flanked by his Navigator and Probationer, a sense of pride and fulfilment swelling in his massive chest. Project M was proving to be a complete success. Glory for himself, glory for the Dominators. This surely meant promotion to the Dominant Echelon.

The trio came to a halt before a pair of massive metal doors.

'Through here, Director, lies the fruit of our labours,' rumbled Navigator Deka with pride.

'Open,' growled Vaar. 'I am impatient.'

'Command accepted.' Probationer Azbo pressed a chunky switch and the doors slid open with a smooth hum of astutely-managed power.

They revealed a vast concrete-floored hangar with a corrugated metal ceiling, sloping down to meet breeze-block walls. The place was unlit, to conserve energy, but on either side of the chamber massive shapes could be seen; metal tubes, driven into the concrete floor at an angle, pointing up like the muzzles of enormous cannon towards circular hatches in the ceiling. From the ends of these tubes, shining silver nosecones could be seen. And around the bases, thick coils of ridged, semi-transparent tubing curled, like giant snakes crushing their prey. The tubes pulsed with an eerie green luminescence, the only source of light in the chamber, which cast everything in a sickly green glow. These tubes all led to a central console, manned by a solitary Quark. The whole place throbbed with the thrum of unimaginable and deadly energy.

'Observe the process of conversion in process... Er, *progress*,' said Azbo. 'Must we continue to converse in this strange language, Director? With our objective so close to completion?'

Probationer Azbo mumbled his agreement with this.

'Negative!' Director Vaar rounded on his two subordinates. 'Nothing must compromise Project M! We may still need to deal with the humans. Four cycles represents one week on this world. That is plenty of time for the humans to interfere! Now – take me to the prisoner. It is about time we made use of his abilities.'

— CHAPTER THIRTEEN —

Safe as Houses

The next morning, Lethbridge-Stewart woke bright and early, and much refreshed. The pain in his head had subsided, and he didn't think he had concussion – but then you never knew, and he had smacked his head hard on that dratted, if aptly-named, rock.

He dressed quickly and went down for a leisurely if lonely breakfast of sausages (decent ones, local fare), bacon, eggs, and toast served by the landlord Cyril. He was the only tenant at *The White Hart*, Emma and Mike having decided to spend the night in their camper van.

After breakfast he wandered outside, impatient for the cavalry to arrive; eager to get to work, to get into Dominex and rescue Chorley, if the man was still alive. He considered giving Hamilton a quick call but had resisted, as he had nothing more really to say; the call would have just been something to do to ameliorate the anxiety of waiting.

The street outside was empty. It was only half eight on a Thursday morning and there was no one about; not even the milkman, who had come and gone hours earlier. With nothing else to do, Lethbridge-Stewart took in the two pints left by the front door of the pub and set them down on the bar, where they looked incongruous against the backdrop of ale pumps and spirits. To kill time, he went back to his room and checked over his Enfield service revolver. They'd need far more potent weaponry against the Quarks than his grandfather's finest. Lethbridge-Stewart was confident that Hamilton would provide this on the evidence of his report. Couple of SLRs, a dozen grenades, perhaps a bazooka or two, would put paid to the comical but deadly little robots. Lethbridge-Stewart wished he had more intelligence, knew how many of the things there were.

He moved to the window of the small first floor bedroom, where he could see Emma and Mike's van, in the pub car park next to the landlord's Austin Maxi and his own silver Mercedes. He ran over the plan of action he had sketched out in his mind.

Once the troops arrived, they'd go straight up to the Dominex plant and demand entry – which he had no doubt would be denied. Then they would force entry, and battle would be joined. His heart beat faster at the prospect.

As he watched, the side door of the camper van slid open and Emma emerged, yawning, clad only in a long white dress. Lethbridge-Stewart looked away, momentarily embarrassed. Wouldn't have pegged those two as early risers. When he glanced back out of the window, Mike had joined her, barefoot in ragged flares and a tie-dye t-shirt, and the couple stood hugging in the bright sunlight of the early June morning. Lethbridge-Stewart thought of Sally, then again looked away. He wondered why they were still hanging around. Leaving his holstered gun in the bedside table, he went downstairs and out into the car park, coughing as he opened the door, giving them time to realise they were no longer alone.

'Good morning!' he said briskly and cheerily. 'You

know, there's no need to hang around. You could go and join your friends in Plymouth.'

Mike, still hugging Emma, squinted down at Lethbridge-Stewart from beneath his frizz of ginger curls. 'We're staying.'

'Oh.'

'Yeah, well we wanna find out what's happened to Harold,' said Emma. 'He's one of us.'

Mike snorted.

Emma nudged him in the ribs. 'You know what I mean. He's on our side. Against the likes of Dominex.'

'Dominex,' muttered Lethbridge-Stewart. He turned and gazed in the general direction of the moor. 'You really think they're building nuclear weapons in there? What's your source?'

Emma looked evasive. 'There's been talk at CND meetings, rumours, that's all really. Conspiracy theories.' She frowned. 'You've been down there, you've seen these robot things, you know they're up to no good.'

The low growl of approaching vehicle engines broke the silence of the summer morning.

'Yes, and we'll soon find out exactly what.' Lethbridge-Stewart left the pair and strode out to the front of the pub, to welcome the reinforcements. He was rather disconcerted to see just a single Land Rover and an armoured truck – the covered, windowless kind, used for transporting prisoners. Not the sort of transport you'd convey troops in, in any kind of weather.

The Land Rover came to an abrupt halt outside the pub, blocking the road. The armoured truck stopped behind it. Its doors opened and two soldiers leapt down, boots thudding on the warm tarmac. Lethbridge-Stewart was alarmed to see that they were Military Police. They immediately ran into the car park where they began to manhandle Mike and Emma back towards the truck.

'What the blazes is going on?' Lethbridge-Stewart asked.

'They're being taken in for questioning.'

The voice came from behind him. Lethbridge-Stewart whirled round to be confronted by a familiar face to which he couldn't at that moment attach a name.

'Help us!' screamed Emma.

'Fascists!' Mike was yelling. It took the two MPs to restrain him, which allowed Emma to break free.

She ran up to Lethbridge-Stewart. 'What's going on?'

'I wish I knew.'

Two more MPs had emerged from the rear of the armoured truck and they ran across to haul Emma away.

'Would you mind coming with me, sir?'

Lethbridge-Stewart turned back to the familiar face. Of course – it was Sergeant Johnny Rivers, an old face from Korea.

'Yes, I would. What the devil is going on?'

A couple of young soldiers had got out of the Land Rover and were standing with their rifles across their chests.

'I take it I'm being arrested. Would you be so kind as to tell me why?'

Sergeant Rivers had the good grace to look embarrassed. 'Orders of Major General Hamilton, sir.'

Lethbridge-Stewart's mind raced. Why would Hamilton have him arrested, after all the evidence of his report? Must be pressure from above. Which meant that the energy minister must be in the pocket of Dominex. Which meant

– he didn't know what, but he did know that there was no point in resisting arrest.

'Very well, take me to Hamilton then, I'll have it out with him.'

'You're to be taken to a safe house, sir, for the duration.'

'The duration of what? Come on, Johnny, we've served together. Fought together! Drank together, you name it. Can't you tell me?'

Sergeant Rivers' face remained blank but his eyes were full of turmoil, of the conflict between his orders and his friendship. It was a one-sided battle. 'Please come with me, sir. Don't make me use force.'

Lethbridge-Stewart nodded and sighed. 'Very well. You're only following orders, as you should. I'll come quietly.' He walked towards the Land Rover. The two privates stepped aside. One of them opened the rear door and gestured inside with the butt of his rifle. Lethbridge-Stewart glanced at the armoured truck, which was pulling away, its gears grinding. He turned back to Sergeant Rivers. 'They'd better not be harmed. They haven't done anything.'

'Get in, sir. Please.'

No choice. Lethbridge-Stewart slid into the back seat of the Land Rover and closed his eyes as the tarpaulin flap fell and closed off the outside world.

Soon he was being driven away from the pub, from Buckfastleigh, and from the moor and the mysteries held by Dominex. Away from the battle.

Lethbridge-Stewart caught a glimpse of moorland in the driver's mirror as they took the road out of the town.

'This isn't over,' he muttered under his breath.

*

Harold Chorley, Press and Public Relations Officer for Dominex Industries, sat attentively at his desk, awaiting orders. He felt a surge of warm gratitude to Director Vaar for the wonderful opportunity he had been given. Working for such an innovative, cutting edge company like Dominex, one that was going to bring cheap energy to the whole world! They'd given him a nice little office right in the middle of the Dominex plant, with his own desk and typewriter, even a little bed for when he got tired, and a bucket for – other needs.

There was a weird buzzing in his head, just behind his eyes, but he put that down to excitement. He was just very excited to be here. At the forefront of the nuclear industry. The epicentre, even.

The door slid open and Director Vaar strode in, accompanied by Navigator Deka and a Quark. The Director was back in his business suit once more. How powerful and handsome he looked! And the Quark…

Lancing orange light and pain…

Chorley shook his head. Must have been a dream,

Director Vaar beckoned with a huge finger. 'Come. It is time for your first assignment.'

'Command accepted!' barked Chorley enthusiastically, knowing this was a phrase that pleased his new masters. He then followed their hulking figures – how big were their shoulders! – and the little robot along the shining metal corridors of Dominex. They eventually arrived in a box-like room, one wall lined with complicated-looking equipment, all dials and flashing lights. In the centre of the room stood another Quark.

'Quark! Deploy!' bellowed Navigator Deka.

The front of the Quark began to open like the door of an oven, and Chorley felt another qualm of fear, fear that was quickly replaced by curious excitement. In a recess in the Quark's gunmetal grey body, something familiar glinted in the harsh lighting.

Chorley pointed with a trembling finger at the little robot. 'Is... is that a television camera?'

Director Vaar grinned down at him. 'Correct, human! It is a television camera. For we are going to make a television programme.'

Corporal Sally Wright was worried. She hadn't heard from Alistair in two days, and no one seemed to know where he was. She'd asked around, but to no avail. People either genuinely didn't know, or did know and had been ordered not to say. Well, she understood that. She would do the same, in those circumstances. Didn't make it easier, though, not knowing if he was safe... or in serious danger.

She decided that in order to find out the truth, she would have to go directly to Chelsea Barracks herself. So Sally travelled to London once her duties at Strategic Command had been completed for the day, and cornered Corporal Bishop in the mess hall. The mess was a loud, echoing place; basic furniture, bare walls and scrubbed tiled floor, the clatter of cutlery and the chatter of conversation meaning they needed to lean across the table to converse.

'Are you quite sure you don't know where the colonel is?' she asked insistently. 'Just between ourselves?'

Bishop shook his head, took another sip of tea, and Sally couldn't help but notice the bandage on one hand. Injury sustained during his last field assignment, she knew, much like the light burn still visible on his non-bandaged hand.

'You are his personal assistant! Surely he tells you his movements?'

'Not everything. Need to know. And some things I don't need to know. Most things, actually. I'm a very small cog in a very big… something.'

Sally fought down a feeling of intense frustration. Though she respected the chain of command, and understood the discretion required in Alistair's line of work, it could be brutal where personal feelings were involved. Especially if you were near the bottom of the food chain. Red tape didn't come into it – more like red chains secured behind a lock to which only select people knew the combination. 'Well, when was the last time you spoke to him then?'

Bishop seemed to consider. He took another sip of tea. Her own mug sat untouched on the scrubbed wooden table in front of her.

'Well?'

Bishop looked around the mess hall. 'Do you know how many corporals get to be adjutant to a colonel? None,' he said. Sally understood. He was very privileged to be in his current role, and he didn't wish to jeopardise that. 'So, I'm not telling you this, okay?' he said, lowering his voice further. 'You don't repeat any of this. I'm only telling you because – well. You know why.'

Sally leaned further across the table. 'Go on.'

'It was Tuesday night – I was working late, doing some admin work for the colonel. The phone rang. It was a chap called Harold Chorley. He was screaming, yelling, asking to speak to the colonel. So I put him through to the colonel's home number.'

'And?'

'The colonel thanked me and took the call.' Bishop frowned. 'Strange thing was, despite the lateness of the hour, he didn't sound a bit surprised. Almost as if he was expecting it.'

Sally sat back in her chair. She picked up her tea and took a sip. The implications of Bishop's words swirled around in her mind. 'And the very next day Alistair disappears.'

'I wouldn't worry,' said Bishop, clearly trying to calm her fears. 'He's on some mission somewhere, need to know, like I told you.'

Sally put her mug down. 'If he is acting under orders then why did he take his own car? Why not a Land Rover, or his staff car? You should have driven him!'

Bishop shrugged, ignoring the implied accusation. 'Perhaps it's an undercover assignment?'

Sally sighed. She wasn't going to get anything more out of Bishop. She'd have to go above him. Go to the top – to Hamilton.

The next morning, Sally had staked out Hamilton's office at Strategic Command – as far as her duties permitted – waiting for the general to emerge. It was a long, frustrating wait, but just before lunchtime she was making one of her passes along the corridor when the door opened and the man himself came out.

'General,' she called, increasing her pace to catch up with him. 'I know this is irregular, but I must talk to you.'

'Sorry, urgent meeting, can't hang about.'

161

'It's about Colonel Lethbridge-Stewart,' she said to the back of his neck.

He stopped walking, turned to face her. 'Of course it is,' Hamilton said with a sigh. 'Back into my office.'

Inside the office Hamilton poured himself a tumbler of whisky and sat himself behind his desk. Awareness of Hamilton's rank forced Sally to automatically stand to attention, despite the unorthodox way she had approached him.

'Please, sit down.' Hamilton gestured to a wooden high-backed chair in the corner of the office. She moved it into position and sat down tentatively. Why did she feel that she was about to be put on a charge? Hamilton was just staring at her. 'You're concerned about the colonel?' he said at length.

'Well – yes. I haven't seen or heard from him since Tuesday. Over two days ago now.'

'Corporal Wright, surely you accept that officers of the colonel's rank are sometimes sent on missions where security is of the utmost importance?'

She felt like a schoolgirl being admonished by a stern headmaster, which only made her more determined. 'I accept that, General. Just as I hope *you* accept that the colonel is my fiancé, and if his mission is strictly need to know, then surely I have a right to be included in that.'

'You are also only a corporal, your personal connection to Lethbridge-Stewart does not override the chain of command.'

Sally lowered her head, suitably put in her place. 'Sorry, sir,'

Hamilton took a sip of whisky. 'Damned difficult

situation, this,' he said, mostly to himself. His tone softened. 'Of course, I understand your concern. You're a good officer, you have never let your personal feelings get in the way of the job. But in these circumstances, I fear that keeping you in the dark is preventing you from performing your duties to the best of your ability.'

Sally could barely breathe. Was she about to be placed on medical leave? Or worse – dismissed?

'That being said, I can reassure you that the colonel is perfectly safe.' To her surprise, he laughed. 'Safe as houses.'

Hamilton was acting very strangely. Sally started to feel that there was bad news coming. Perhaps the worst. 'Where is he? What's happened to him? Sir.'

Hamilton took another sip of whisky. He then spoke quickly, quietly, as if afraid of being overheard. 'On Tuesday morning, Colonel Lethbridge-Stewart embarked on a secret mission, with my blessing. The nature of this mission is top secret, very hush-hush. The mission was, largely, a success, and the colonel has now been taken to a safe house, for debriefing.'

'A safe house?'

'A secure location used for debriefing in matters of national security.'

'National security?' Sally blinked. 'Sorry, sir, I seem to keep on repeating things.'

Hamilton smiled briefly. 'And that is all I can tell you.' His usual gruff manner had returned. 'Do not worry, the colonel will come to no harm.' Hamilton smiled indulgently, clearly thinking he'd done a top job of reassuring her.

Quite the opposite. What he'd told her had only made

her even more alarmed. But there was nothing she could do. She rose and saluted. She was about to turn and leave, but found herself saying, 'Please, General, could you not go and visit him? See if he's all right?'

'Not really meant to,' said Hamilton. 'Most irregular. However, I'm curious to find out a few things myself, so I shall see what I can do.'

'Thank you, sir,' Sally said, saluted again, and walked out of the office. Before she reached the door, Hamilton stopped her.

'Just one thing, Corporal.'

She turned to face at him, not liking the look on his face.

'As you know, I have fully supported your relationship with Lethbridge-Stewart, primarily because the colonel is a good officer and knows the line between professional duty and personal feelings. I believed the same of you. However,' Hamilton said, his tone darkening, 'I warn you. Do not give me reason to reassess that opinion and remove my support.'

Sally swallowed. She knew the general had a lot of pull with Alistair, almost certainly more than she did. She nodded, and left the room as quickly as she could. As the door closed behind her she dabbed at a tear. She had gone too far. She just hoped Hamilton didn't tell Alistair. If it came down to her or the advancement of Lethbridge-Stewart's career, she knew she would lose.

— CHAPTER FOURTEEN —

Inside Dominex

The safe house was in Richmond, an affluent area in the midst of parkland bordered by the wide meander of the Thames, well out of the capital, well out of the way.

It was at the end of Lower Grove Road, a long avenue of semi-detached 1930s red-brick houses bordering Richmond Park, or more specifically, the cemetery which occupied the north-west corner of the park. It was a quiet area in which nothing much ever happened. There was hardly any traffic on Lower Grove Road, making it the perfect place to hide people away, yet keep them close at hand, in case they were required.

To the neighbours, and to residents of Richmond, number nineteen was home to Mr and Mrs Morris; a quiet and retiring, professional couple in early middle age. He was an accountant while she worked in a bookshop in the town. Both jobs were, of course, a cover, as Mr and Mrs Morris were government agents. They lived solely on the ground floor, where there was a front room, a small kitchen, and a back room with the bunk beds in which they slept. The upper floors were reserved for guests of the safe house and their minders. 'Mr and Mrs Morris' weren't married; their relationship was purely professional. Edgar Morris often worked from home, sometimes driving out in his cream-coloured Ford Cortina to visit clients (in fact, to pick up or deliver messages from or to a drop box, or attend a debriefing session). Wendy Morris went out every weekday to the bookshop. Their real names were known only to themselves and their handlers.

For a day and a half, life in the safe house ran to a mind-numbingly regular, unchanging routine. Lethbridge-Stewart woke up early, as soon as it got light, and lay in bed, thinking, planning. At oh-six-hundred he rose and performed some cardio exercises, to keep himself in trim: fifty push-ups followed by as many sit-ups and squat thrusts (the size of the room made these tricky, but he managed). Then he showered and dressed. At oh-seven-fifteen there was a knock at the door, and Wendy Morris bought in breakfast. Lethbridge-Stewart had tried his luck against the beefy minder, whose name he learned was Jeff, and had the bruises to show for it. Anyway, even if he did manage to subdue Jeff, there would be a minder lurking in the corridor outside and on the floor below, and then Edgar Morris on the ground floor; not to mention all the locked doors and windows. If by some miracle he did get outside, he wouldn't get far before they tracked him down.

After breakfast, and after Wendy came to collect the tray, Lethbridge-Stewart would read. Thankfully he didn't have to endure *An Early Bath for Thompson* as he had asked for and received a surprisingly good selection of books from Wendy Morris. There would be a knock on the door at midday, and lunch was brought in at twelve-fifteen. Then more reading, and thinking.

It was a tolerable routine Lethbridge-Stewart knew he'd get used to, after a few days imprisoned at the safe house, but regardless he would continue planning his escape.

At nineteen-hundred he had a visitor.

Lethbridge-Stewart was lying on the thin, hard bed when there came a knock at the door. The next fifteen minutes passed in an agony of anticipation, during which Lethbridge-Stewart paced the room, imaging all sorts of scenarios. He was about to be freed! They were bringing him a cup of tea. They were bringing him more books. They had come to fix the dodgy flush.

At nineteen-fifteen-hours the door opened to reveal the figure of Major General Hamilton.

Conflicting emotions raced through Lethbridge-Stewart. Anger, chiefly, but also relief. Anger and resentment at the way he had been treated, but relief at the sight of a familiar face. It was the first time he had seen his superior since the meeting Wednesday morning before he had travelled down to Buckfastleigh. Though they had spoken on the phone, of course.

'Come to check up on me, have you?' He was unable to keep the bitterness from his voice. 'Well, I'm all right, all things considered.'

Hamilton had the good grace to look embarrassed. He coughed. 'May I come in?'

'As if you need to ask,' said Lethbridge-Stewart, and stood aside to let the general in. Hamilton commandeered the solitary, tattered chair by the dressing table. Lethbridge-Stewart moved to the bedroom door, but even before he reached it he could hear Wendy turning the key. He folded his arms, and slumped against the locked door. A glimmer of hope – had Hamilton come to release him? That hope sank with the general's next words.

'I'm very sorry about all this, Colonel. But it's necessary.'

'Orders from above, no doubt.'

'My hands are tied.'

Lethbridge-Stewart regarded his superior and bit back his instinctive response. 'What's the cover story?' he asked, keeping his tone level.

Hamilton shifted uncomfortably in the shabby chair. 'You're on a top secret mission, hush-hush, need-to-know.'

Lethbridge-Stewart snorted. 'And are people buying that?'

'They seem to be. After all, it is plausible, and not too far from the truth.'

'What about Sally? She knows why I went down to Devon. She'll be going spare.'

'I told Corporal Wright the truth,' said Hamilton plainly. 'That you're being held here to prevent you stirring things up with Dominex. It was her idea that I came and see you today. Well, mostly her idea. There is another reason.'

Lethbridge-Stewart suppressed a smile at the idea of Sally telling Hamilton what to do. The general was being kind. He didn't take orders, or suggestions, from junior NCOS.

'I've got something to show you.' Hamilton rose and went to the door, upon which he knocked four times. The door opened and a trolley was wheeled in by Edgar Morris, with one of the ever-present minders lurking in the corridor outside. On top of the trolley was a black and white television set, underneath which sat a bulky machine the size of a suitcase which Lethbridge-Stewart recognised as one of those new-fangled video recording machines. Once the trolley had been wheeled into the room and squeezed in opposite the bed, Edgar Morris retreated without a word, locking the door behind him.

Lethbridge-Stewart watched as Hamilton fiddled with the machine, muttering under his breath.

'Home pictures time, is it?

Hamilton sat back down on the bed, saying nothing, gesturing to the screen.

There was a fanfare of busy brass music and the familiar logo of the *Inside Out* documentary programme appeared. Then the words *Inside Dominex with Harold Chorley* appeared on the screen in bold black letters against a background photo of the Dominex plant.

Lethbridge-Stewart raised his eyes and glanced at Hamilton. The general was intent on the screen, his face creased in a frown of concentration.

The familiar face of Harold Chorley appeared in close-up. The first thing Lethbridge-Stewart felt was immense relief that the fellow was alive, and appeared to be unharmed. Or at least had been at the time of the recording.

'I have been granted exclusive access inside one of the most radical, novel, and, yes, dangerous enterprises in the country and, indeed, the world,' Chorley was saying in hushed, portentous tones. Was there something a bit off in his manner? A glassy, dazed look in his eyes? A strange, sweaty pallor to his face? Chorley went on, 'From their Dartmoor base, Dominex Industries collects the waste products from the nuclear power plants across the country and turns it into power which they predict will, within five years, provide fifty percent of the UK's energy needs.'

The scene changed to a montage of nuclear power stations, pylons, factories, schools and hospitals. Chorley continued in voice-over, 'In a unique deal with the British Government, Dominex Industries are pioneering their process in the UK giving us a clear advantage over our competitors. What's good for Dominex is clearly good for the country.'

The picture cut back to Chorley. 'I am the first and only reporter to be granted exclusive access inside the Dominex plant down here on Dartmoor, just outside Buckfastleigh. Obviously in such an installation as this there are areas where I am not permitted access, due to the top-secret nature of the Dominex process, and of course the danger of dealing with nuclear waste. But here I am in one of the monitor control rooms which keeps an eye on the levels of radiation in the nuclear waste containment chambers.'

The camera panned back to reveal that Chorley was standing in a grey-walled room lined with complicated-looking equipment busy with dials and blinking lights.

'And here is Dominex boss, Dominic Vaar, who has recently returned from a London meeting with Energy Minister Sir Anthony Bufton, and who you may have seen being interviewed by Robin Day on Monday's *Panorama* programme.'

The massive figure of Director Vaar stepped into shot.

'The face of the enemy,' whispered Lethbridge-Stewart.

Hamilton said nothing, just kept staring at the screen.

'Director Vaar, what are Dominex's plans for the future?'

Vaar looked directly to camera. Lethbridge-Stewart shivered. 'We hope to commence importing waste from other countries all over the world, and we hope to sell the energy from our process to fund our expansion, and provide cheap power for the whole planet!'

'A laudable and charitable objective,' said Chorley obsequiously. 'I'm sure we are all grateful to Dominex

Industries. Director Vaar, I'm sure the viewers would be interested to hear about your personal background.'

'I am from a poor family of farmers,' said Vaar smoothly. 'I worked and studied hard for many years to get where I am today.'

'A fine example and inspiration to us all,' Chorley wheedled.

Hamilton reached forward and stopped the tape. 'What do you think?'

'Why did you show me this?'

'Come on, man. Chorley! What's your assessment?'

'Man's been bribed. Or threatened. Or brainwashed,' Lethbridge-Stewart said, and then paused to make his final point. 'Or all three.'

'Or he could be telling the truth.'

'He was there in the cavern with me. He broke, or at least twisted, his ankle running away from the Quarks. They have clearly captured him, and turned him somehow, and are using him for propaganda.'

'Hmm...' Hamilton looked as if he was struggling with a big decision.

'Sir, you've heard my account of what happened down there?'

'Yes.'

'And you believe me?' Lethbridge-Stewart stared earnestly into Hamilton's eyes. 'You do believe me?'

Silence.

'I think you need some fresh air!' said Hamilton in a bluff, breezy tone that took Lethbridge-Stewart by surprise.

'Sorry?'

Hamilton stood up and made for the door. 'Fresh air!'

171

he bellowed. He rapped on the door. It opened to reveal the hulking form of Jeff, clad in his customary flared blue jeans and orange singlet.

Hamilton gestured over his shoulder at Lethbridge-Stewart. 'He tells me that he hasn't had a breath of fresh air since arriving yesterday morning.'

Jeff folded his muscular arms across his chest. Lethbridge-Stewart winced. Black hair sprouted from his armpits. Singlets might be in fashion, but they did the chap no favours – not that it looked like he cared. He glared indolently at Hamilton. 'So?'

'So, come on, man, this fellow's a political, being kept here for his own safety. It's not as if he's going to try to escape. Let me past, man!'

Without waiting for an answer Hamilton somehow managed to barge past the minder. 'You can take the equipment away whilst you're here,' he called back over his shoulder.

Lethbridge-Stewart slipped past the minder, who, ignoring Hamilton's orders, followed them both down the stairs. What the devil was Hamilton up to? Lethbridge-Stewart expected to be grabbed at any moment, but was allowed to walk unimpeded down the first flight, alert for any chance of escape. As they passed the landing and descended the second flight towards the hallway, the bearded face of Edgar Morris popped out from the kitchen doorway.

'What's going on?'

'Taking him outside for a breath of fresh air,' Hamilton blustered as he breezed past.

Lethbridge-Stewart made to step into the kitchen –

172

maybe there was a way out – but Edgar Morris stepped out in front of him. He heard Jeff come to a halt behind him and did his best to look downbeat and desperate for fresh air.

'What's going on?' Wendy Morris's voice came from further back in the kitchen, her words echoing those of her fake husband's.

Edgar turned to answer her and Lethbridge-Stewart took the opportunity to slip past. He followed Hamilton down the short hallway to the rear of the house. Hamilton unbolted the back door and stepped out, ushering Lethbridge-Stewart after him.

They were in a small yard, bordered on one side by the back of the house and on three sides by a high brick wall. Lethbridge-Stewart gratefully gulped in lungfuls of fresh air and gazed up at the darkening summer's sky. The frosted glass window of his room gazed blindly out from under the eaves. Set in the outside wall was a green-painted wooden gate. He tried the latch. Locked.

Hamilton stepped towards him, and spoke quickly and quietly directly into his ear. 'I've decided. Get the hell out of here, Colonel, get down to Dartmoor, rescue Chorley, and find out what Dominex are really up to. And if it's bad – stop them.'

Jeff the minder loomed out of the safe house, his massive, hairy frame filling the doorway. Lethbridge-Stewart leaped forward and shoved the man in the chest. He staggered backwards, swearing profusely. Lethbridge-Stewart slammed the door shut after him.

'Hurry! Over here!'

Lethbridge-Stewart stepped over to the back wall where

173

Hamilton was stooping, hands laced together. Without stopping to think, Lethbridge-Stewart placed his foot on Hamilton's hands and let himself be boosted up over the wall.

'Now you really are on a top secret, hush-hush, need to know mission!' gasped Hamilton.

Lethbridge-Stewart just had time to glimpse the minder emerge roaring from the house with Edgar Morris close behind him before he dropped down the other side of the wall.

He found himself in the back garden of the adjoining house, between two enormous rhododendron bushes. A ginger cat, which had been prowling up on the birdbath in the centre of the lawn, stared briefly at him before running pell-mell up the side of the house. From the other side of the wall came shouts and sounds of fisticuffs. Hoping that Hamilton would be all right, and thanking him under his breath, Lethbridge-Stewart set off in the direction the cat had taken.

He slipped through the front garden, keeping his head down, and out the front gate. He was now on Queen's Road, a wide, tree-lined thoroughfare of townhouses. His first instinct was to lay low, and hope that the search for him which would soon be underway would pass him by. Dangerous urge, had to resist.

Lethbridge-Stewart ran along the pavement, using the trees and parked cars as cover. His second instinct was the station – also dangerous. Protocols were in place to deal with those fleeing a safe house, protocols which were undoubtedly being acted upon right at that very moment. Lethbridge-Stewart hoped that Hamilton had managed to throw a spanner in those particular works, but he couldn't chance it. Best assume that the station would be watched.

He glanced behind. No sign of pursuit. Would they send the minders after him? Or use agents already in the field? Would there even be any, for such a low-risk category prisoner as himself? All he could do was keep on running. He needed to reach the capital, where he could lose himself and put his plan into action. When, of course, he had a plan. Now his only priority was flight.

He crossed the road at random and slipped down a side street – Park Road. He broke into a run, hoping that people who saw him would think he was a jogger, or late for his train, rather than a wanted man. He took a quick dog-leg into Onslow Road, heading east, towards the river. He jogged along Richmond Hill and soon passed from the residential area of the town into the centre. Thank the Lord they'd put him in civvies – his uniform would stand out a mile.

He slowed down as he came into a street with cafes and antique shops on his left and a small park to his right. To his disquiet there weren't many people about, but enough, he hoped, to be able to mingle and hide. A bus passed and he briefly toyed with the idea of hopping on, but resisted. Buses, like trains, would also be watched.

He need help, as well as some kind of information.

He ducked into a phone box and routed through the directories which hung to the right of the phone. He finally found the number he wanted and placed a reverse-charges call to journalist Larry Greene, friend and confidante of Harold Chorley.

CHAPTER FIFTEEN

On the Run

General Hamilton straightened up, wincing as pain shot through his lower back. *Getting too old for this sort of thing.* 'Good luck, old chap,' he muttered, as the sound of Lethbridge-Stewart's running footsteps receded into the distance.

Strong hands gripped his upper arms. Hamilton shook himself free and spun round to be confronted by the glowering face of the minder, whose gaze shifted towards the wall over which Lethbridge-Stewart had scrambled. Before the fellow could take a single step in pursuit, Hamilton punched him, hard, in the stomach, and he went down, gasping.

'What the blue blazes is going on?' Edgar Morris had appeared, arms akimbo, in the doorway.

'Escaped,' hissed the writhing minder, struggling to his feet.

'Friday 13th, old man, bad luck for some,' Hamilton said with a grim smile.

'Bird's flown!' shouted Edgar Morris over his shoulder. 'Alert Control.'

The minder grabbed Hamilton's arm again. 'You – inside.'

'Get your hands off me, you blasted ape!'

'Be gentle with him, Jeff.' Edgar sneered, and gestured inside with a thumb. 'Coming quietly?'

Hamilton allowed himself to be steered back inside the safe house and guided gently but insistently into the small kitchen. He found himself seated opposite Edgar Morris at the Formica kitchen table. Jeff stood guard at the doorway opposite him, while Wendy Morris stood, arms folded, against the cooker, regarding him coolly.

'You've caused us a great deal of trouble,' said Edgar Morris. The man's attitude was truculent, superior; typical of these Intelligence wallahs. 'It was bad enough you coming here in the first place. Had to concoct some story about a family friend in the military.'

'My heart bleeds for you.'

'And then aiding and abetting our guest's escape! What kind of game are you playing?'

'It's no game, I assure you. And Lethbridge-Stewart was not a prisoner here. He was being kept here for his own safety.'

'Safety you've compromised by turning him loose!'

'He won't stay loose for long,' put in Wendy with a smirk.

Hamilton felt anger rise within him. Damned Intelligence johnnies! Though they were ostensibly on the same side, it sometimes felt as though they were deadly enemies. 'We'll see about that. My man's pretty good.'

'Your man?'

Now it was Hamilton's turn to smirk. 'I'm his CO. How much do you know about your "guest", as you put it? Do you even know why he was brought here?'

Edgar Morris bristled. 'We're only told basic details. Need to know. All we know is that the colonel was being held here for political reasons. And now you tell us it was for his own safety. Safety from what? From who?'

Hamilton decided to ignore this question. 'You know nothing about the real situation.'

'Whatever it is, it's clearly something you don't agree with,' said Wendy primly. 'Really, you should have registered your disapproval through official channels. You're in a whole heap of trouble now.'

Hamilton slapped the table. 'I have my reasons, which I refuse to divulge to the likes of you. Suffice to say, in freeing your "guest" I may have ensured the safety and security of the country, if not the world.'

Edgar snorted. 'Are you feeling all right, old chap?'

'Perfectly fine.' Hamilton rose to his feet, as did Edgar Morris. He heard Jeff take a step behind him. 'You can't keep me here.'

Edgar bunched his fists, leaned on the table, thrusting his face towards Hamilton. 'You've broken God knows how many rules, you won't tell us why – for all we know, you could be a Russian agent!'

'Hogwash!' Hamilton turned to leave. 'Have me followed, tap my phone, interfere with my mail, turn all your damned dirty tricks on me, and you won't find a thing.' He tried to step past Jeff, but the fellow barred his way.

'You'll be court martialled for this,' said the minder.

'Out of my way.'

Jeff stood firm.

'If I don't report back by twenty-thirty hours, squads of soldiers will descend on this place and you'll be blown wide open.' Hamilton turned to regard Mr and Mrs Morris. 'It must have taken a hell of a lot of time, work and patience to build this place up and establish your cover. What a shame if you had to start all over again.'

Impasse.

At length, Edgar sighed, and said, 'Okay, Jeff, let him past. But you haven't heard the last of this!'

Without a backward glance, Hamilton shouldered his way past the glowering Jeff and out into the summer night.

Lethbridge-Stewart didn't like this, but he had little choice in the matter. The safety of the UK was on his shoulders, and at that moment only he had the latitude to do what was needed. And he wasn't above using whatever means he had at his disposal.

He continued to scan the faces of those in *The Halfway House*. If what Hamilton had told him previously was true, he'd recognise Larry Greene easily enough. He just hoped Greene wouldn't take too long. He was attracting attention, sitting in the corner on his own with just a glass of water before him; any money he had, had been left at the safe house when he escaped. The barman hadn't been happy when Lethbridge-Stewart had asked for some tap water, and he could see the barman was getting ready to come over and tell Lethbridge-Stewart to hop it. It was a pub, not a shelter for the homeless.

Fortunately it was then that Larry Greene chose to enter.

For a moment Lethbridge-Stewart thought he was looking at Chorley. Same sharp haircut, same thick glasses, same suit. Only his face, which bore a much more friendly expression, and the less-assured manner with which he carried himself, set him apart from Chorley. As the man approached him, Lethbridge-Stewart wondered if Greene and Chorley were brothers.

Greene went to offer his hand, but Lethbridge-Stewart spoke before he could do so. 'I suggest you get us both a pint, Mr Greene. Before the natives become restless.'

Greene looked around and grinned. 'Ah yes, brilliant. Right you are. Back in a jiffy.'

Lethbridge-Stewart waited, and motioned Greene to sit down as soon as the man returned. Lethbridge-Stewart took a deep draught of his beer. While he did Greene spoke.

'I tried to find you a couple of months ago, you know. Enlisted by your General Hamilton. That it is before he dropped me like a pair of old boots.' Greene narrowed his eyes, waiting for Lethbridge-Stewart's response. There was none, he was too busy savouring the taste of the beer. Greene continued, 'So I contacted Harry, and we began our own investigation. Didn't get far before we got slapped with the Official Secrets Act, mind, but far enough to work out that your disappearance had something to do with the peculiar capsules and the soldiers who believed it was still 1914.'

'Yes, I had heard something about that,' Lethbridge-Stewart said, after he had placed his half empty pint glass on the table. He would have loved to get into this some more, since Greene may have answers Lethbridge-Stewart needed, but right now there were more important things to deal with than what had happened to him in East Germany. 'Have you heard from Chorley lately?'

If Greene was curious, he didn't let it show. 'Not since Tuesday night.' He leaned in closer. 'This something to do with the Dominex thing?'

'It is indeed. I was hoping he'd told you, and since there

hasn't been even a murmur of it in the papers, I'll take that as proof of your credentials.' Lethbridge-Stewart was taking a risk, after all Greene was still a journalist, and one who had proven himself of dubious integrity a couple of months ago, but Lethbridge-Stewart needed to remain below the radar for as long as possible, so his options were limited.

'What do you need, Colonel?'

'A place to stay for the night, and money,' Lethbridge-Stewart said simply, his tone making it clear that Greene didn't have a choice.

'On one condition,' Greene said.

'Go on.'

'You tell me exactly what happened to you two months ago.'

'Very well.' It was an easy promise to make, since Lethbridge-Stewart still didn't really know what had happened.

In the Dominators' control chamber deep within the Dominex plant, Director Vaar was supervising the final stages of Project M. 'Soon,' he growled to himself. 'Soon. Then we can leave this pitiful world, and proceed to glory.' He strode over to where Navigator Deka was monitoring the communications console. 'Is the ship fuelled and ready? We must be prepared to leave this world the moment Project M is ready for deployment.'

'Yes, Director Vaar.'

'Excellent. We are now in the final cycle. Project M will be initiated the day after tomorrow.' Vaar turned away.

'Director, some unwelcome news.'

Vaar swung round. 'Unwelcome? It had better not

present a risk to Project M!'

'It may present a... minimal risk,' said Deka, clearly struggling with the Tellurian terminology.

'Report!' barked Vaar.

'The human that escaped from the nuclear waste storage chamber and was imprisoned on the orders of the human politician, has since escaped from his place of incarceration and is now at large.'

Probationer Azbo stepped away from the bank of instruments he was monitoring. 'He must be found and destroyed! He knows too much.'

'Silence!' roared Vaar. 'You are a fool, Probationer Azbo. If we were to send Quarks to hunt him then we would be revealed and Project M compromised!'

'We should have destroyed him when we had the chance,' Azbo rumbled sullenly.

'And wasted vital Quark energy!'

'Then what should we do, Director?' Deka asked.

Vaar considered. 'Nothing. Project M is one cycle closer to launch. We cannot waste resources on this single human.'

'But what if he tells the other humans?'

'Silence, Probationer! There is nothing this single human can do to prevent the completion of Project M! He has been disgraced and discredited, remember? The other humans will not believe his story. He is a fugitive, on the run from his own people.' Vaar waved a dismissive fist. 'He poses no threat to us. Now return to your duties!'

'Command accepted,' mumbled Deka and Azbo in unison.

The next morning in Croydon, Lethbridge-Stewart awaited

the arrival of his 'forces'. He had got as much information out of Greene he could regarding the events of late April, while furnishing Greene with what he knew (which was still very jumbled in his mind). Satisfied, Greene had allowed Lethbridge-Stewart the use of his phone to call in a few favours. And now, sufficiently rested and with some funds, Lethbridge-Stewart waited.

The park in which he waited was a small urban patch of sooty grass bounded by boxy concrete residential developments on either side, the corrugated iron wall of a warehouse at the back, and the main road, separated by iron railings with flaking blue paint, at the front. Despite the sunny morning the park was shrouded in shadows cast by the surrounding hulks. It was not the ideal place for a park, but it was the ideal place to meet more or less in secret. Within the park two yew trees grew, adding to the gloom of the place, and at the back, before the red brick wall separating the park from the warehouse, was a children's playground. Powell and Hooper had already arrived, and in the distance Lethbridge-Stewart saw the third member of his new time slouch towards them.

Jason Stevens, had been a corporal in the Parachute Regiment before being granted an early service discharge. He had served the British Army well enough and was highly regarded by Pemberton, but it turned out that military service didn't suit him as well as he suited it. Nonetheless, he owed Lethbridge-Stewart a favour or two – or rather he owed them to Pemberton, but Old Spence wasn't around to collect. Lethbridge-Stewart was, and he intended to do so.

'Hello, Stevens.'

'Good morning, sir,' Stevens managed to say, looking

around furtively. 'Sorry, bit late. Tube.'

Lethbridge-Stewart glanced at his wristwatch. Stevens was exactly on time. They shook hands briskly and firmly.

Lethbridge-Stewart narrowed his eyes. 'How are you doing?' he asked, more out of fealty to Pemberton than any real interest. Stevens may have been granted an honorary discharge, but to Lethbridge-Stewart's mind that was not so far from desertion. He knew full well Pemberton had agreed with that sentiment, and took it personally. A fact of which Lethbridge-Stewart was to remind Stevens on the phone last night.

'Fine. Started autobiography. Writing – tough lark.'

'I'm sure.' Lethbridge-Stewart turned to the Hooper and Powell. 'Stevens, this is Flight Lieutenant Ken Powell,' he said, indicating to the older of the two. Powell was in his mid-fifties, with a weather-beaten face and curly, sandy hair that belied his age. 'Ex-RAF, now runs a car showroom in Penge. Knew my father.'

Powell stepped forward and shook Stevens' hand.

'And this is Corporal Brian Hooper, ex-Royal Engineers, Bomb Disposal. Knows all that's handy to know about things that go bang. Now on... well, shall we just say, gardening leave.'

'You could call it that,' Hooper said. 'Truth of the matter is I was given Medical Discharge, on account of this.' He lifted his right hand, which was missing two fingers and a thumb. 'Hazards of the old job. Never mess with gelignite!'

Lethbridge-Stewart coughed. Well, indeed. 'Before that he saved my hind in Korea, more than once.'

Stevens shook hands with the explosives expert, whose bearded face and bright blue eyes shone with intelligence.

'Just the four of us?' Hooper asked.

'Yes. I was rather pressed for time. And...' Lethbridge-Stewart glanced around at the faces of the other men. '...it should be enough.'

'Enough for what?' Powell had a gruff Yorkshire accent.

'I'll explain in more detail later,' said Lethbridge-Stewart. 'First of all, we're off on a nice day-trip down Devon way.'

— CHAPTER SIXTEEN —

Objective: Dominex

As he drove the commandeered furniture van out of Croydon, Lethbridge-Stewart allowed himself a moment of satisfaction. The real test, of course, was yet to come, but right now he let himself enjoy the luxury of being content with the way things were turning out. Luxury, however, was something his team were not at present able to enjoy. Crammed in the back of the van between the tables, chairs, dressers, mattresses and other assorted items of furniture, they were having to make the best of it. Lethbridge-Stewart grinned as he heard them burst into a verse of a familiar, ribald army song about the virtues of certain inhabitants of Inverness. Against such spirit, what chance did the enemy have?

He took the van onto the M3 London to Basingstoke motorway, and recalled the last time he had made this journey; only a few days ago, although it seemed like a lifetime. He'd driven his silver Merc – which was, presumably, still parked up at *The White Hart* – full of doubt about Chorley's incredible story. How different now – he had seen the Quarks in action first hand, and would be engaging them in combat soon. But they were not just up against the Quarks and their mysterious masters, but an entire government who had fallen foul of Dominex's

186

promises of cheap energy for all. And now Chorley was their pawn, spreading their propaganda. Lethbridge-Stewart hoped they'd be able to rescue the poor chap.

Once outside London, Lethbridge-Stewart kept to the minor roads, taking them through Salisbury and then Yeovil. It was now just past midday, but he didn't want to chance the motorways or A-roads as the furniture van may have been be reported stolen by now. Lethbridge-Stewart kept well within the speed limit, alert for any sound of sirens or tell-tale flicker of flashing blue lights. It was therefore almost thirteen-thirty by the time they reached the outskirts of Exeter. He was ravenous – as, no doubt, were his team, who had kept up a near-constant barrage of bawdy songs, stories and jokes for the entire journey. Apart from one quick comfort stop in a lay-by, they'd been cooped up in the back of the lorry with all the furniture for a good three hours. There was nothing for it, he'd have to chance a stop.

He crossed the Exe at the small village of Cowley and took the road south towards the town. He knew the town fairly well, so was able to negotiate a route around the outskirts and out through Matford. Although his stomach was rumbling in protest he made himself drive a few miles down the A38 – for once risking a major road – until he found a small road leading off, barely more than a muddy track. There he parked the van up, well out of sight of the main road, disembarked and opened the back.

Four faces gazed at him expectantly out of the gloom.

'Half an hour here, chaps. We're almost at our destination.' He placed the bag of provisions on the floor of the van, taking a Cornish pasty for himself.

'Which is?' asked Powell as he eased himself down out

of the back of the lorry, grabbing a Scotch egg from the bag. Hooper extricated himself from between a sideboard and an easy chair and disappeared out of the van and into the darkness. Stevens began some stretching exercises up against the side of the lorry.

'A place called the Bunker. Hope Cove Bunker, to be more precise.'

'That's our target?' said Stevens,

'No, it's our staging post.'

'So what's our target?'

'I'll tell you when Hooper gets back from his ablutions.'

They had been very patient so far; in their position he'd be dying to know what the mission was. Hooper returned, looking much relieved, and grabbed a pork pie. Stevens had finished his exercises and was tucking into a slab of cheese between two hunks of bread.

'Our target is the Dominex installation on Dartmoor,' Lethbridge-Stewart explained when everybody had settled a bit.

'Holy Moly,' said Stevens through a mouthful of bread.

'The nuclear recycling place?' Hooper asked. 'Blimey. It's the most dangerous business on Earth.'

'What exactly is our mission?' Powell asked, frowning. 'I take it this is completely unauthorised?'

'Why else do you think the colonel would call in favours?' Stevens said, and Lethbridge-Stewart had to smile. It was a rather stupid question from Powell. Perhaps the ex-RAF was a bit old for this kind of adventure.

'I am acting alone – under the approval of my CO, Major General Hamilton,' Lethbridge-Stewart said, and added, 'but against the wishes of the government.' He let that sink in for a moment. 'This mission is completely unofficial and unsanctioned. Dominex have the blessing of the energy minister.' He went on to detail what he had learned so far, and his experiences in Devon and at the safe house. 'So,' he concluded, 'if any of you want to back out, now's your chance.'

To their credit, all three men shook their heads.

'No way,' said Stevens. 'After what Old Spence did for me... Well, this is my chance to pay him back.'

'Our mission,' said Powell again, impatiently. 'Come on, man!'

Lethbridge-Stewart explained and the men listened. He told them about the cavers, about what Chorley had discovered, and the current state of play.

'What was the nature of these hostile forces?' asked Hooper.

So far, so simple. Now it came to the part that was less believable. Lethbridge-Stewart took a deep breath. 'This bit is going to be rather hard to take. Unfortunately, I do not have any photographs, so I'll just have to describe them to you. They are robots – automata – machines. They are small, and somewhat comical-looking, like overgrown toys, but their appearance belies their firepower. I warn you now, do not underestimate them. Their masters call them Quarks. They have square bodies, round spiked heads, and feet like shoeboxes.'

As he expected, the three soldiers burst into peals of derisive laughter.

'As I said, their appearance is somewhat whimsical, but don't be deceived. They possess retractable arms which fire a sort of directed energy beam which is utterly deadly.

Moreover, they can transform themselves – unfolding like, as Chorley put it, a Swiss army jack-in-a-box. They are thus able to change from a small robot not much bigger than a pillar box to a towering thing the height of a house, and deploy a wide range of weapons. The existence of these Quarks – and the advanced process that Dominex use – indicate that there could be alien influences at work behind Dominex.'

'You mean the Russkies?' Powell asked.

In for a penny, in for a pound. 'No. Alien to this world. Extra-terrestrial.'

He let them laugh and scoff for a moment. 'I know it sounds incredible, unbelievable even, but I've encountered such things before. The recent evacuation of London...'

'Where Old Spence was killed,' Steven said.

Lethbridge-Stewart nodded. 'Yes, he gave his life to save the UK. Did you hear the reason behind the evacuation?'

Stevens frowned. 'Gas leak, wasn't it?'

'I'd heard that bears escaped from Regent's Park,' put in Hooper.

'Hard to get to the truth after a D-notice has been issued,' added Powell.

'The reason for these conflicting reports is because the cause was alien activity in the London Underground. Something called the Great Intelligence had established a bridgehead there, and was using robotic servants resembling, ah, Yeti as its foot-soldiers.'

Again the laughter and exclamations of disbelief.

'Laugh you may,' said Lethbridge-Stewart sternly. 'These creatures may sound ludicrous, and in the case of the Quarks, even look ludicrous – but underestimate them

190

at your peril. I lost good men down in the Underground, and five people have died at the hands of Dominex. So I advise you to take the threat very, very seriously.'

Hooper shook his head and laughed again. 'If this was coming from anyone but you, I wouldn't credit it.'

'You said these Quark things have masters,' asked Stevens. 'Who are they?'

'Dominex management. You may have seen Dominic Vaar both on *Inside Out* and *Panorama*. You have probably assumed, from his heavy features, that he is a Slav or a Russian. But I believe he is an extra-terrestrial, sent here for some devilish purpose not yet known. There may be more like him within the Dominex plant – or it may be just an army of these Quark things. We don't know. But we must be prepared to face them too.'

'This is a lot to take in, lad,' said Powell, reaching for a Scotch egg. 'For an old soldier like me.'

'I realise it is, but you must trust me. I picked you because I know you all well, and know that I can trust you under fire. And you know me well enough to know that I am the last person who would go around making up seeming nonsense like this.'

'All right,' said Hooper, scratching his beard. 'We believe you. So what is the mission?'

'The mission is primarily one of rescue. Our first objective is to find Chorley and get him to safety. Our secondary objective is to find out what Dominex are actually up to, and, if it's inimical to the interests of the country, stop them.'

'What with?' Stevens spread his hands wide. 'We ain't got any weapons!'

'That's why we're going to Hope Cove first.'

'What is Hope Cove? Where is it?' said Powell.

'To answer your last question first, it's in South Devon, on the downs outside Salcombe. It was built, in secret and at great expense, in the '50s as part of the RAF's ROTOR radar detection programme.'

'I remember that,' said Powell. 'It was meant to detect Russian bombers creeping up on us. Over-elaborate mess, a throwback to the war – they brought in Linesman to replace it, I seem to recall.'

'True, and in 1954 Hope Cove Bunker was all set to take its place in the ROTOR network. But radar technology, as you pointed out, moves quickly, and the type of radar the Bunker was going to use became obsolete, so the place never became part of ROTOR. It was used as an RAF base for a few years until ten years ago, when it was converted into a nuclear fallout shelter for regional government officials.'

'So why the hell are we going there?' said Powell.

'One, as a base of operations. And more importantly, I know for a fact that Hope Cove has a fully-equipped armoury.'

'How are we going to get in to such a place?' said Powell. 'They're hardly going to let us walk in and take their guns!'

Lethbridge-Stewart thumped the side of the furniture van. 'That's where this will come in handy. Here's the plan...'

— CHAPTER SEVENTEEN —

The Bunker

Another dull morning in the Bunker, thought Sergeant Richard Bell, stifling a yawn as he locked the door to the generator room. The generator, a Meadows 375kva unit fed by an underground diesel tank, was working perfectly, as it had been since well before his posting, and would until well after he'd gone. He trudged along the narrow corridor of cream-painted brickwork and green doors which ran through the centre of the lower, underground floor of the Bunker. Only another four weeks of mind-numbing routine and then it was back to the Siggies, his beloved Royal Corps of Signals, which he thought of as home. Back to some proper technical work, not this boring housekeeping.

He stifled another yawn. Well, he only had himself to blame – he'd volunteered for this posting, after all. The decommissioned ROTOR kit was still stored at the Bunker and that was why he'd come here. He spent all his free time tinkering happily with the stuff. Obsolete it may be, but it was still fascinating, and he was learning a lot about radar systems, something he'd known little about before the Bunker posting.

He climbed the narrow stairway to the upper, above-ground floor of the Bunker. An almost identical corridor awaited him. They were so alike that in his absent-minded moments Bell sometimes forgot what floor he was on, and spent many minutes looking for a room that wasn't there.

He wandered back to the control room situated at the front of the top floor near the entrance. Skeleton crew, that's what he was. Just him, at present. Meant to be two but due to cutbacks they'd decided that one was enough, although it didn't occur to them how stir crazy one chap might get down here on his own. But Bell had the ROTOR kit to keep him company, and that was enough to keep him sane. 'I haven't started talking to myself yet, at least,' he said to himself as he entered the tiny control room.

Though windowless, there was an exterior view, via the four cameras mounted on each corner of the concrete rectangular block that constituted Hope Cove Bunker.

He sat down and twisted the dial on the monitor so that the screen showed the view from the camera above the Bunker entrance. The black-and-white picture snow-stormed and changed to show a straight gravel track leading from the Bunker entrance to the perimeter fence. There, on the other side of the gate, was a truck – civilian, by the looks of it – with a man standing beside it with his finger on the entrance buzzer.

This was the most exciting thing to have happened to Bell in the entirety of his posting – even more exciting than his discovery of a stash of certain magazines in the storeroom.

He clicked the intercom switch. 'Hope Cove Bunker, Sergeant Bell speaking, please state your business?'

The tiny speaker crackled, then a voice said, 'Furniture delivery.'

'Just a moment.' Bell pushed his glassed back up his nose, slid open another drawer, and took out a folder containing the Bunker schedule. He knew even before he checked that there were no deliveries planned for the day. Suspicion began to rise. 'There's nothing in the schedule,' he said into the intercom. 'What furniture?'

'For the conference room,' came the voice again. 'New chairs!'

Bell frowned. He'd just been in the conference room. The chairs seemed all right. In fact, he'd never really noticed the chairs. They were just, well, *chairs*.

'Look, I've come all the way from Exeter for this!' crackled the voice again.

Bell's suspicion began to curdle into confusion. A mistake could have been made, he supposed. Lines of communication could have become muddled. Some Home Office civil servant had forgotten to tick a box and so Bell hadn't been informed of this delivery. Even so, a smidgeon of suspicion remained. 'I'll need to check with HQ.'

'You do your checking, mate, but get a wriggle on. I've got other deliveries to make.'

'Right.' There was something odd about that voice. Sounded too posh to be a delivery man.

A quick phone call confirmed that there was indeed no delivery scheduled for today, in fact nothing all week, or indeed for the remaining duration of his posting. Bell passed this information on to the delivery man, expecting it to be the end of the matter.

'Must be some sort of mistake. Contact Major General Hamilton on this number.' The delivery man gave a number that Bell wrote down on his desk blotter. Who the hell was Major General Hamilton? Bell rang the number.

'Hamilton,' came the clipped tones of a member of the

officer class.

'Sergeant Bell at Hope Cove Bunker,' he began, and explained the situation.

'Yes, bit of a mix-up this end. Breakdown in communication. I'm on the Nuclear Shelter Steering Committee, really should have told you chaps about this delivery. Pretty crucial, sort of thing.'

Chairs? Crucial? 'Yes, sir,' mumbled Bell. 'Thanks for clearing that up, sir.'

The voice on the other end of the line coughed. 'Carry on, Sergeant.' The line went dead.

'Well? Did you check?' came the other disembodied voice, impatient and still curiously not working-class.

Only slightly reassured, Bell felt he really had no choice. Orders were orders. New chairs for the conference room it was. He pressed the switch for the electronic entrance release, and watched as the wire mesh gate swung silently open. 'Enter.'

He watched as the delivery man clambered back into the van. A moment later the vehicle began to trundle slowly along the gravel drive towards the bunker entrance. Bell rose and made his way down the central corridor of the Bunker's upper level towards the entrance bulkhead. The corridor ended in a massive grey-painted blast-reinforced door secured with a combination lock. With practiced ease, Bell spun the combination and heaved on the handle. The door swung open to connect with the wall with a dull clang. He stepped over the threshold into a small, windowless ante-chamber. The outer door was the twin of the inner door and once again Bell spun the combination, thinking that despite all this palaver, at least he would get a glimpse of daylight and a face full of fresh air out of it.

Unlike its brother the outer door was mounted on a sliding mechanism and Bell heaved on the handle, wincing as the heavy door protested against its bearings. Job for later – get the oilcan out.

As soon as the gap was wide enough to admit a man, a figure burst through and slammed Bell against the side wall. Bell kicked out against his assailant, succeeding only in sending a fire extinguisher clanging and rolling across the tiled floor. Bell felt a hand grip his throat and found himself staring into a pair of frowning, malevolent brown eyes. He tried to speak but the hand gripped tighter. And tighter. He kicked out again, the blood pounding in his ears. Stars flashed across his vision. He was going...

'All right, Stevens, put the man down.' The voice belonged to the delivery man – the posh, fake delivery man.

Bell's assailant let him go and he slumped against the wall. Three other men had entered, crowding messily into the tiny ante-chamber. They were all in civvies. A bearded chap slid the outer door closed and spun the combination. An older chap helped Bell to his feet.

Bell at last found voice. 'What the – what the hell is going on?!'

The fake delivery man, who wore the blue serge overalls and flat cap of a real delivery man, but sported an unmistakably military moustache, said, 'Don't fret, Sergeant Bell. We're not terrorists, or Russians – or furniture delivery men, for that matter.'

'I knew it,' muttered Bell. 'There's nothing wrong with the chairs in the conference room!'

Bell found himself bundled out of ante-chamber and

back along the corridor. Despite their civilian attire, Bell could tell they were, or once had been, soldiers. Something in the way they moved with smooth, powerful economy. Something in the way they looked to the man in overalls, clearly their leader. So who were they? Mercenaries? And what did they want at the Bunker?

As if in answer to these unspoken questions, the leader spoke. 'I'm Colonel Lethbridge-Stewart, and I'm head of a top-secret taskforce on a mission of national importance, and we're requisitioning this Bunker.'

'You're bonkers,' Bell blurted out.

'That's as maybe.' They reached the control room. 'Inside.'

Bell obeyed, feeling as if he was in a bizarre dream. His first thought was the panic button beneath his desk, but before he could reach it Lethbridge-Stewart darted between him and the desk. Bell felt Stevens' hands grasp his shoulders.

'Sorry, can't have you calling the cavalry,' Lethbridge-Stewart said. 'Stevens, Hooper – you're on weapons detail. Key?'

Bell blinked. 'W-What?'

Lethbridge-Stewart clapped his hands. 'Get with it, man! Armoury key!'

In a daze Bell went over to the key press, spun the combination and took his time looking for the appropriate key. He was on his own now. They weren't armed, as far as he could make out. Could he try to jump them? No way. There were four of them and the bald bloke looked like a right nutter.

'Come on!'

Bell picked out the armoury key and handed it to

Lethbridge-Stewart, who tossed it to the bald chap, Stevens, who then disappeared down the corridor with the bearded fellow – Hooper, presumably. Bell was left alone with Lethbridge-Stewart and the older chap.

Lethbridge-Stewart sat down at Bell's desk, and smiled. 'Now, how about a nice cup of tea?'

Tea drunk, Lethbridge-Stewart and the older chap – Flight Lieutenant Powell, ex-RAF – marched Bell to the conference room. They'd sat him in a corner, out of the way; not treating him as a prisoner, but there was no doubt in his mind what would happen if he tried to make a break for it. The ex-Para, Stevens, scared him. Something dangerous in his eyes. The other chap, Hooper, was an explosives expert, a technical fellow, and in other circumstances they could have been mates.

Not these circumstances.

Lethbridge-Stewart had found a swagger stick from somewhere, and spread out an Ordnance Survey map of South Devon on the conference table. A little yellow flag indicated the Bunker, and a red flag indicated – as far as Bell could make out – a spot on the edge of Dartmoor, near Buckfastleigh.

'What did you find in the armoury?' Lethbridge-Stewart asked once Stevens and Hooper had returned.

Stevens indicated a pile of cases that he'd brought in and dumped at the far end of the conference room. 'Guns: couple of Armalite AR-18 automatic rifles, pair of Browning semi-automatic pistols, all with ammo. Artillery: four dozen Mills fragmentation grenades, and a Thumper with a box of two dozen 40x46 mil grenades.'

'Thumper?' queried Lethbridge-Stewart. 'Not sure I'm familiar with that particular piece of ordnance.'

Stevens grinned. 'Never officially found its way over here, but clearly that doesn't bother those who run the Bunker. Used by our American cousins over in Vietnam, so I guess nobody's told them about this stock pile. It's more commonly known as the M79 grenade launcher. Called Thumper because of the sound it makes.' He walked over to the crates, opened one, and picked up a stubby weapon resembling a sawn-off shotgun with a thick muzzle and a polished wooden stock. 'Single shot, which means that you have to reload each time, but it's got a good, long range, and those 40x46 grenades are high explosive.' He broke it open, exposing the breech. 'Grenade goes in here. Simply aim, and fire. *Thump!* Should do a lot of damage.'

The smile on Stevens' face chilled Bell's blood.

'Just remember whose side you're on, Stevens,' Lethbridge-Stewart said, the warning *very* clear.

Stevens frowned. 'Of course, sir.'

'No other explosives, though,' said Hooper, after a moment's silence. 'Pity.'

'Should be enough for our purposes,' said Lethbridge-Stewart.

Their purposes? There was enough ammo there to take down a small town! Bell wondered what he'd found himself in the middle of.

'Communications?'

'Standard handheld RT,' said Hooper.

'Excellent. Now it's time for a final briefing before we go in.'

'Hang on,' said Powell, frowning over at Bell. 'What

about speccy?'

Lethbridge-Stewart glanced in Bell's direction. 'Oh, he can stay and hear the briefing. After all you're on our side, aren't you, Sergeant?'

Bell nodded. Best play along with these lunatics. First chance he got, he'd press that panic button, and no mistake.

Lethbridge-Stewart frowned for a moment. 'Do you have a sister in the service?'

'Cousin – Carol. Well, Caroline, but she prefers Carol.'

Lethbridge-Stewart smiled. 'She served with me a few months ago for a short time.' He nodded and continued. 'Good. Now, gentlemen, as you know, our objective is Dominex.'

Dominex. The name rang a bell. Then Bell realised, and his mouth went dry. Oh no. Oh God, no! The nuclear waste reprocessing place on Dartmoor – he realised now what the red flag indicated. The lunatics had taken over the Bunker! Only... Bell had spoken to a general, who was clearly in on this, and Lethbridge-Stewart had served with Carol. But he could have been lying, trying to gain Bell's trust. Bell swallowed. This wasn't looking good whichever way you painted it.

'We need to get in there unobserved,' Lethbridge-Stewart was saying, 'if at all possible. The caves are out, as the way in is blocked by the aforementioned rock fall, and even if we could get past that, there would probably be enemies waiting for us on the other side. So we're going to cut our way through the perimeter fence. Sergeant Bell, is there any cutting equipment on site?'

They were going to cut their way in to a nuclear waste reprocessing plant? Bell nodded dumbly.

'Excellent. Now then, as a distraction, we're going to need some fireworks. Hooper, Powell, you'll be responsible for those whilst Stevens and I cut our way in. Radio silence until we're inside. Once in we'll rendezvous and make our way into the complex, try to locate Chorley. Take a look at this plan – see the large rectangular building in the centre? That's what we'll make for.'

They all leaned over the plan. 'Hang on,' said Powell. 'What if we're wrong? What if Dominex are on the level, what if they really are producing cheap energy, and doing good?'

Lethbridge-Stewart looked pensive for a few seconds, then shook his head. 'I hope you're right, but I don't think so. In any case I'll take full responsibility.'

'What about these Quark things?' Stevens asked.

'Yes, well their firepower is deadly – and they have the ability to transform, as I've already described.'

The only quarks Bell was aware of were elementary particles. Firepower? Transformation? He felt as if he was slipping into a nightmare, or madness.

'But they do have one significant weakness – a weakness we shall exploit. When I encountered them in the caves, they stopped firing. I only worked out why after I came to. They're machines, and like all machines, they need to recharge. So, if we are confronted with them, the best option is to draw their fire – drain their energy – so they have to stop and recharge. Then let them have it with the grenades.'

'Just one thing,' Hooper said. 'How will we know when the things are recharging?'

'Well, for one thing, they'll stop firing,' said Lethbridge-Stewart with calm authority. 'And whilst they are recharging, they, er, wave their arms about, and make a high-pitched burbling noise. Part of the process, I assume.'

Bell expected the others to burst into laughter, but they just looked at each other, and nodded, as if they'd accepted this madman's theories as Gospel.

'Dominex is twenty miles north from here. We'll set off at twenty-hundred hours, under the cover of darkness. We'll hide the van, yomp up to Black Tor...' – Lethbridge-Stewart rapped his swagger-stick at a point on the map – '...for a recce, then hike down into the valley, and to Dominex.' He turned his gaze on Bell. 'So, we have five hours to spend in the company of the redoubtable Sergeant Bell.'

Four pairs of eyes converged on Bell. He felt he had to say something. 'I still think you're all bonkers.'

Lethbridge-Stewart clearly chose to ignore this. 'I take it there are sufficient provisions to go round. We're going to need food. Other than that, it's merely a matter of keeping ourselves occupied until the off. Do you have any board games?'

'Board games,' repeated Bell. There was a big stack of them in the common room. He'd never had need of them, of course, being here all Billy No Mates. Now he had plenty of people to play with, but he wished to God this wasn't so. 'Yes. *Monopoly, Risk*...'

Lethbridge-Stewart rubbed his hands together. 'Excellent. And appropriate. More tea?'

They'd gone. Thank God, they'd gone! Gone, and taken their madness with them.

They'd asked him to come with them, but he'd politely declined. Somehow, the thought of breaking into a nuclear reprocessing plant didn't appeal to him. It was a dangerous business, the most dangerous he could imagine, and any trespassers would be met with ultimate force. They'd understood, of course they'd understood. Colonel Lethbridge-Stewart had been most sympathetic and most apologetic as the Para maniac Stevens had tied him to one of the chairs in the conference room.

That was an hour ago. It was now twenty-one-hundred hours, according to the clock on the wall of the conference room. They would be at the Dominex installation now. They would be breaking in.

The lunatics!

Lethbridge-Stewart had said, in his reassuring patrician voice, that they would send someone to release Bell 'when it was all over'. Something about the man's manner had reassured Bell, despite the lunacy of their so-called top-secret hush-hush mission. But that sense of reassurance had completely vanished within two minutes of their departure.

When what was all over?

They were about to break into a nuclear waste processing facility! In fact, they probably were at this very moment.

Unable to move, Sergeant Richard Bell kept an eye on the clock, and waited for the balloon to go up.

— CHAPTER EIGHTEEN —

Destroy! Destroy! Destroy!

It was a deep and musky summer night. The moor brooded, keeping its secrets close to its mossy bosom. Overhead, the stars shone like pinpricks in a vast canopy of bruised blue. The moon, a pitted yellow coin, reflected its light down onto the rolling hillocks and slopes, onto the gorse and bracken and heather, onto the eternal stones, and onto the valley beneath Black Tor. And onto the Dominex installation, an illuminated grid of metal and concrete, an artificial thing, an alien thing, its brightness a brutal defiance of the moonlight, its very presence an affront to the ancient land upon which it lay.

Black Tor itself was a jet-black clenched fist of rock, raised as if in defiance of the gleaming complex below. In its shadow, gazing down upon the lights of Dominex, four men stood, clad in khaki battle dress and boots, with rifles slung around their necks. Their faces were pale and serious in the moonlight.

'Well, there it is,' said Lethbridge-Stewart softly.

The men stood in silence for a few moments. There was no sound at all, except for that which they made themselves. Their breathing, the shuffling of their boots. After a while, Powell coughed. 'Best get on with it then.'

Lethbridge-Stewart allowed himself a smile. Powell's

lugubrious, down-to-earth attitude was precisely what was needed at times like this. 'Right. Maintain radio silence until you're in position, then contact me when you're ready to fire.'

'Yes, sir!' Hooper grinned and hefted the grenade-launcher, which he carried in addition to a Browning automatic pistol and bag of high explosive 40x46 grenades.

'Very well. Off you go'

Hooper and Powell saluted, and made off down the slope towards the Dominex installation.

Lethbridge-Stewart turned to Stevens. The man looked eager, ready for anything. Lethbridge-Stewart hoped that Pemberton was right about him. 'Right, we'll give them ten minutes to get into position, then move down.'

'Yes, sir!' Stevens was, in addition to a hi-powered self-loading rifle, carrying the bolt-cutter they'd liberated from the Bunker.

'Ten minutes.' Lethbridge-Stewart peered down the incline. The figures of Powell and Hooper were still just about discernible, dodging about the humps and tumps of the lower slope, almost lost to view in the gloom. 'Ten minutes and we're going in.'

The twenty-mile drive from the Bunker had been a solemn affair. There was none of the singing and ribaldry of their journey from London. Powell sat up front with Lethbridge-Stewart, and was even more quiet and taciturn than usual. The two younger men were in the back with the weapons and kit. All had changed out of civvies into the khaki gear that Powell had found at the Bunker, and in doing so, a subtle change had come over all of them. Now they were in uniform, they were in earnest. They were soldiers with a job to do. An unsanctioned job that would probably land them all in prison, but a job nonetheless.

Lethbridge-Stewart took the main B-road through Kingsbridge until they reached the small village of South Brent, at the southern extremity of Dartmoor, at sunset. As it would remain light until almost twenty-one-hundred hours, they proceeded onto the moor and parked up to wait out the remainder of the daylight.

When it was dark enough, Lethbridge-Stewart drove the furniture lorry further into the dark and rolling moorland, and parked in the very same secluded overgrown farm track he had used before the ill-fated expedition into the caves. There Lethbridge-Stewart issued his team with a final briefing, and issued the weapons and supplies. Powell and he had the handheld RT transmitter-receivers, while Stevens and he had the SLRs. Powell had the Heckler and Koch, and Hooper had charge of the M79, as well as one of the Browning semi-automatic pistols. Lethbridge-Stewart had the other Browning, and they all carried half a dozen Mills bombs each. Enough to give the enemy some trouble, he hoped.

They had then moved up the steep slope towards Black Tor under the light of the new moon.

And now ten minutes had passed. Lethbridge-Stewart nodded to Stevens. It was time to go.

Hooper and Powell jogged across moonlit moorland, the lights of Dominex glittering in the distance. Hooper ran awkwardly, the grenade launcher slung across his back, the bag of grenades hanging heavy in a pack on his belt. As planned, they had skirted round the perimeter of the Dominex plant to approach it from the south; Lethbridge-Stewart and Stevens would be making their entrance on the side facing Black Tor to the west.

They came to a copse of stunted trees, and Powell called a halt. They crouched down amidst the trunks. Hooper could see a sheen of sweat on the older man's brow. 'You all right?'

'Course I am, lad!' snarled Powell. Then, contemplatively: 'Are you sure about this?'

Hooper sighed. Not again! 'Look, we've been over this. We both trust the colonel. We both know him, we both owe him.'

'It was his father I knew,' said Powell. 'Gordon Lethbridge-Stewart. Served under him in Africa during the last lot.' His eyes assumed a faraway, reminiscent look.

There wasn't time for this. 'So, like father, like son. You came when you got the call, didn't you? Why are you having doubts now?'

A wry smile softened Powell's craggy features. 'Aye, son, you're right. I came when he called. What else could I do? I'm sixty in a month. My best years are behind me. This is the last chance I'll ever have to recapture my glory days.'

'Right. So we're okay to go, yeah?' Hooper unshouldered the grenade launcher and checked it over.

'What's the range of that thing?'

'Three hundred fifty metres.'

Powell gazed over at the shining lights of Dominex. 'We're too far away.'

Hooper slid the barrel locking latch and broke the M79 open. He took a grenade from the pack, slid it in place and closed the weapon with a sturdy *click*. 'We'll move in to three hundred metres, drop one on the fence, move forward and drop another one further in. Should stir things up a bit.'

'Right you are, lad.'

Hooper grinned, hefted the launcher, and set off at a crouching run across the moor.

On the western side of the Dominex installation, Lethbridge-Stewart and Stevens made their way cautiously across the moorland, keeping low, using gorse bushes and bracken for cover. When they were about a hundred yards away, Lethbridge-Stewart called for a stop.

Stevens hunkered down beside Lethbridge-Stewart and the two men slithered forward on their bellies, taking advantage of a slight hummock for cover. The summer night was rich with the musk of heather and the sweet coconut tang of gorse. Ahead of them, the lights of the Dominex installation flickered through fronds of bracken.

'This is near enough, I think,' whispered Lethbridge-Stewart. He unclipped the handheld RT from his belt.

Stevens nodded in the direction of Dominex. 'Do you think they've seen us?'

'I think we're too far away. Or at least, I hope. In any case, won't be long now, until...'

'Boom!' Stevens grinned maniacally.

'Er, yes, indeed.'

They settled down to wait, eyes fixed on the lights of Dominex.

'Right,' said Hooper, dropping into a crouch behind a substantial gorse bush. 'This is near enough.'

Powell slumped down beside him, breathing heavily. Hooper hoped the old geezer wouldn't slow him down.

'Do you think they've seen us?' the older man panted.

'Doesn't matter if they have,' said Hooper grimly, brandishing the grenade launcher. 'They'll soon know we're here.' He stood clear of the bush until he had a clear line of sight at the Dominex installation. The chain-link fence ran left to right across his field of vision about three hundred metres ahead of him. Lit at intervals by bluish-white lights, it shone and shimmered like a giant silver necklace.

There was no way he could miss. 'Make the call.'

'Mayhem One to Mayhem Leader,' said Powell into the RT. 'We're in position.'

A burst of static, then Lethbridge-Stewart's voice. 'Mayhem Leader; fire when ready.'

Hooper slid the safety catch and hefted the M79, nestling the stock into his shoulder. He looked along the barrel, aiming low, braced himself for the recoil, and pulled the trigger. There was a stout, hollow *'thub!'*. The stock kicked into his shoulder, and with a searing hiss the grenade was away, whistling through the starry night. Hooper held his breath. One second, two seconds, then–

A white-orange explosion blossomed in the middle of the fence and there was a distant crump, followed by a metallic clattering as bits of fence flew through the air and rained down.

'Bloody Nora!' came Powell's excited shout. 'That should wake 'em up!'

Hooper reloaded the launcher, ran forward fifty metres, fired again. The second grenade landed some distance inside the Dominex plant, atop an outhouse. There was another explosion, another rain of debris. Sirens blared.

Hooper reloaded, grinning, and gestured to Powell. 'That was the easy bit.'

Even though he'd been expecting it, the explosion still made Lethbridge-Stewart duck. It happened away over to their right, on the south side of the Dominex plant, as they'd planned. He watched the orange fireball expand, flying debris picked out sharply against the glare. An acrid smell of burning now merged with the heady nocturnal scents of the moor.

Lethbridge-Stewart turned to Stevens, but the man was already on his feet and running towards the Dominex plant, bolt-cutters in hand. Lethbridge-Stewart leapt up and ran after him. As he caught up there was a second explosion, this one from inside the Dominex plant, that made them both hit the ground. Up and running again, and at the chain-link fence. Bright white lights above. They would surely be seen – but then surely the distraction would have worked. Stevens was working at the fence with the bolt-cutters like a man possessed. Within minutes he had cut a jagged L-shape through the wires, which he then pressed aside, allowing them to squeeze through.

Lethbridge-Stewart unshouldered his SLR.

They were in.

Director Vaar opened his eyes. Something was wrong. An alarm was sounding within his recharging chamber, a tiny yet insistent buzzing. Groggily, he pressed the release switch and the lid of the chamber swung open. He stepped out, and clenched his fists. Being roused from recharging was dangerous, and meant that he wouldn't be operating at full capability until he re-entered the chamber. But his underlings would not dare to wake him without good reason. Project M must be in danger! Director Vaar snarled, and stomped from his private quarters towards the control chamber.

'Navigator Deka! What is the meaning of this?'

'We are under attack!' Deka thundered as soon as Vaar entered.

'Report!'

'Two explosions on the southern perimeter. High explosive, massive damage. Armed humans loose within the complex!'

'We must deploy Quarks to destroy them!' shouted Azbo.

'Silence!' Vaar thought quickly. Most of the Quarks were stowed on the ship, ready for take-off. Only ten remained on the complex, there to carry out the final checks and duties before departure. But if they were under attack, that departure would be compromised. 'Status of project M?'

'Project M is ready for deployment,' said Navigator Deka with admirable pride.

'Navigator Deka, you will accompany me to the ship. Probationer Azbo – you have your wish! Take the remaining Quarks, find the attacking humans and destroy! Then join us at the ship. We will then launch, and activate Project M from orbit.'

'Destroy!' rumbled Azbo. 'Command accepted!' So saying, he lumbered from the control chamber, bellowing for Quarks.

'Deka – with me!'

'Command accepted. But what about the human,

212

Chorley?'

Vaar snarled with irritated impatience. 'He will burn like the rest of his species once Project M is unleashed! Come!'

Harold Chorley, Press and Public Relations Officer for Dominex Industries, couldn't sleep, but who needed sleep? He was far too busy to sleep! These press releases wouldn't write themselves. No! That was his job, and he loved it. Loved working for Dominex! Loved Director Vaar! He even – no, especially – loved the Quark that stood guard in the corner of his room. It stood there now, its arms retracted, twittering to itself, watching him scrawl. Watching him write! The typewriter had broken hours ago – he had a vague memory of throwing it to the floor in a fit of screaming terror, then crawling into the little bed with a thumping headache, but that must have been a dream, why would he do that? So instead, Chorley was using a felt-tip pen he'd found in his jacket pocket to carry on his writing. He'd also run out of paper, so he was writing on the wall, the lovely cold metal wall of his prison cell. No! His room! His room, his lovely room that Dominex had provided.

He was writing a biography of Director Dominic Vaar.

The race that came to be known as the Dominators were once a human-basic tribe of hunter-gatherer-warriors dwelling on the planet Drahb in the Phi-Ralix galaxy. A naturally warlike species, they quickly became the dominant life-form on the planet, and developed a highly industrialised technological society based on atomic power. They mastered space flight through the use of negative mass flux absorption – utilising radiation for power – and conquered first their home solar system, and then the entire Phi-Ralix galaxy. A massive achievement for any race.

Their ancestors were stocky, pale-skinned bipeds with dark hair, as vulnerable and naked as the Tellurians of Earth. During the conquest of their home solar system, they experimented with physical augmentation. They made themselves taller, toughened their skin, and encased their bodies in armour plating. They eradicated the messy and tedious business of sexual reproduction and instead became a mono-gendered species who reproduce by parthenogenesis. They altered their bodies to remove the need for food and obtained their energy from radiation, extending the normal Dominator lifespan by several hundreds of years. In every way, they are better than you!

As their conquest of the galaxy expanded, word of the fearsome conquerors spread from planet to planet. They became the Masters of the Ten Galaxies!

Planets and star systems fell to the Dominators. As their empire expanded, so did their command structure, with a clear chain of command from the lowest ranks (Probationers) up to the middle ranks (Navigators, Tacticians, Engineers) to the top ranks (Directors) and the Dominant Echelon of the War Fleet.

The need for power was their one constant problem. During the conquest of the Phi-Ralix galaxy, they found their resources were spread thin. The Dominators therefore cultivated a strict culture of power conservation. Waste of energy was considered a capital offence, and Probationers were rigorously trained in the techniques of power management. In addition, Dominators made use of enslavement of the conquered to help build their empire, and also constructed a tool to assist in their programme of expansion; a robotic slave force they call the Quarks.

Quarks were designed by Dominator Engineers to be readily transportable and adaptable: their cuboid bodies could be easily stored and transported, and the spherical, spired heads assembled from packs stored within a cavity inside the main casing. On low power, Quarks were able only to move very slowly, conserving their energies for their weaponry. A squad of high-powered Quarks, however, is a versatile and lethal tool, able to transform and expand into various configurations as the situation demanded it.

Such measures allowed the Dominators to expand and conquer their home galaxy. Now they require new sources of power, to expand their empire ever further. Negative mass flux absorption required nuclear energy – radiation found in space, e.g. solar radiation, was not sufficient – therefore task forces were created to find new methods of acquiring negative mass flux energy. Director Vaar is the head of a special task force sent to the Milky Way galaxy for that very purpose.

His eyes blurred as he read the words he wrote... No, they made no sense. He had written about the Director's humble upbringing on his father's farm, the trials and tribulations of his youth, his bashful teenage romances, the evidence of his early entrepreneurial skills, his rise to power and prominence... But the words before him...

He frowned. The writing was getting paler and paler. His felt-tip pen was running out! Desperately, he licked the end. No use! Made it worse. Vinegar! He needed vinegar! That always revitalised felt-tip pens! But where was he going to get vinegar?

Chorley staggered to his feet. Pain throbbed through his head. 'Quark. Get me some vinegar! Quark!'

The Quark shuffled forward, its blocky arms swinging outwards. 'Vin-e-gar?' it trilled.

Chorley clutched his head. 'Yes! My pen – it's run out, and – ah!' The pain suddenly subsumed his head and he slumped to the floor. 'My writing,' he moaned. He twisted round so he could admire his work.

Chorley gasped in shock.

The words made no sense. And at the bottom of the wall, running from wall to floor was one word, written over and over again: *MAD!*

He crawled to the bed and sat sobbing, head in hands. 'What's happening to me?'

The Quark emitted a trilling sound, like a metallic bird call, and began to shuffle from the room.

'Where are you going?' cried Chorley. He couldn't bear the thought of his little friend leaving!

'Other duties,' burbled the diminutive robot.

Chorley leapt up from the bed. 'I'll come with you!'

The Quark swung round, extending its energy weapon. 'Do not move! Do not move or I will destroy!'

Chorley sat back down on the bed. He suddenly had a very clear memory of his blue Hillman Imp being consumed in a fireball. Better do as the Quark said. He watched it sullenly as it shuffled to the door, which slid open to let it out, then closed behind it.

Chorley sat on the bed, nursing his throbbing head. He stared fearfully at what he had written on the wall. Mad.... Mad... no, not mad, but MAD. Capital letters. MAD. An acronym! But what did it stand for? He remembered Director Vaar talking to the other Dominators about it. Project M, project MAD. But what did it stand for?

Oh no.

Chorley stood up, wobbly on his feet. He had to get out of here. Had to get out! He went over to the door, and pressed all the buttons on the panel next to it. To his surprise, the door slid open. He stepped out of his room, his

216

office, his prison cell, and ran down the corridor. 'Quark!' he called. 'Wait! We have to get out of here! Your masters are mad! They're going to unleash MAD!'

But the Quark was nowhere to be seen.

Chorley stopped running. There was no point. MAD would destroy everything!

Hooper and Powell picked their way expertly over the burning remains of the fence. All around them, the dry moorland foliage burned, white smoke curling into the dark blue sky, making them cough. Glowing orange filaments drifted through the air. Sirens shrieked. Ahead of them, the looming blocks of the Dominex complex. Grenade launcher cocked and ready, Hooper moved across the concrete apron into the cover of an outbuilding, Powell behind him, rifle at the ready. The two men kept into the cover of the building and peered round the edge. Nothing was moving, except them. They ran down an alleyway between two corrugated iron sheds. Rounding a corner, Hooper glimpsed two figures in the distance – two huge, towering figures, like Frankenstein and his brother in shoulder pads.

The two men ducked down behind some barrels.

'What the hell are they?' called Powell over the incessant sound of the sirens.

'Must be the chaps in charge,' answered Hooper.

'Mayhem One to Mayhem Leader,' said Powell urgently into the RT set, cupping his hand around the microphone. 'We've sighted a couple of suspicious-looking chaps, big fellows, potentially Dominex top brass.'

Hooper watched impatiently as Powell listened to the reply. 'Well?'

'The colonel says to follow them, see what they're up to. He and Stevens are going to try to find this reporter chap.'

'Right.' Hooper hefted the grenade launcher. 'So let's go.'

Keeping to the shadows, they followed the two hulking figures.

Probationer Azbo smiled in grim satisfaction as the remaining Quarks within the complex assembled outside the concrete fortress that housed the Dominator's control chamber. Their box-like bodies jostled together and they chirruped in anticipation. Azbo's black heart almost burst within his barrel chest. At last, he was doing the job a Dominator was meant to do!

'Quarks! New task! There are humans loose within the complex. They must be found – and destroyed!'

The Quarks burbled happily to themselves.

Azbo raised his arms above his head. 'Now, go! Destroy! Destroy! *Destroy!*'

Lethbridge-Stewart and Stevens, rifles at the ready, prowled through the concrete and steel canyons of the Dominex plant, alert for any movement. Sirens blared, masking any other sound, so they communicated by hand signals. Lethbridge-Stewart had memorised the plan of the Dominex installation, and he led them both deeper and deeper into the complex. Presently they came to a series of stout square buildings formed of bare, unpainted breeze-blocks. Though he did not know their purpose, he knew that they bordered the central area. He pointed to a gap between the nearest two buildings, and Stevens ran on ahead, keeping low, scanning from side to side.

With a quick look around, Lethbridge-Stewart followed him into the narrow gap between two of the buildings; just wide enough to admit a man. He squeezed through, the rough breeze-blocks scraping the shoulders of his khaki battle-shirt. The passage reeked of oil, and at the far end, bright white spilled along the narrow space, casting Stevens' shadow back towards him.

All at once the sirens stopped, leaving an eerie silence. Lethbridge-Stewart caught up with the ex-Para and they crouched at the end of the passage, surveying the scene before them.

As Lethbridge-Stewart had guessed, there before them was the centre of the installation: a vast fortress of grey concrete. Lights shone from its roof, illuminating the wide concrete apron that surrounded it and a line of Quarks that stood before the hangar, casing blocky shadows across the concrete apron. Beyond them, a tall, powerful figure stood, clad in black armour built up around the neck. Its face was pale and its black hair glistened in the artificial light. It was gesticulating at its robotic servants, its guttural voice echoing up and down the concrete canyon. Lethbridge-Stewart squinted. The features were difficult to make out at this distance. Director Vaar, or another like him?

Suddenly the figure raised its massive arms above its head. 'Destroy! Destroy! *Destroy!*' it bellowed, before stomping off around the side of the building and disappearing from view.

'Destroy!' repeated the Quarks, their tinny metallic voices grotesque echoes of that of their hulking master's. They turned round, shuffling on their shoebox legs, their weapon arms extended, and fanned out across the concrete.

Their master folded his arms, nodded in satisfaction, and strode off, disappearing around the edge of the building.

Lethbridge-Stewart and Stevens watched as the Quarks advanced.

'Destroy! Destroy! We – will – *destroy!*'

— CHAPTER NINETEEN —

Launch Capability

This was it. Stevens had forgotten what it was like, why military service intoxicated him. Why it was so bad for him. He always got caught up in it – too much so. That was why he'd left. He'd tried to explain to Old Spence, but the colonel never understood. The heat, the excitement of battle, it did things to him. Bad things.

He watched the Quarks as they advanced across the concrete, their angular shadows reaching out towards him. It didn't matter to him that the enemy were squat, block-like robots with spiked heads. In fact he hardly even noticed. They were the enemy, to be destroyed. And he was the meanest, hardest bloke in the service. They had no chance! He made to run from their narrow hiding place between the two breeze-block buildings, but he felt Lethbridge-Stewart's restraining hand on his shoulder.

Stevens grimaced, turned to face the colonel. For a moment it wasn't the stern face of Colonel Alistair Lethbridge-Stewart looking at him, but the angry visage of Colonel Spencer Pemberton. 'Lemme go!'

'No, man! They clearly know we've broken in to their base – but they haven't seen us. Wait until they've passed by and we'll get into the main building. We have the advantage of surprise!'

Stevens shook his head, clearing both his vision and his head. He had let down one colonel, intentionally or otherwise, he wouldn't do so to another.

There was a cacophony of chirruping blecps. Stevens swung back around. Three Quarks were approaching their hiding place, and, beyond them others were converging.

'Well, they've seen us now!' shouted Stevens, the heat taking over once more. Dropping to his knees, he raised the SLR, aimed, and fired, moving the barrel in a smooth raking motion along the line of Quarks. Bullets whistled through the air, hit their targets with a metallic spatter. The zing of ricochet, the kick-back of recoil, – all this was music to Stevens.

'Have it, you titchy tin twerps!' he yelled, loosing off another round.

Again the restraining arm. 'It's no use! Look!'

The Quarks were still advancing. They weren't even marked! Not a chip on their lead-grey casings.

'Remember what I said – try to draw their fire, drain their energy! Now – when I say run, make for that tower over there.'

Stevens looked to where Lethbridge-Stewart was pointing. A cylindrical silver tower topped with a conical canopy stood a hundred yards away.

'Now, go!' A hand slapped his back.

Stevens ran, boots thudding on concrete, glimpsing the Quarks turn to cover him. Suddenly there was a sound like a hot iron being plunged into icy water, and Stevens staggered as a blast of heat jetted past his left ear, and a streak of orange light like compressed, directed fire lanced into the distance. Stevens staggered, recovered, and ran on a zig-zag course towards the tower. Further blasts of searing energy laced the air around him. Chest heaving, he at last reached the tower and scrambled round to its far side.

Discarding the SLR, he fumbled for the grenades on his belt. Grasping one in his fist, he peered round the edge of the tower. The Quarks were advancing – they were slow, but they were machines, which meant they wouldn't give up until their power was drained. But how long would that take? What if they were fully-charged? What if the colonel's strategy failed? The colonel! Where was he?

Stevens scanned the ground between the breeze-block buildings and the hanger. All he could see was the line advancing Quarks. A hand on his shoulder made him gasp, and he slid back into cover.

The sight of the colonel's face made him giggle with relief.

'Thought you'd bought it, sir!'

That reassuring smile; there was something about it, something that reminded Stevens of Old Spence.

'Not quite yet, old chap!' Lethbridge-Stewart peered around the edge of the tower, then at the grenade in Stevens' hand. The smile disappeared. 'Let them have it.'

Stevens yanked out the pin, leaned around the edge of the tower, its metal surface cold against his cheek, and lobbed the Mills bomb at the nearest three Quarks. He ducked back into cover, held his breath and–

There was a satisfying crump and the cylindrical tower reverberated with an alarming clangour as bits of exploded Quark peppered its sides.

Stevens looked. 'Yes!'

One Quark lay in pieces, completely destroyed. But the

others were still advancing. Nine of them, still.

Did they have enough grenades?

'Fire in the hole!'

Stevens felt himself dragged back into cover as the Quarks fired. He crouched on the gritty concrete with Lethbridge-Stewart as searing orange bolts of energy shot past their hiding place, slamming into the buildings on the far side of the complex.

Lethbridge-Stewart got to his feet, and to Stevens' horror, stepped directly into the line of fire.

Stevens leaped up to haul him back – and collided with the colonel as he dodged back into hiding, just as the Quarks unleashed further bolts of deadly fire. The two man lay there panting.

'And I thought I was a nutter!' gasped Stevens.

After a while, he realised that the firing had stopped. An eerie silence hung over the complex. Lethbridge-Stewart stood and beckoned him to follow. Peering round the edge of the cylindrical tower, Stevens saw that the Quarks had stopped. They were waving their arms and emitting a strange burbling.

'They're recharging. Now!'

Stevens and Lethbridge-Stewart ran from cover, almost right up to the recharging Quarks. Stevens had never felt so alive. He unpinned a Mills bomb, rolled it underneath a Quark; out of the corner of his eye he saw Lethbridge-Stewart do the same.

One – two – three – boom!

Stevens ducked to the ground as the two Quarks exploded in a fountain of metal fragments. He dodged past another pair of Quarks and, giggling, slid two more grenades into the space between their waving arms. Behind him, another explosion. Stevens rolled into cover, surveying the scene. Six Quarks lay shattered, but three remained. Their arms had stopped waving about. Did this mean they were now fully charged? Where was the colonel?

There – by the entrance of the main building.

Stevens started to run over toward him.

'Look out, man!'

Stevens swung round.

The three remaining Quarks were changing.

Their legs extended until they towered over him, and from their box-like bodies extra arms unfolded. Arms ending in the blank, black mouths of what were unmistakably weapons.

'Destroy!' they trilled – for although now massive, their voices remained the same. 'Destroy!'

Stevens felt completely calm as the giant alien robots towered over him.

He knew what he had to do.

Powell and Hooper paused as the sounds of battle reached them. The two figures they were following also stopped, looking back towards the centre of the complex.

'Sounds like all hell's breaking loose back there, lad.' Powell said. 'We should go and help them.'

'The colonel can take care of himself, and as for that Stevens… No, we follow these two, as ordered.'

They followed the two hulking figures until they came to a concrete hangar. The hatch, which took up the whole of the front of the building, began to slide slowly upwards with a chatter of rattling aluminium. Its progress was clearly too slow, as the figure on the left grasped the bottom of the hatch and heaved on it, roaring in impatience. With a protesting shriek the hatch came to a juddering halt and refused to move. It had only opened five or so feet, enough to admit a man, but not these – whatever they were. The two figures began to argue, their stentorian voices echoing through the night. Then they both crouched down, and, with enough dignity as they could muster, dropped to their knees and crawled through the gap into the darkness within. Presently, bright white light snapped on, shining brightly through the gap. The hatch remained open, presumably stuck.

Hooper glanced at Powell.

Powell sighed. 'Well, lad, never look a gift horse, and all that.'

The two men ran over and ducked into the hangar. They found themselves in a bright, wide space with white-painted walls and a corrugated iron ceiling with a circular hatch in its centre.

Below this hatch stood what Hooper could only describe as a flying saucer.

'Bloody hell!' Powell hissed. 'The colonel was right!'

Supported on four struts, the huge craft's segmented underbelly was fringed by a sequence of circular lights which pulsed steadily. The silver upper canopy shone as if polished and was ringed by slitted cowlings. The thing was topped off by a – cockpit? Hooper wondered – that resembled a flattened pillbox. A ramp let up to a hatchway in the craft's underside. An almost sub-aural thrum of power filled the hangar.

Standing in front of the saucer were the two hulking

figures of the masters of Dominex. Seen in bright light, they were an unsettling sight; their huge, tree-like limbs were clad in armour that glittered bluish-purple, and their shoulders were encased in ridged, jet-black armour that completely hid their necks – if they even had any! Their faces were deeply lined and ghastly, like the faces of fresh corpses.

And those faces were glaring directly at Powell and Hooper.

Hooper hefted the grenade launcher. A high-explosive blast in here might knock them all out. At his side, he could see Powell raise the Hechler and Koch. Powell fired, but the bullets pinged off the armour, ricocheting against the whitewashed concrete walls, clanging off the corrugated iron ceiling.

'Pathetic humans!' bellowed the figure on the left. 'What can you do against the might of the Dominators?'

'Dominators, eh?' yelled Powell. 'Well, you won't be dominating us!'

The Dominator grinned ghoulishly. 'We will not need to. Soon we will destroy your world!'

'Not if I can help it, mate!' Hooper shouted.

'Quark!' the other Dominator barked.

The saucer's hatch opened, revealing, at the top of the access ramp, a squat robot with a spiked, spherical head. Block-like arms swung in their direction. Obviously one of the things the colonel had described. And yes, it did look kind of odd, but Hooper wasn't in the mood for laughing.

'Quark, destroy!'

Hooper raised the grenade-launcher, aimed, his finger caressed the trigger–

There was an unearthly, pulsating, throbbing sound, and

the air between the Quark and the two men seemed to shimmer. Hooper dived to one side, but Powell was too late. He screamed as alien energies consumed him. His skin glowed white, so white it hurt Hooper's eyes, and then seemed to blister like photographic film thrown into a fire. And then Powell was *gone,* simply gone, not there, vanished, destroyed without even a scream.

Enraged, Hooper leapt to his feet. He aimed the M79 straight at the Quark, and fired.

On his way to the hangar where the ship waited ready for lift-off, Probationer Azbo paused, black-gloved fingers twitching. He could hear the sounds of battle behind him.

Surely there was time? Time to watch his deadly Quarks in action, before Project M was unleashed?

With a ghoulish grin, he turned round and stomped back towards the battlefield.

Lethbridge-Stewart watched in horror as the three surviving Quarks, now giant crane-like creatures, towered over Stevens. He reached for his SLR – but realised he must have dropped it in the heat of battle. All he had left was the Browning. More powerful than his trusty Enfield, but still only a pistol. It would have to suffice.

He stepped out from cover, aimed, and fired. The bullets simply pinged off the Quarks' casing, as he'd expected. Cursing, he ran towards Stevens. 'Run, man! Get out of there!'

But Stevens just sat there as the three robots brought their weapons to bear on him. What was he doing? Lethbridge-Stewart came to a halt as he realised. Stevens had a grenade in each hand. With slow, deliberate movements, he removed the pins, and placed them on the ground between the three Quarks. He produced another two grenades, and did the same.

Then he ran.

The three Quarks fired at the exact same moment that the three grenades exploded. Arcs of orange energy blasted towards Stevens, and there was an enormous concussion as the grenades went off. Lethbridge-Stewart threw himself to the ground and debris rained down around him. After a moment he looked up. The Quarks were still active, but their legs had been completely smashed. They lay on the concrete, emitting a pathetic, low burbling, their arms waving feebly.

Of Stevens there was no sign.

'Human!' roared a voice from behind him.

Lethbridge-Stewart swung round. Framed in the doorway was a massive figure. It stomped onto the battlefield, glaring at the damaged Quarks with a scowl of disbelief and anger. It uttered some words in a guttural, alien tongue, then swung round to Lethbridge-Stewart. 'Destroyed! Destroyed! You have destroyed my Quarks!' it bellowed. 'Now, I will destroy *you!*' With a growl of fury the giant being lunged forwards.

Lethbridge-Stewart fired the Browning, but as with the Quarks, the bullets just bounced off. He aimed for the creature's face, but the bullets were swatted away as if they were mere insects.

There was nothing for it. Lethbridge-Stewart turned and ran, the enormous alien in pursuit.

The grenade streaked past the Quark and into the interior

of the saucer. Hooper hit the deck, and watched with satisfaction as the blast blew the small robot right out of the hatchway and against the far wall, which it hit with a resounding clang. It fell to the floor, inert. The two Dominators had also been thrown backwards by the blast, and were now picking themselves up. Hooper discarded the M79, unholstered his pistol, aimed, and fired. The bullets simply bounced off their armour. He took a headshot and smiled grimly as one of the blighters went down, purple blood issuing from a wound in its temple. The other Dominator ran for the ship and was inside before Hooper could take aim.

Hooper walked over to where Powell had been standing. There was nothing there, not even a scorch mark. The handheld RT set lay to one side, undamaged.

He picked it up. 'Mayhem One to Mayhem Leader! Powell's dead. The enemy have a vessel – a flying saucer! I'm going in!'

No reply. Just a crackle. Had the colonel heard him? The door of the saucer began to slide closed. Discarding the RT set, Hooper sprinted across the hangar and up the access ramp, just making it through the narrowing gap. He found himself in a circular control room thick with smoke and the trilling sound of dozens of alarms all sounding at once.

He coughed, put a hand over his mouth. The grenade had clearly done some damage. A massive figure loomed through the smoke. Before Hooper could bring his Browning to bear, the Dominator gripped him by the shoulders and slammed him against the wall. Hooper kicked out, his booted feet striking the Dominator's armour. A cadaverous face, contorted in anger, was thrust into his own.

'Foolish human! You have compromised Project M!'

The Dominator let him go and Hooper expected to crash to the floor, but some strange force kept him there, spread-eagled against the wall. He struggled but he could not move – it was as if he was glued there.

Helpless, he watched as the Dominator staggered over to the centre of what he supposed must be the flight deck of the saucer. Massive hands stabbed at buttons, pulled levers. The Dominator turned round, grinning in triumph.

'We have launch capability!' it bellowed.

CHAPTER TWENTY

Project M

Director Vaar groaned and hauled himself to a sitting position. He put a hand to his head. Blood – his own blood. He was not fully recharged, his body weaker than it should be. Yet he was alive – the projectile had only grazed his skull. Nevertheless, some sort of head armour was clearly a necessary addition to Dominator armour. He would put it to the Dominant Echelon, when he returned to the War Fleet...

A rising howl of energy emanated from the ship, and there was a clanking, rattling sound as the hatch in the ceiling of the hangar slid open. Vaar staggered to his feet, fists clenched in anger. Deka was leaving without him! He would never return to Drahb, never see the look on the Domina's faces when the Dominators won! He would die on this miserable world once Project M was unleashed!

The ship began to rise slowly, the air beneath it shimmering. Vaar backed away from the wave of heat emanating from the ship's engines, and staggered from the hangar before it got too much.

His anger seeped slowly away. Logically, what else could Deka have done? With his Director shot, presumed dead, and humans running amok on the base, the Navigator's first priority would be Project M. So, although he would die,

Project M, would succeed, for the greater glory of the Dominators!

Vaar watched as the ship rose from the hangar, a shining silver emblem of victory etched against the canopy of starred blue. Although he knew Deka could not hear him, he cupped his gloved hands to his mouth and shouted, 'Navigator Deka! Activate Project M! Destroy this miserable world! *Destroy!*'

Lethbridge-Stewart ran through the Dominex complex, the enraged Dominator hot on his heels, desperately seeking some weapon or somewhere to hide. If the thing caught him, it would tear him limb from limb, he had no doubt – no point even trying to engage the brute in hand-to-hand combat. He rounded a corner, and saw ahead of him the open end of a storage shed, piled high with crates and barrels. Around the upper edge of the shed ran a railed gantry, accessed by ladders. The germ of an idea began to form.

Gasping, Lethbridge-Stewart hauled himself up the nearest ladder.

On his belt, his RT set crackled. 'Mayhem One to Mayhem Leader! Powell's dead. The enemy have a vessel – a flying saucer! I'm going in!'

No time to answer. The footsteps of the pursuing Dominator clanged on the rungs horribly close behind him.

Lethbridge-Stewart reached the top and ran along the gantry, trying not to notice the vertiginous drop. Snarling, the Dominator hauled itself up onto the narrow metal walkway, its weight making the whole thing sway alarmingly. Lethbridge-Stewart grabbed the rails on either side with both hands, but stood his ground. The Dominator ran towards him with alarming speed. Lethbridge-Stewart found himself caught in a vice-like hug, the air being squeezed from his body. The chemical stench of the Dominator's breath made him retch.

'Probationer Azbo!' came a voice from below. Not the voice of a Dominator – a human voice! 'I'm not gonna let you do it, I'm not gonna let you blow up the world!'

Grunting, the Dominator relaxed its grip, and turned its head to peer down at the source of this interruption. Seizing his chance, Lethbridge-Stewart slid downwards and grabbed the Dominator's legs, hauling it up and over the low railings. The Dominator's low centre of gravity was his undoing, and Azbo plummeted, yelling, to the concrete floor, landing with a slam that shook the entire building.

A dishevelled figure ran up to it and did a little victory dance.

Lethbridge-Stewart blinked. 'Mr Chorley?'

Chorley's bespectacled, unshaven face looked up. Fellow looked deranged. 'Oh, so the cavalry's here at last!'

Lethbridge-Stewart descended the ladder as Chorley raved and gibbered over the body of the Dominator. Ignoring Chorley for the moment, Lethbridge-Stewart inspected the alien, drawing his Browning just in case. He grimaced. The back of its head had connected with the concrete. Purple blood pooled around its head and shoulder armour, spreading out across the floor.

'Dead as a – Dominator,' muttered Lethbridge-Stewart. He winced. His ribs still hurt. He turned his attention to Chorley. Looked like the chap hadn't bathed, or shaved, for a week. 'Are you quite all right?'

'I'm fine!' yelled Chorley. 'Look, now you're here, you've got to stop Dominex! They're not here to help us! They're aliens! They...' He stopped, looking around. 'Their ancestors were stocky, pale-skinned bipeds with dark hair, as vulnerable and naked as the Tellurians of this world,' he mumbled, still looking around like some wild animal. Lethbridge-Stewart stepped closer. 'During the conquest of their home solar system, they experimented with physical augmentation. They made themselves taller, toughened their skin, and encased their bodies in armour plating. They eradicated the messy and tedious business of sexual reproduction and instead became a mono-gendered species who reproduce by parthenogenesis.'

'Chorley, man, what are you talking about?'

The journalist didn't answer, he just continued on spouting what, to Lethbridge-Stewart, seemed like pure propaganda. 'They altered their bodies to remove the need for food and obtained their energy from radiation, extending the normal Dominator lifespan by several hundreds of years. In every way, they are better than you! As their conquest of the galaxy expanded, word of the fearsome conquerors spread from planet to planet. They became the Masters of the Ten Galaxies!'

Lethbridge-Stewart had enough. He grabbed hold of Chorley and shook him. 'Snap out of it, man! What's wrong with you?'

Chorley looked at him, his eyes wide. 'They want to destroy us! They mean to unleash Project M!'

'What the blazes is Project M?'

Chorley began to prance up and down, gesticulating wildly. 'Project M! Project MAD! Project M-A-D! Mutually assured destruction!'

Lethbridge-Stewart frowned. Mutually assured destruction – the policy of nuclear deterrence by which the use of nuclear weapons by either side would cause the complete destruction of both. It had helped prevent full-scale nuclear conflict since the end of the Second World War.

'What's that got to do with these Dominator johnnies?'

Chorley stopped pacing and faced Lethbridge-Stewart, suddenly calm. 'Everything. The hippies – Mike, Emma! – were right; they *are* building nuclear weapons down here. They plan to launch them against Russia! The counter-strikes and escalations will set off a full-scale nuclear war!'

Lethbridge-Stewart glanced at the prone figure of the Dominator. He shook his head. 'Why? What's in it for them?'

'They want to turn this planet into a radioactive wasteland. Fuel for their space fleet!'

Maybe it wasn't all propaganda after all. Lethbridge-Stewart narrowed his eyes at Chorley. 'And how do you know all this?'

Chorley waved a hand dismissively. 'I overheard everything. Everything! Only… It doesn't all make sense.' He shook his head, clearly confused. 'They gave me a job. I wrote press releases for them.' His tone brightened. 'Did you see *Inside Out* the other day? Good, wasn't I?' He laughed a laugh which didn't fill Lethbridge-Stewart with much hope for his sanity. 'Anyway, I'm okay now.'

Lethbridge-Stewart very much doubted that. 'How many more of these Dominators are there?'

'Two – Director Vaar and Navigator Deka.' Chorley grabbed Lethbridge-Stewart's sleeve. 'Come on! We've got to stop them!'

On the Dominator ship, Hooper watched helplessly as the Dominator manipulated controls. There was a small explosion on a console and the huge Dominator staggered backwards. 'Out of control!' it bellowed. Another explosion, and Hooper dropped to the floor.

He was free! The systems holding him in place must have got damaged.

Drawing his Browning pistol, he crawled round the central console, trying for a clear shot at the Dominator's head.

'Halt! Do not move!' trilled a voice behind him.

He scooted round to see a Quark advancing, weapon-arm pointing right at his face. Cursing, he scrambled out of the way. The Quark fired.

'No!' cried Navigator Deka. 'You will only cause more damage!'

The floor gave a sickening lurch and Hooper slammed into a bulkhead. Acrid smoke curled around him.

'Out of control! Out of control!' yelled the Dominator.

Hooper saw the Quark tumble backwards, crashing into a control panel. There was a shower of sparks. Another explosion. The floor gave another lurch, and then seemed to fall away completely.

Hooper held on for dear life.

It was as if a massive fist smashed into him. Everything went black.

Lethbridge-Stewart and Chorley ran from the shed back towards the control chamber. From above came a howling sound like a jet out of control.

'Look!' cried Chorley, pointing into the sky.

Above them, rising into the blue starry sky, was an astonishing sight. An aircraft, without wings, shaped like two silver bowls joined together. An alien ship. It wasn't the first alien spacecraft he had seen, but still Lethbridge-Stewart gazed at it with awe.

'You have failed, humans!'

Returning his gaze to earth, Lethbridge-Stewart saw Director Vaar staggering towards them. There was a gash in his temple, from which purple blood oozed.

The Dominator leader limped towards them. 'Project M will succeed! Soon, nuclear weapons will rain down on your enemies in the east, and they will respond in kind! Mutually assured – *domination!*'

Lethbridge-Stewart raised the Browning and fired without hesitation, aiming at the wounded Dominator's face. But when he pressed the trigger, there was merely an empty click. He was out of ammo.

Vaar's lip curled in a slow, demonic smile and he looked up at the ship.

'They've won,' wailed Chorley miserably. 'They can set off the missiles from the ship!'

But something was wrong.

Now far enough above them to appear the size of a shilling, the ship had stopped, and was listing to one side. Then it began to return to Earth, slowly at first, and then with increasing speed, descending diagonally through the night sky.

'Nooooo!' Director Vaar roared.

Black Tor had stood for untold centuries. Rain, wind, sleet, snow had weathered it, the endless years moulding its shape.

The Dominator ship hurtled down from the heavens and smashed into the black fist of the Tor. There was an immense explosion, and rock, metal and plastic flew out in every direction over the moor.

The sound of the explosion reached the Dominex installation, rattling the corrugated iron warehouses and sending shock waves through the concreted ground, making Lethbridge-Stewart and Chorley stagger.

'Hooper,' muttered Lethbridge-Stewart. 'He went onto that ship. Must have sabotaged it in some way.' He looked around. 'Hang on, where's Vaar?'

'He'll have gone to the missile silo – he can launch them from there!'

Lethbridge-Stewart and Chorley ran through the complex as blazing debris began to fall from the sky, landing with crashes and bangs all around them. Chorley led Lethbridge-Stewart into the main Dominex building and along a wide central corridor, which ended in a doorway opening into a vast concrete-floored hangar with a corrugated metal ceiling, sloping down to meet breeze-block walls. On either side, metal tubes had been driven into the floor at an angle, pointing up like the muzzles of enormous cannon towards circular hatches in the ceiling. From the ends of these tubes, shining silver nosecones could be seen. Around the bases of the tubes, thick coils of ridged, semi-transparent tubing curled. These tubes led to a central console, at which stood the figure of Director Vaar, regarding them coolly.

'You just are in time to witness the end of your planet,

and species. All I need to do is press this button...' – his finger jabbed down towards a patiently glowing green circular panel – '...and the missiles will launch.'

Lethbridge-Stewart walked towards the Dominator, shrugging off Chorley's restraining hand. He had to stall Vaar. He spread his arms to show that he was unarmed. 'Why do this?'

'It was my idea!' Vaar snarled. 'The Dominant Echelon had decreed that new methods needed to be found, to keep the fleet fully fuelled. I came up with Project M, a radical, even dangerous project, fraught with risk. But what is risk to a Dominator? Negative mass flux absorption requires nuclear energy, and you foolish humans have plenty of it.'

'And so you start a war?' Lethbridge-Stewart asked, continuing forward slowly.

'Normally we send a ship with two Dominators and a consignment of a dozen Quarks to assess a planet for its suitability for conversion into fuel, and its inhabitants are used as a slave force to achieve that end. But not this time. This time we have Project M!'

'You'll die too, you know, in the conflagration.'

'That does not matter. Our fleet will be refuelled, and the Dominators will go on, to conquer, and destroy!'

'What's the point?' Lethbridge-Stewart edged closer. If he could jump the fellow, get him away from the console. 'Why do you need to dominate?'

'It is the law of the universe!' bellowed Vaar. 'Dominate, or be dominated! You are a military being, you must appreciate the logic. Are you not prepared to destroy, in order to survive?'

'For survival, yes,' said Lethbridge-Stewart. 'But to

destroy an entire planet, kill all those millions of people? Just to refuel your fleet?'

'Project M was approved by the Dominant Echelon! It was deemed to be the most energy efficient means of achieving our ends. Turn the weapons of a primitive planet upon itself!' Vaar laughed. 'And we – *I* have succeeded!' His hand moved towards the button.

Lethbridge-Stewart sprang for Vaar, and grabbed his arm with both hands, pulling it away with all his strength.

'Ha! Try to stop me, human! Go on – try with all your might!' Vaar snarled. 'You cannot – because you are weak! Puny, insignificant worms! You deserve to be dominated!'

His free hand closed around Lethbridge-Stewart's neck. Stars flashed in Lethbridge-Stewart's vision. His grip on Vaar's arm loosened. Suddenly Vaar flung him clean across the room. Lethbridge-Stewart landed against one of the missile tubes, winded.

'Chorley! Stop – him!' Lethbridge-Stewart gasped.

But Chorley was gazing at Vaar like a rabbit caught in the headlights. What was wrong with the man?

'Mr Chorley will not attack me! For I am his employer – am I not?'

'Y-yes, sir,' stammered Chorley. Then, with more certainty, 'Yes, sir! What would you like me to do?'

'Die!' roared Vaar. He stepped towards the console and his hand reached for the button that would activate Project M.

'Hold it *right there,* you big-shouldered bozo!'

Lethbridge-Stewart twisted round.

Stevens!

His khaki kit was charred, and his face was covered in

dried blood from which his eyes glared hotly. But in his hands he held his SLR, and he was pointing it directly at Vaar.

'Pathetic hu—' Vaar's words were drowned out by the deafening chatter of rifle fire. Round after round slammed into the Dominator's chest, sending him reeling away from the console. Stevens marched forwards, still firing.

Vaar staggered backwards, roaring with rage.

Firing the SLR with one hand, Stevens unholstered his Browning, and tossed it over to Lethbridge-Stewart.

Lethbridge-Stewart caught the pistol, leapt to his feet and closed in on Vaar. Stevens had stopped firing, and the huge Dominator was on his knees. Lethbridge-Stewart ran between the console and Vaar. Vaar looked up, snarling. Lethbridge-Stewart aimed the pistol right between his eyes.

'It's over, Vaar.' His finger tightened on the trigger.

'You do not possess the courage,' growled Vaar. 'That is the failing of your species. You can only go so far, then you come up against your own limitations.'

'Don't count on it. You were prepared to destroy my world. Kill millions of people. Do you really think I would hesitate to kill you?'

Vaar's green eyes narrowed. 'Hmm. I revise my statement. I do believe that you could kill me.' A ghastly grin. 'You have the capacity to destroy, so there is hope for your species after all!' Vaar turned his gaze away in a gesture of arrogant indifference. 'No matter. Do as you will. I have failed, so my existence is irrelevant.'

Lethbridge-Stewart tensed himself. The Browning felt hot in his hand. Just pull the trigger, end a life. But there had been enough death, enough destruction. 'No. I'm taking you prisoner. I'm sure there's a lot we can learn from you.' He turned away before Vaar could respond. 'Stevens, cover him.'

Lethbridge-Stewart walked over to Chorley. The man was sitting cross-legged on the floor of the hangar, his face completely blank. Lethbridge-Stewart waved a hand in front of Chorley's eyes; no response. 'Mr Chorley? Hello? Are you in there?'

Still nothing. *Casualty of war*, Lethbridge-Stewart thought, controlling himself with difficulty, half-wanting to go back and shoot Vaar in the face. Instead he walked out of the missile hangar and back along the central corridor to the main control chamber, checking for Quarks, but all had seemingly been destroyed. He walked back outside, into the summer night. Or rather morning – a glance at his watch told him that it was well past midnight.

Smoke drifted slowly across the complex, from the explosion of the Dominator ship. Lethbridge-Stewart closed his eyes. Powell and Hooper, two more men lost; two more deaths. He opened his eyes again. It was over now. No more death, no more destruction, at least not today.

Lethbridge-Stewart walked back into the missile chamber, to where Director Vaar still fumed, Stevens' SLR aimed right between his eyes.

Vaar glared up at him. He had the aspect of a captured animal, a dangerous predator, something that had to be contained, at all costs. Lethbridge-Stewart looked down at the captive alien. This being, this monster, had considered the lives of every single person on the planet of no consequence. Lethbridge-Stewart felt nothing but contempt. His heart felt cold, heavy in his chest.

'Well, Director Vaar. How does it feel to be dominated?'

'You will never dominate me!' snarled Vaar. 'The Domina could not control us, and neither will puny Tellurians! You had better destroy me. Before I destroy you!'

'I've had quite enough of this,' said Lethbridge-Stewart. 'You're my prisoner. Your plan has failed. There's nothing more to say. Apart from – Stevens, keep him covered.'

'Yes, sir!'

Lethbridge-Stewart turned his back on the defeated alien and walked away.

Dogs of War

A lone in his flat, Harold Chorley stood at the window, staring out at the view over Albert Bridge. He held a tumbler of port, but he hadn't touched it, and after a couple of minutes, put it down on the glass-topped coffee table. *Best not to take any mind-altering substances,* he thought, *however benign.* Had to get back to normal. Normal... whatever that was. After all that Dominex business. He frowned.

What exactly had happened? He remembered going down into the caves with Lethbridge-Stewart. They had found something... hadn't they? He remembered Director Vaar, his boss, his job as public relations officer with Dominex. And meeting Lethbridge-Stewart again, the exploding ship... and then what?

He couldn't remember.

Scared now, he picked up the port, desiring its calming effect, and resumed his position by the window. The alcohol burned his throat. What the hell had happened to him down there? What the hell was wrong with him?

He looked out over, but did not really see, Harold Chorley's London.

'So,' said Major General Hamilton, leaning back in his chair. 'After all that, there's quite a few loose ends to tie up.

Whisky?'

Lethbridge-Stewart glanced at his watch. It was just gone oh-nine-hundred on Monday, the day after he, Stevens and Chorley had returned from Devon. Stevens had gone back to his flat in the Isle of Dogs, with the air of a man with a job well done. His last words to Lethbridge-Stewart had been, 'You know where I am if you need me.' Would he need Stevens again? Lethbridge-Stewart had a feeling he might.

'Yes,' he said to Hamilton, 'why not?'

Hamilton poured them a tumbler each.

'Here's to those who didn't make it,' said Lethbridge-Stewart. 'Ian Cawdery and his brother, the two hikers, Keith and Marie, Corporal Hooper, Flight Lieutenant Powell...' They raised their glasses in a toast, then sipped in silence for a moment.

'Without them it could have been a whole lot worse,' said Hamilton. 'The whole planet destroyed, just to fuel some alien war fleet.' He shuddered. 'The world owes you, Colonel. You deserve a medal, but due to the secret nature of these things...'

'I don't want a medal, sir. You know what it is that I want.'

'Yes, well, I'll be getting round to that in a moment.' Hamilton coughed, rubbed his hands together. 'Now, let's get down to the unfinished business. The small stuff first. Your car has been brought back from *The White Hart* and is now stationed at Chelsea Barracks awaiting collection. The furniture store has been recompensed. Everything's been straightened out and neither of us will face a court martial for the business at the safe house.'

246

'There's a relief,' said Lethbridge-Stewart, taking another sip of whisky. 'How much do they know?'

'No more than anyone else. Must be infuriating for those intelligence wallahs. Not knowing,' said Hamilton with clear relish. 'Now, Sergeant Bell has, er, been released from Hope Cove and is now being debriefed. He's being told that he played a vital part in the mission.'

Lethbridge-Stewart smiled at the memory of Bell's bemusement, and his stoicism in the face of what must have seemed a bizarre situation. 'Might be a good chap to keep around.'

'The two civilians picked up when you were taken to the safe house, Miss Emma Hindmarsh and Mr Mike Thomas, have been released without charge, as per your request. They have been persuaded not to pursue damages.'

'Good – on both counts.'

'Now this brings me to the matter of Harold Chorley. The charges of civil disturbance he picked up in Little America have been dropped, after a little pressure from myself.' Hamilton shook his head. 'Chap's in a bad way. The brainwashing has shaken him up pretty badly.'

Lethbridge-Stewart remembered Chorley in the hangar, the blank look on his face. He'd remained like that for the whole journey back to London, only seeming to come to himself as they'd reached the capital. 'If it wasn't for him, that Dominator would probably have crushed me to death. And he tipped me off about the enemy's plans.'

Hamilton nodded. 'Yes, fellow came through in the end, despite the brainwashing. Which was hardly his fault. I daresay the same thing would have happened to you, had you fallen into the enemy's hands. We've a lot to thank

Chorley for. It was he who brought Dominex to our attention in the first place. And bally brave of him to venture down into those caves with you. So we have, at the very least, a responsibility for the fellow's welfare.'

Lethbridge-Stewart sighed. But Hamilton was right. They owed him. 'I'll make sure he's looked after.'

'Now, onto bigger matters. Firstly, and thankfully, the Russians remain in complete ignorance that nuclear missiles were about to be launched against them from our country, and that will remain so. I've no need to remind you of complete secrecy in this affair.'

'Of course, sir.'

'The energy minister, Sir Anthony Bufton, has, of course, resigned. He will doubtless make a more than comfortable living from chairing various committees and accepting professorships.' Hamilton sighed. 'That's the way it goes.'

'Shocking, sir. Absolutely shocking.'

Hamilton took another swig of whisky. 'What else can be done? No one will ever know of his complicity. The Dominex affair is buried under D-Notices and level upon level of secrecy. The official line is that Dominex closed down due to a fault in their process. Saturday night's mayhem has been attributed to that.'

'What's going to happen to the Dominex plant?'

'It's being taken over by the Ministry of Defence, turned into a training camp. At least, that's the cover story. In reality we'll be looking at the technology the Dominators left behind, see what we can make of it. The surviving Quarks have been taken to the Vault. They're in a bad way, but we should still be able to learn something from them.'

Lethbridge-Stewart didn't like the idea of Quarks still

active, and even less that the Vault had them. He'd have to put in a call to Miss Travers.

'Damn shame their spaceship was destroyed. We could have learned a lot from that.'

'And Director Vaar?' Lethbridge-Stewart asked.

'Yes, Director Vaar.' Hamilton stood up and moved over to the window. 'He's been taken to a high security prison. Can't tell you where, I'm afraid. There he'll be interrogated, and imprisoned for the rest of his natural life. However long that may turn out to be.'

The thought of the hulking Dominator, ensconced in a cell somewhere, disturbed Lethbridge-Stewart. But sparing his life had been the right thing to do, he was sure of it.

'Now, I've saved the best for last. The Dominex affair, coupled with recent events at Fang Rock, has given Gilmore and I, and our supporters, the leverage we've been waiting for.'

'Music to my ears!' Lethbridge-Stewart drained the rest of his whisky, despite the earliness of the hour.

Hamilton raised his glass. 'Mine too! It's been a long, damned hard struggle, but we got there at last, Colonel.'

In the midst of a barren rocky plain on the distant planet Drahb, in the galaxy of Phi-Ralix, stood a gigantic city of cylinders, cones and blocks of shining metal and grey stone. It dominated the skyline, as it should, for this was Vobus, capital city and the seat of power for the Domina, the infamous Star Maidens of Drahb.

Deep within the tallest, most imposing edifice in Vobus was a vast domed chamber. Its arched windows gave stunning views over the city, and its ceiling was decorated with a stylised map of the ever-growing Drahb Empire. A map which grew with each passing phase of the Drahbin sun. Beneath it was an ovoid conference table carved of ebon rock, around which, in high-backed stone chairs, sat the august members of the Domina.

At the head of the table, in the largest chair, sat the Prime Domina, Trix. Her cladding was inset with purple jewels, and her head, unlike those of the rest of her race, was clean-shaven. Her green eyes glittered with intelligence, and anger. She was listening to a report from Communicator Bera.

'After losing them at Dulkis, we have finally traced the Dominator *War* Fleet. It has been seen passing through the Sol System of Mutter's Spiral.'

'The fools!' Domina Maga hissed. 'Do Vaar and the Dominant Echelon think they can escape the Domina for long? They continue to spread their lies, their propaganda!'

'Enough!' bellowed Trix. The other Domina fell into silence. She looked at each of them. 'They represent a grave error, and the error was ours. We allowed the men to have equal power, and now they mock us. Belittle the Drahb Empire. But no more. We will send out our own fleet, find out why they visited the Sol System. The Dominators must be destroyed!'

Hamilton put his glass down and took out a buff brown envelope from a desk drawer. 'Your official transfer orders to commander of the Home-Army Fifth Operational Corps, on paper a special forces unit attached to the Scots Guards, but in reality... Well, *we* know otherwise. Of course, for the time being you will need to operate out of Chelsea Barracks until Dolerite Base is ready.'

Lethbridge-Stewart took the envelope and raised an eyebrow. 'Dolerite Base?'

'Yes, we have procured the old LONGBOW facility beneath Edinburgh Castle for our purposes. It's going to take a couple of months to refurbish the place.'

Scotland. Yes, Lethbridge-Stewart could live with that. He'd have to pay his grandfather a visit while there, show Sally his family's estate perhaps. He had enough Scottish blood still in him to know he'd enjoy living in Edinburgh for a time.

'What of my troops? The list you gave me…'

'Best we can manage, I'm afraid. Too many questions would be asked if we transferred the best of the British Armed Forces to the Corps, so you get the best of a bad bunch. However,' Hamilton said, holding up a hand. 'You can pick your command staff, within reason. I've already reassigned Lieutenant Colonel Douglas to be your 2-in-C, and Miss Travers will transfer from the Vault at the earliest opportunity.'

'Very well. I want both Stevens and Bell, for a start,' Lethbridge-Stewart said. Stevens was a risk, but he felt the ex-Para would be worth it. And Lethbridge-Stewart felt he owed it to Sergeant Bell after his resilience at the Bunker.

'As you want.' Hamilton stood up, their business concluded for now. 'Bring Bishop in, too, of course. I believe he's redacted all the Corps' old files by now.'

Lethbridge-Stewart smiled. Bishop was doing a good job. He'd be a lance sergeant before he knew it. Lethbridge-Stewart saluted and left Hamilton's office with a renewed sense of purpose.

Aliens had come before, and would come again.

But next time, Colonel Alistair Lethbridge-Stewart and the Home-Army Fifth Operational Corps would be ready for them.

Thanks

Thanks go to: Andy Frankham-Allen, for giving me this opportunity and for his brilliant editing work, without which this book would not be as good as it is. Peter Anghelides, Paul Leonard, John Rivers and Paul Vearncombe for their advice and support during the writing of this book. Terrance Dicks, for without whom none of this would have been possible. Denise Di Caro, for unflagging support and encouragement during the writing of this book.

Candy Jar Books thank Kevin Nolan for military advice and Gareth Starling for the 'secret plan'.

Lethbridge-Stewart will return in Spring 2016.

Read on for the exclusive preview of the next title:

Moon Blink
by Sadie Miller

Daughter of Doctor Who legend,
Elisabeth Sladen.

Moon Blink by Sadie Miller

— PROLOGUE —

Colonel Alistair Lethbridge-Steward hadn't planned to remain at the Chelsea Barracks so late but time had got away from him and now he was all alone in his office with only a weak whisky soda and a collection of Top Secret files for company. He knew he only had just over a month left until Dolerite Base was operational, and until then he had to continue to work out of the Barracks in London, trying his best to maintain his tenuous cover. He eyed the stack of files wondering where to begin. There was still much work to be done; a *lot* of homework for him to get through before he officially took command of the Home-Army Fifth Operational Corps.

He opened the first manila file and scanned its contents. The "Space Race", as it was euphemistically called by the press. It seemed that the Soviet and American space programmes had developed into something far more advanced than merely a schoolboy rivalry over who would be first to put man on the moon – they were *already* there, despite the very public mission being undertaken at the moment by *Apollo 11*.

He sipped his whisky and took a deep breath. No wonder these files were top secret. He returned to the documents, reading with something akin to shock.

They showed evidence of mining activity specifically with the intention of creating nuclear reactors using the excavated lunar material. He turned the page. The Russians had even gone so far as to install a complex gravity imitation system on their base making it possible for men to work there just as easily as inside a nuclear control room back on Earth. The Americans, it seemed, had soon copied their technology with nothing staying secret for long even on the moon.

As if that wasn't surprising enough, the files continued to explain about the *British* Space Programme run by one Professor Ralph Cornish and the British Rocket Group, which was aiming beyond the moon – to Mars itself. Only recently they had launched *Mars Probe 5*.

Lethbridge-Stewart looked up from the file. This was incredible. He hadn't even known there was a British Space Programme, never mind that it was arguably more successful than that of the Americans and Soviets. RHIP, he supposed. In this case the privilege was the knowledge of secrets that could get a man killed.

He took another sip of his whisky and enjoyed for a moment its warming sensation as he looked out of the window across to the concrete towers that housed some of the Guards Regiments four companies. The dusky summer light dappled across the desk and he closed the file.

It is already late, he thought. *No need to rush.*

The sun had not quite finished setting but already the moon had appeared in the sky. Lethbridge-Stewart watched as they shared the horizon for a moment. He found himself calling to mind the words of Sally Wright, his fiancée. She wasn't one for silly sentiment but her last parting words had struck a chord with him. *Whenever we are apart know that we are looking at the same moon.*

That's all very well, Lethbridge-Stewart thought. The more pertinent question is who on the moon is looking back?

He shuddered, knowing he'd never look at the moon the same way again.

Demetrius' feet rang out as he walked quickly through the corridor. He didn't dare run; there was no running aboard the lunar base. Besides, if he ran someone would know something was amiss and Demetrius knew he couldn't risk anyone finding out something was wrong.

The base had been completed six months ago. Back in Odessa he had been one in a long line of builders working on the shipyards, and his family had been one of the first to utilise the connection between nuclear power and the propulsion of ships. He had had no idea he was working on a lunar base until he had woken up there several months back and now he knew he was trapped there until whoever was running the base decided they could return to Earth.

Helium-3 had been mined successfully from the lunar surface and now he was helping to build the fusion reactors. Things had been going to plan until the Soviets had realised that they were not the only ones who had discovered the Helium-3 rich crater crusts. Now an American base was stationed just the other side of the Terrae, visible but far enough away to not have caused any problems for them – yet. But the Americans were not the only ones on the Terrae. There had long been rumours of aliens, spacemen living on the moon too, but it wasn't until the week before that Demetrius had realised that one of those stories was actually true.

He hadn't been hard to lose, Demetrius thought as he continued his pursuit. Why did it have to look exactly the same? Why couldn't it have been green with strange shaped heads and eyes like the stories he had heard as a child? But these aliens were nothing like anything he had ever read about as a little rebenok. This one had wanted him to know it was an alien, it had left out the special powder and ever since then it was all Demetrius could see. Now Demetrius kept his head down as he made his way through the maze of corridors, keeping his eyes low as he watched the alien figure nimbly slip its way past the others on board.

No one seemed to take any notice of him and Demetrius quickened his pace. He could call out, get someone to stop it, but he didn't want to be known as the man who let one of them escape. He needed to be here, his bosses had made sure he knew his family were counting on him to complete the mission otherwise they would never see a ruble of his salary payment.

The alien came to the exit and Demetrius saw it reaching for the door handle, struggling when he found it locked. Quickly Demetrius reached for his respirator, sliding it over his mouth and breathing in the oxygen, his lungs expanding gratefully as he stepped forward to the pull the alien back from the door, but the figure was too quick for him. The door suddenly gave way and the figure stumbled out onto the rocky, uneven surface.

Once outside the confines of the base, the figure moved nimbly, almost gliding across the otherwise impassable surface. Demetrius closed the door quickly, the warning alarms signalling that a door had been open. Helplessly he watched as the figure climbed over the divide and ducked under the bridge, making his way towards the US Base.

'*Chto zdes proishodit?*'

Someone was shouting behind him. Demetrius shrugged his shoulders, casting one last glance across the now deserted Terrae. The alien was somebody else's problem now.

On the US Base across the other side, the figure straightened itself, its clothes suddenly matching the uniform of the new base, fading from blood red to a deep royal blue. It was not the first time it had walked between the two sides, it knew exactly how to manipulate its appearance so as to be accepted without question. All at once it became a male with pale eyes and tanned skin, complimented by thick blond hair; the all-American poster boy. He passed through the corridor unnoticed, making his way into the control room.

'Where did you get to, Bobby?' Nick said, turning away from the control panel he was manning, the younger man at his side turning around too, the multiple screens behind them all blinking as one as the machine interface continued to control and monitor the critical operations on base.

'Just fancied a walk,' the newcomer said to his erstwhile colleagues. 'Stretch my legs.'

'Thought you might have cut out on us there,' Nick said, looking Bobby up and down with an air of suspicion, as he always did. Cabin fever was beginning to set in, and for Nick it was worse than most.

'Not far to walk to,' Jed muttered morosely, thinking longingly about the long stretches of road and river in his

Mid-Western hometown.

'What did I miss?' Bobby said, taking up his seat beside them.

'Nothing much, Bobby, just working on the moon, no big deal.' Nick reached out to punch him playfully in the ribs, but Bobby moved easily out of his reach.

'Freeze dried strawberries?' Bobby said, dryly.

'Naw, I'm sick of all this rehydrated crap, I want some real food!'

'Cool your chops and listen up,' Nick said. 'I've got something you're going to want to hear. A rumour.'

'What kind of a rumour?' Bobby said a little too quickly.

Nick paused and stretched out his jaw. 'There's going to be a lunar landing, on TV. I overheard one of the commando communications. They're going to film it, have everybody watch.'

'The Russians?' Jed baulked.

'Naw silly, the Americans of course! But they're not going to show them what's really going on here. We're not going to be making our TV debut, it'll just be a couple of astronauts, guys making more dough.'

'Oh,' Bobby said, his face relaxing slightly.

'You thought I was going to say something else, huh?' Nick got to his feet, his hands rising to his thick hips.

Bobby shrugged. 'Possibly. But I don't mind being wrong.'

The colour flamed in Nick's cheeks. 'You trying to say something about me? That I always got to be right?'

'Not at all.'

'No, I can take it. Lay it on me.'

'Stop it, Nick,' Jed said, shifting in his seat. 'Ain't no

point lip flapping when we all have to be here 'til who knows when.'

'There are others you know,' Nick said darkly. 'And I'm not just talking about guys like us! Others.'

'Don't go saying stuff like that,' Jed said nervously, his eyes bulging with fright. 'There's no one here except us and those guys across the way.'

Nick turned to Bobby. 'Where did you say you came from again?'

Bobby blinked at him. His eyes darted around the room quickly, avoiding Nick's gaze. Nick began to pace around the small, cramped space.

'You see, me and Jed here were working at the same plant in Monroe, Michigan. I was there when the odium cooling system malfunctioned, caused a partial core meltdown – I've seen things you wouldn't believe.'

Bobby said nothing. He was still looking around him, his eyes searching for a name, anything that could give him an alibi, buy himself some time. He should never have tried to fit in with them, he realised. He had only wanted to know who these men were that came to his planet, but it was too late now. Beneath Jed's uniform he could just about see the stamped blue logo of one of his t-shirts from home; *Funk Brothers: Detroit Michigan.*

'Detroit,' he said quickly.

'What nuclear plant you been working at there?' Nick scoffed. 'None that I heard of!'

'I was working in a laboratory,' Bobby said, confident with the word. Nick narrowed his eyes.

'So if you're really a Michigander, what's your team? I'm a Wolverines man myself. Who's yours down in

Detroit? Go on,' Nick pressed. 'Who's your team?'

Bobby remained silent; he could see from the pulsing muscle in Nick's cheek that he was about to lose his temper.

'Pistons or Titans! Could have gone for either one! So if you're no Flatlander, who are you really?'

Bobby didn't respond.

'I bet your name isn't really even Bobby either, is it?'

Suddenly Bobby got to his feet, his hands shaking as he grappled in the pockets of his uniform, searching for something.

'What you doing, Bobby?' Jed asked him nervously, but Bobby didn't answer. Jed turned to Nick like a child looking for reassurance. 'What's he doing? Hey, Bobby, what's the matter with you?'

Jed shook him, but Bobby didn't answer. Then all at once his hands stopped shaking; he had found the item in his pocket he was looking for. He looked across at Nick and Jed in silence. Suddenly, the very small room felt even more claustrophobic.

'I'm scared,' Jed said, his protruding teeth biting down onto his lower lip. 'Do something, Nick! Make him talk!'

Nick stepped forward, his hand balled into a fist, but Bobby held his hand up, signalling for him to wait. Nick held back confused for a moment.

'Take this,' Bobby said, stepping forwards suddenly and handing something to Jed. 'It will make you feel better. It will help you see them, then you won't need to be afraid anymore.'

'Don't touch nothing from him!' Nick said, charging over to get between the two of them. 'He's one of them, I know he is! He's going to try and kill you!'

Jed looked up at Bobby and then down to the small parcel in his hand. It was a rock, purple in colour, a hard centre with a crumbling exterior, which was leaving a white cast on his palm. In the confined space he began to see the powder rising into the air, feel it tickling at his nasal cavities. Behind him Nick started to wheeze.

'What the heck...?' He gasped.

The powder was glistening and sparkling like a biotitel. Jed stared at it and then looked back up to Bobby. His mouth hung open in surprise and fear as he saw the eyes in Bobby's head beginning to widen.

'Holy–' Nick began, darting across to the wall of the small room, his hand reaching for the emergency lever. Bobby stood in front of Jed, his true self beginning to be revealed, his hand outstretched in friendship.

'Don't!' Jed called after Nick. 'It's still just Bobby, he doesn't want to do us no harm!'

But it was too late. The emergency sirens were already going off, the red lights flashing across the whole of the station. Jed looked back at Bobby. There would be no escape for him now.

— CHAPTER ONE —

The Eagle Has Landed

The location of the Vault was innocuous enough, none of the very infrequent passers-by would ever have dreamed of the terrible secrets that lay beneath the sweeping vista of green and yellow slopes that straddled the Anglo-Scots border. Anne Travers had learnt a lot since joining the Vault and seen many things, some of which she wished she hadn't. Now she was beginning to feel restless again, longing for the freedom to work under her own steam. She held her handbag close to her, the telegram and its message concealed safely inside. A trip to see her father was a welcome distraction, despite his strangely urgent and cryptic message.

One of her colleagues at the Vault had dropped her off at the nearest train station to the Cheviot Hills. The traffic moved quickly, it seemed no one wanted to be on the roads tonight. There was a strange calm in the air that Anne couldn't quite put her finger on. By the time they reached the station to catch the last train of the evening, the platforms were empty and there was no one to share her carriage with, which Anne was grateful for.

As the train pulled away from the station, Anne took a moment to look out of the window and watch the station disappear into a cloud of steam before settling down to examine the telegram again. Her father was often sending her odd requests, which usually called for Anne to go and see him in person to fully appreciate their meaning, but something about this one seemed different. She noted he had sent it to Alun too, though there was no explanation yet as to why.

The journey didn't take long but Anne was exhausted, her body now kept underground in the darkness all day at the Vault only to come out into the night at the end of it. She slept fitfully in the empty carriage; the rocking motions of the train soothed her into a brief dreamless sleep.

It was very late by the time Anne's train had pulled into Kings Cross Station, She hailed a taxi, which took her in no time at all right to the doorstep of her father's home. As she opened the door she could already hear her father clattering around inside, the house in total darkness. She sidestepped across a pile of papers and a stack of books, the top volume in Nepalese with a title that Anne could roughly translate through the dim light as meaning *Mountain Man*. She felt along the hallway for the switch and then suddenly the space was flooded with light.

'Hello?' Anne called out. There was no reply. She looked around her father's house. It was so chaotic, not like the order she insisted on at her small bungalow in Kilham. She wondered how her father could think straight living there.

'Hello?' she called out again. 'Is anyone home?'

She made her way into the back of the house. Her father was racing around the living room frenetically, items of clothes and open books strewn about on every side. She wondered what time Alun had arrived and felt annoyed that he hadn't tried to make some kind of order. She glanced at the walls, which were natural calico, unmarked. At least it looked like Isobel wasn't there.

As she made her way into the living room she could see her father was hunched over; his hair at odd angles as his busied himself with an object on the side table.

'Father?' she said. It took a few more moments for him to realise she was there. As soon as he turned and saw her, he stood and ran towards her in one motion.

'Anne!' he said, clasping her close to him. 'You made it!' Childish delight spread across his heavily lined face. Anne looked at him quizzically, wondering what on Earth could have come over him. 'I'm so glad to have the opportunity to share this moment with at least one of my children!'

Ah, Anne thought ruefully, *that explains the mess.* So Alun clearly hadn't made it after all. He was never the best at managing his own time, much preferring to stay firmly ensconced in the past.

'Yes,' Anne said. 'I got your message. Your very urgent message,' she added pointedly, pulling out the telegram from her handbag. Her father nodded, his face becoming suddenly serious.

'Indeed,' he said. 'I have a surprise for you.'

He stepped to the side so that Anne could see into the cluttered room behind him.

'Behold!' he said with a flourish.

Anne was nonplussed. 'What am I looking for?' she asked. She really did not enjoy these eccentric games her father liked to play, especially not in the small hours of the morning.

'This!'

Anne eyed the nineteen-inch colour TV on the table behind him.

'I took the liberty of purchasing it for the occasion. What do you think? Oh! I'm forgetting my manners! Would you like something to eat, drink? I suppose it must be getting very late, I must admit I do lose track of time these days, not much of it left for me now so important to make the most of it! How's the secret job going? Alun was most put out you wouldn't fill him in. Spending lots of time in that dark inhospitable place I presume?'

'Yes actually.'

Her father chuckled with delight. He didn't know how right he was, Anne thought. He continued to bustle around her, asking her question after question before she could make any answer.

'Sorry, you must forgive me, it's been so long since I saw you and there's so much I want to ask, but take a seat, my dear Anne, you must be tired. Take a seat,' he pressed.

'Just you and me then, is it, Father?' Anne asked looking around her to see if any of her father's guests were still in evidence.

'Yes, just us two,' he confirmed, sitting down next to her.

'Alun won't be joining us then?' Anne asked. 'Your telegram mentioned you had invited him also.'

'Well it's a long way, isn't it, for him from Oxford?' her father said. 'I'm sure he's far too busy with teaching work in any case.'

'While Northumberland is just around the corner,' Anne remarked.

'Besides,' her father said, ignoring her comment and

reaching out to squeezing her hand conspiratorially, 'Alun will be teaching about today for years to come I shouldn't wonder.'

'I think you'll find I'm the one who looks to the future, Father. Alun is much more interested in what has come before. The real world doesn't sit so well with him.'

'Perhaps not,' her father mused. 'But we make history in every moment, Anne. Besides, history tells us so much about what the future will bring. You just have to look closely enough.'

He got to his feet a little unsteadily and made his way over to the bureau at the edge of the room, squashed into an alcove it shared with a stack of boxes piled up high on each side. He selected one of the half-filled decanters, pouring out a tumbler of the dark liquid for both Anne and himself. He returned to his chair and passed across her the drink. Anne took it and the two of them chinked glasses in an almost silent cheers.

'Good health,' her father said after swallowing down a couple of gulps. 'Ah, I needed that after struggling with that monstrosity over there for half the evening. Who would have thought such a small box could be so much trouble?'

'What time is it?' Anne asked, looking around at the clocks which all showed different times, then glancing down at her wristwatch for confirmation.

'Almost time!' her father said excitedly, getting to his feet again and smiling at her with delight. 'We're nearly ready, Anne!'

Anne watched him make his way across to the television and, after a few fumbling moments, switch it on. The screen crackled for a moment, then the blackness lit up with moving pictures.

'What is going on, Father? You didn't make me come all the way down to London to show me a new television set.' Anne was beginning to get a little exasperated with him.

'On the contrary! I called you here to witness tonight's important event with me, a once in our lifetime experience to be shared together!'

Suddenly the penny dropped loudly in Anne's tired mind.

'The moon landing,' she said quietly. With spending all her days underground she had almost forgotten it was happening.

'Can you believe it?' her father was saying over and over, more to himself than to Anne.

'No,' Anne replied dryly. 'At least, I can't believe they're putting people on the moon and letting the whole world watch.'

'But of course,' her father replied. 'The Americans are the winners of the "space race" as they liked to call it, they want to show the whole world the victory over the Russians!'

Anne sank down further into the plush old armchair, dislodging a stack of papers and a rather angry cat that had been dozing underneath the cushion.

'Careful now,' her father said crossly. 'I didn't bring Sasquatch all the way back from Tibet to have her meet a sticky end now!'

The small black cat glared at her, its amber eyes wide with unconcealed malevolence. Anne made a hissing noise at it under her breath, and the cat jumped down to the floor, still looking at her darkly. Her father reached across to squeeze Anne's hand.

'I had hoped that you of all people could appreciate the joy of this momentous occasion, to see how far we have come as a species, that we may actually one day find ourselves colonising another planet!'

Anne's mouth felt suddenly dry. She sipped at her tumbler of whisky and wondered what turn tonight was going to take. Her father was still lost in his own world, his eyes shining with all the possibilities he was imagining in his mind.

'We are so fortunate,' her father began, 'To have experienced first hand the wonders of alien intelligence wouldn't you agree, Anne?'

Anne's mind flickered to the darkest corners of the Vault, the unclaimed bodies and the extra-terrestrial secrets she had uncovered.

'Of course, Father,' she said. 'But don't you think that perhaps humanity is safer living within the comfortable and blissful ignorance of Earth?'

Her father nodded but he was only half listening to her now.

'*Those seized with fright by the full moon are visited by a goddess.* Do you know who said that, Anne?'

'Hippocrates.'

'Ah! Yes indeed. Father of modern medicine and even he could not explain away the allure of the moon.'

'He also said *there are in fact two things, science and opinion; the former begets knowledge, the latter ignorance.* These moon landings may prove more problematic than enlightening. People are not always ready to receive the information science reveals to us,' Anne pointed out.

Her father coughed. 'Yes, well perhaps so but I think

that's enough for now,' her father said, tiring quickly of quotes when he was not the one espousing them. 'Get yourself comfortable. Should be almost time now.'

He got up to change the channel then resumed his seat, sipping at his tumbler of whisky as he watched the screen with unblinking eyes. Anne found her eyes drawn to Sasquatch who was cleaning herself rather theatrically on the carpet. Anne found herself strangely drawn to the spectacle, as she wasn't quite ready yet to see what the moon had in store for them tonight.

'Oh, Anne, you look so tired and terribly pale – go and take a look in the kitchen, I made some awfully good meatballs with grape jelly for Sasquatch, if I do say so myself. I'm sure there must be some leftover.'

'No thank you,' Anne said. 'There was a buffet car on the train. Besides I–'

'Sshh!' her father hissed, holding his finger in the air to silence her. 'Look! It's starting!'

Suddenly, the pictures began to form on the television screen. Her father turned to her, his face shining. Sasquatch eyed them from her position on the floor. Anne looked from her father to the television screen. The picture was grainy, the audio crackling making it hard to hear exactly what was being said between the Eagle lunar module and Mission Control Huston. Anne watched as the Eagle lunar module touched down in the southwest Marie Tranquillitatis.

'I'm going to step off the LM now.'

Astronaut Neil Armstrong was taking his first steps onto the moon.

'That's one small step for man. One giant leap for mankind.'

It was so unbelievable it didn't look quite real, though Anne was in little doubt that it was. There was no way the Americans would risk doing something so dangerous as falsifying a moon landing; public opinion would never recover. Anne glanced down at her wristwatch. 3.56am, but she felt wide awake.

She watched as Armstrong continued to take his first steps across the lunar surface, which looked to her as if it was both hard and soft at once, powdery in texture rather like a desert. He moved slowly, bouncing from side to side a little like drunks at closing time. There was plenty of back and forth between Armstrong and Mission Control, most of it seeming to be directed at his sample collecting. Anne squinted to try and get a better look but the picture quality was just too poor. She wondered what discoveries lay in wait in the deep craters, wide as football pitches.

Armstrong was not alone for long. Fellow astronaut Edwin 'Buzz' Aldrin soon joined him.

'Beautiful view,' Mission Control commented as Aldrin moved across the surface.

'Isn't that something? Magnificent sight out here,' Aldrin responded.

'Beautiful,' Anne found herself echoing in spite of herself. 'Isn't it, Father?'

She glanced across at her father, but his eyes were closed, his chin sinking down to meet his chest as his belly rose and fell rhythmically, the air rushing in and out of his nostrils making a soft, sonorous sound. Anne smiled to herself. All the preparation and he had tired himself out, falling asleep at the most crucial moment. She reached across and covered him with the throw, Sasquatch dutifully pottering over and making herself comfortable on the toes of his slippers.

Anne got up and clicked off the television, the image resonating on the back of her eyelids for a moment. She closed the living room door and took the creaking steps one by one up to her old room.

She crept into bed for the night in her childhood bedroom, though the lights of early morning were already starting to creep through the curtains and across the carpet. She got up and went to open them a chink to look up at the moon, which looked so unbelievably bright and far away. She had seen so many things, and yet she couldn't quite comprehend the idea that there could still be men up there, walking and working along the surface just like she was doing down in the depths of the Cheviot Hills. The boundaries of scientific discovery were expanding rapidly, and it both thrilled and cautioned her.

The sky was lightening from navy to blue, the moon still visible as the sun started to make its approach towards the horizon. Anne could understand the wide spread appeal of the moon landings but for someone like her, who had already experienced more than her fair share of alien life, she couldn't help but feel a little apprehensive. It was all very well going to other planets, but what if another planets occupants decided to come here? She didn't have much more time to think about the matter as the promise of the warm bed called to her and soon Anne found herself once again giving in to the irresistible lure of sleep.

The next morning Anne was up early. She made her way downstairs to find her father still in the living room. He was struggling with the television, which he had nestled in his lap, several cups of tea surrounding him, all which looked as if it had gone cold.

'Missed it!' he kept muttering to himself. 'Bloody missed it!'

'Everything all right, Father?' He didn't respond, his attention still engrossed in the back of the television. She asked again.

'Why didn't you wake me?' he said, turning to her with the pursed lips of a petulant child.

Anne laid her hand on his arm. 'I didn't realise you had fallen asleep,' she said.

'Asleep? I was just resting my eyes,' he countered gruffly. 'No, it's this blasted television set! Must have tuned it to the wrong channel. Missed it!'

Anne stood and watched him for a moment but said nothing. She didn't want to ruin it for him by telling him in reality he had slept through the whole thing.

'Well it's been lovely to see you, Father, but I really must be getting back to work now.'

Anne moved to the hallway to collect her things, the single bag she had brought with her resting against the leg of the hall table, Sasquatch sitting on it territorially. Her father appeared beside her, his eyes blinking at her through his spectacles, his hair still wildly clumped on one side as if he had slept in the chair all night.

'Not staying for breakfast? You must take care of yourself, Anne, you never know when someone might come and take you away from all this work you do in the deep dark hole.'

'Yes, Father.' She agreed with him about the Vault, but she wasn't about to give up on her solo scientific endeavours quite yet. 'But I don't want to miss my train.'

'Oh, come now, there will always be another one. Can't tempt you to a tea? You must have something before you go, it's not good for the mind working on an empty stomach.'

At the mention of food Anne could feel her insides starting to growl, and after a moment's hesitation she let her father take her back towards the kitchen, where he began hunting through the cupboards which were filled with jars and specimens that belonged in a laboratory rather than a domestic kitchen.

'Porridge?' he offered finally. 'There's a bag of Scottish raw oats, no milk mind, but it's just as nice with water. Your mother used to make it beautiful with just water, do you remember?'

Anne didn't reply. She didn't often like to think of her mother, it was like a jarring shard of light piercing through the darkness of her memory.

'Let's get the kettle on – oh, I seem to have used all the mugs.'

'Just porridge is fine,' Anne said distractedly as she started to move around the kitchen distractedly. She didn't particularly want to get back to the Vault, but an evening with her father was about as much as she could take. As she made her way around the kitchen island something caught her eye. She walked across to the fridge and then paused to look at a postcard pinned behind a rather gaudy magnet of Mount Everest.

'What's this?' asked Anne as she retrieved the postcard from the fridge.

'Oh that came for you,' her father said distractedly.

Anne turned it over in her hands. It was from the

Kennedy Space Centre Complex, built in 1939, Florida. She sat down at the table and began to read.

Dearest Anne, it began. *Have taken a trip down from Washington to the sunshine of Florida for vacation, heading up to Huston soon. Apollo 11 mission commencing in two weeks. Heading across the pond week after, can't wait to see those Northumberland hills. Fondest love, Patricia.*

'When did you say this arrived?' Anne asked glancing at the postmark.

'Hmm? Oh a fortnight ago perhaps, I forget now,' her father called back, stirring the hot pan full of the thickening oats. 'Nothing important I presume? Nothing important gets sent on a postcard.'

'I'm not sure,' Anne admitted. With all the hub of space activity going on in the States, she couldn't imagine why Patricia would choose now as a time to come and make a trip to England.

Anne studied the postcard again. Perhaps she ought to head back to the cottage first before going back to the Vault, she thought to herself. It looked as if she was about to have a visitor.

Available from Candy Jar Books

LETHBRIDGE-STEWART: THE FORGOTTEN SON
by Andy Frankham-Allen

For Colonel Alistair Lethbridge-Stewart his life in the Scots Guards was straightforward enough; rising in the ranks through nineteen years of military service. But then his regiment was assigned to help combat the Yeti incursion in London, the robotic soldiers of an alien entity known as the Great Intelligence. For Lethbridge-Stewart, life would never be the same again.

Meanwhile in the small Cornish village of Bledoe a man is haunted by the memory of an accident thirty years old. The Hollow Man of Remington Manor seems to have woken once more. And in Coleshill, Buckinghamshire, Mary Gore is plagued by the voice of a small boy, calling her home.

What connects these strange events to the recent Yeti incursion, and just what has it all to do with Lethbridge-Stewart?

"A solid start to the series. The Brigadier is such an integral part of Doctor Who mythos, it seems right and proper he now has his own series." – Doctor Who Magazine

ISBN: 978-0-9931191-5-6

Also available from Candy Jar Books

LETHBRIDGE-STEWART: THE SCHIZOID EARTH
by David A McIntee

Lethbridge-Stewart was supposed to be in the mountains of the east, but things didn't quite go according to plan. On the eve of war, something appeared in the sky; a presence that blotted out the moon. Now it has returned, and no battle plan can survive first contact with this enemy.

Why do the ghosts of fallen soldiers still fight long-forgotten battles against living men? What is the secret of the rural English town of Deepdene? Lethbridge-Stewart has good reason to doubt his own sanity, but is he suffering illness or injury, or is something more sinister going on?

Plagued by nightmares of being trapped in a past that never happened, Lethbridge-Stewart must unravel the mystery of a man ten years out of his time; a man who cannot possibly still exist.

"McIntee turns in a fine Who-based thriller that harkens back to the era in which it's set while also exploring ideas and concepts more modern. It's a fast paced tale that makes for a wonderful addition to this new series." – Warped Factor

ISBN: 978-0-9933221-1-2

Also available from Candy Jar Books

LETHBRIDGE-STEWART: BEAST OF FANG ROCK
by Andy Frankham-Allen
Based on a story by Terrance Dicks

Fang Rock has always had a bad reputation. Since 1955 the lighthouse has been out of commission, shut down because of fire that gutted the entire tower. But now, finally updated and fully renovated, the island and lighthouse is once again about to be brought back into service.

Students have gathered on Fang Rock to celebrate the opening of the 'most haunted lighthouse of the British Isles', but they get more than they bargained for when the ghosts of long-dead men return, accompanied by a falling star.

What connects a shooting star, ghosts of men killed in 1902 and the beast that roamed Fang Rock in 1823? Lethbridge-Stewart and Anne Travers are about to discover the answer first hand...

ISBN: 978-0-9933221-7-4

Also available from Candy Jar Books

Tommy Parker: Destiny Will Find You
by Anthony Ormond

When Tommy Parker packs his bag and goes to his grandpa's house for the summer he has no idea that his life is about to change forever.

But that's exactly what happens when his grandpa lets him in on a fantastic secret. He has a pen that lets him travel through his own memories and alter the past. Imagine that! Being able to travel into your own past and re-write your future.

Tommy Parker: Destiny Will Find You! is an exhilarating adventure that redefines the time travel genre.

You'll never look at your memories in quite the same way again...

ISBN: 978-0-9928607-1-4